Lieutenant Syreen thinks of herself as a skilled spaceship pilot in the Duchy Fleet. When another stellar nation invades her home system, her skills are put to the ultimate test. Before long, all her wingmates are shot dead, all their other space-ships are destroyed, and she soon she finds herself as Fleet's only survivor on active duty. How is she supposed to fight the already victorious enemy battleships all alone?

Giving up is not an option, at least not for her. Forced to with-draw and find new answers, she must also keep control of her own body that begins to demand warm blood.

After her escape, she starts looking for support for her cause. However, no other nation wants to become the invaders' next target. Instead of support, she only finds a few lucky survi-vors, and a researcher who will at least fund her while follow-ing his own goals. His mention of the remnants of an ancient race triggers her curiosity — because the invaders were also looking for a relic of an ancient race. Could these two goals be related?

Time of War
Copyright © 2020 Valerie J. Long
ISBN: 978-1-4874-2931-7
Cover art by Martine Jardin

Published by eXtasy Books Inc or
Devine Destinies, an imprint of eXtasy Books Inc

Look for us online at:
www.eXtasybooks.com or www.devinedestinies.com

TIME OF WAR
FORGOTTEN PEOPLE BOOK 1

BY

VALERIE J. LONG

DEDICATION

For the oldest still active ski jumper. Your happy attitude rocks!

Part One—Coming Out

CHAPTER ONE

A red light flashed over the door. Syreen jumped up and grabbed her bag and was out of her bunk before the klaxons went off. *Not this time, no more disciplinary penalties for being late.*

Half a centicycle later she met her wingmates on the flight deck.

"Get in your gear," Cap barked, "this is not an exercise!"

Not? *Aw shit.* Syreen dashed toward her skirmisher — basically a seat, a power plant, an engine and one light pulse cannon wrapped in a thin, spindle-shaped metal sheet — and let herself drop into her cockpit. *Okay, let's give 'em raiders a good time, shall we?*

She ran through her routine. Buckles, headgear, data glove, flight stick, stimulator. She waited for the short prick of the syringe in her right thigh. *Ouch. I so hate needles.* Her status went green.

"Silver Seven?" she heard her wingleader on the private line.

"Check."

"Syreen . . ."

"Don't worry. I'll be there, I won't chicken out." *Not while we're doing real business. That's not me.*

"I didn't want to imply that."

Oh yes, you did. "Trust me, Cap. Now where's the target?"

"You'll get your fun soon enough. Silver Wing, prepare for launch in five."

A little wave of heat shot through her right leg, and the

psyjuice started its work. The colors around her looked brighter, the fine hissing sound of the oxybox became a rhythmical melody. There was a brief moment of dizziness before her body adapted to the drug. She began to enjoy the warm presence of the stimulator and adjusted herself in her seat. Not for the first time she wondered what it would feel like for the males, but obviously she lacked some imagination.

"One – go!"

Like a gush of sperm, her wing's slender skirmishers were shot out of Base Four's launching tubes. Her tac came to life with a scatterplot of purple icons. *Oh heck!* At least five dreadnaughts, the obligatory wake of cruisers, and a cloud of stingships. Who had ever seen dreadnaughts, the largest warships ever built, in operation? This was not the expected raid they had been preparing for, this was full-scale invasion.

"Silver Wing, here's our order. We'll engage Daddy Five's escort and make room for the tanks. Score well!"

Daddy Five's icon turned yellow together with its escorts.

This is madness. You think I have issues with discipline? Nope. I have issues with stupidity, and to think our three outdated destroyers plus eight wings of skirmishers could stop this armada is outright stupid. But Fleet won't retreat, that's a given. She sighed. *So be it. At least we'll die on the crest of ecstasy today.*

She didn't need much of her concentration to stay in formation. Cap – Silver Leader – wasn't very creative. He flew by the Books, fought by the Books, and he would die by the Books, as their enemy quite certainly knew the rules just as well.

Unless I can do something about it. No, she wouldn't be able to win this battle. But a few unconventional maneuvers – which she was infamous for – might buy her wing some time, perhaps even enough time for someone with brains to stop this massacre.

"Combat config," Cap commanded.

"Check." Her headgear picked up the spot her glance was

focusing on and triggered the reconfiguration. Delicate antennae reached out of the main hull to weave the protective shield, which could deflect stray shots and thus might let them live a few centicycles longer. No way a skirmisher could survive a direct hit from one of the tanks — be it a destroyer, a cruiser or a dreadnaught.

As if to prove her thoughts, behind her Base Four silently melted away. Poor bastards — they had been a sitting duck for the dreadnaughts' long-range missiles. The other bases followed within millicycles. They might have had a chance to launch their own score of missiles, but those would be wiped out by the enemy cruisers' tight mesh of countermeasures.

"Bandits — outer seven," Cap noticed. "Keep positions."

Sure. Give 'em easy prey. You know you'll be the last — your wingmates' shields will amplify yours. Bandits will start shooting the tips — that is, me — and work inward. Meanwhile you get your chance to return fire.

A slight pull on the flight stick, and her skirmisher pranced around the almost invisible beams of energy which crossed in the position she had assumed until a blink before. *Fuck yourself, bastards. And take this.* She triggered her own pulse cannon and struck home. "Score!"

Her tac acknowledged the kill. Her stimulator pulsated joyously inside her crotch. *Ah! More of that!* She aimed and fired again. "Score!" *Now dodge, gal, it's never good to stay in one place too long.* Her shield flickered. *That was too close. How dare you, bastard? Take this!* "Score!"

Cap yelled something about formation and discipline and rules. Meanwhile she plucked another hostile stingship from space. "Score!"

In all simulations, she had been the best. Now she could show her talent. *If Cap wouldn't get so busy quoting the rules, he'd score as well.* "Score!"

Sadly, this had been the last bandit. A few wingmates had scored as well. She felt the stimulator slow down. *No! I want more!*

More kills, more stimulation. So simple. To get more kills, she'd have to engage more enemies. With one swift move, she reassumed her position next to Silver Six.

"You've left formation," Cap accused her over the private line. "You've weakened Basil's defense."

"True. I've dodged three hostile beams. If I was hit, I'd have weakened Basil, too — but permanently. I've promised to cover your ass, so I'd better survive."

"We're at war, Syreen. This is no game."

"I know. I don't play games. And that's what's in the Books. Games."

"Syreen —"

"You can't whip me now. Let's make a deal — if you score better than me, you'll chastise me. If I score better, I get away with it. If it matters at the end of this tencycle, that is."

"I can't teach you better now."

"Good that you understand, Cap."

CHAPTER TWO

"Score!" *Ah.* Another ecstatic pulse in her snatch, and Syreen came. "Ahh!" she cried out her lust.

When the waves of her orgasm ebbed away, she checked her tac again. But the stingship she'd hit had been the last in her vicinity. Most of the enemy's small craft had long reconfigured for atmospheric flight and started to engage planetary defenses. Only one enemy wing had been left behind to swat the few obnoxious skirmishers that had survived their first assault.

Daddy Five was no more — a cold comfort compared to the annihilation of four orbital stations, three brave destroyers and now eight skirmisher wings. Or, in short, all of Fleet except for one skirmisher. Hers.

A small icon in the tac's upper left corner declared Syreen's skirmisher as Fleet's current flagship and its pilot — her — Fleet Commander in Charge. *Oh heck.*

Time for SitOps, she thought. *Situation — normal, all fucked up. Options — slow death from starvation or a quick death from an invader's pulse cannon. Skirmishers can't go dirtside. Skirmishers' pulse cannons can't hurt a dreadnaught. Syreen, face it — you're ultimately screwed.*

The thought made her move in her seat. But her stimulator had stopped vibrating and wouldn't come to life again until her tac registered valid targets. Which had better happen soon, as the continuous flow of psyjuice still made her horny.

If you can't win, change the rules. That was what life had taught her. That was what had kept her alive until now, that was what made her outlive each and every one of her Fleet mates.

She couldn't go dirtside, she couldn't return to her base, she couldn't leave the system without hyperdrive, and she couldn't win the battle in her spacecraft. What she could do was return to a different larger ship for her life support. What she could do was—board one of the enemy tanks.

Chapter Three

After having eliminated an entire stingship wing, Syreen couldn't expect the enemy to have forgotten about her, just the opposite. However, she had a brief open time window before any of the other stingships could be recalled to open space.

Together with a flashing red symbol on her tac, she felt a welcome vibration inside her crotch — one of the enemy cruisers had acquired her as target. Six missiles were homing in on her. That was bad, as those missiles came in fast, but Syreen welcomed the opportunity — and accelerated her skirmisher toward the enemy tanks.

Approaching a tank with a single skirmisher was pure insanity. With the enemy's telemetry already tracking her, it was sure death — or should be. While her shield was battered and wiped away by at least a dozen grazing shots, Syreen dodged energy beam after energy beam, following a crooked, winding path toward the nearest dreadnaught.

Her crazy idea proved right — the cruiser had to cease its fire to not endanger the larger ship, while the behemoth's automatic countermeasures registered the oncoming missiles as the more dangerous threat and began to help her get rid of her pursuers.

All the time, the stimulator was heavily vibrating inside her, while fresh waves of psyjuice kept her alert. She wouldn't fool herself — this time, she wouldn't reach orgasm. Before the dreadnaught's close-range defense could take her tiny ship apart, she had to exit.

Her gaze fixed on a symbol she never wanted to use, while her hand on the flight stick pulled her tiny ship into another nearly impossible dodge. *Slow down, gal! There's no point in greasing that hull.*

The evac symbol flashed. She reconfirmed her order with a determined glare.

The continuous flow of psyjuice stopped. The syringe was retracted, as was the stimulator. The sudden emptiness between her legs felt strange, but the lack of drugs felt stranger. Syreen knew of other skirmisher pilots who needed cycles, if not tencycles, to overcome the withdrawal symptoms. She had never known such trouble. A brief phase of concentration, and she was mentally and physically clear again — as she never had suffered from the other side effects. Psyjuice caused enhanced reflexes, lower inhibitions, quick decisions, but often also reduced initiative and imagination. Perhaps that was a reason why Cap and the others had preferred to fly by the Books?

It hadn't helped them. They were dead, and Syreen soon would be — unless she found entry to the dreadnaught ahead.

First, she had to escape her doomed *flagship*. The fabric of her seat snuck under her belts, wrapped around her body, transparent only over her face, pulled her arms and legs tight, and then the skirmisher canopy was blown away and her seat with tac and oxybox catapulted into space.

Her skirmisher, now on a straight, predictable trajectory, evaporated in the beams of at least six close-range-defense guns. Syreen congratulated herself for her last maneuver — it had shot her seat not only toward the dreadnaught but also out of the direct line of fire. While the large ship's defenses were unlikely to register her as a threat, they surely wouldn't take chances with a hostile skirmisher only to save an unidentified object.

By the Books, she was supposed to trigger her evac transponder now and wait to be picked up by any evac team looking for survivors of both sides. However, as the bases' annihilation had also hit Fleet's own evac teams before they could even start, this would imply surrender, and she didn't feel the least inclined to turn herself in.

Chapter Four

The built-in seat rockets slowed Syreen down before smashing into the large ship — too late for close-range defenses to acquire the target, but not too late for being spotted. Marine infantry would now be deployed for a warm welcome.

She unbuckled and pushed herself away from the seat before it smashed into the hull. Only tac and oxybox remained with her.

Ugh.

The impact was harder than expected. Syreen checked herself, but found no signs of broken bones or cuts in her suit. *Lucky me.* She spotted a maintenance airlock only twenty legs away. *Lucky me!* she repeated, and cautiously started to feel her way to the outer hatch.

Sticky fluid at fingers and toes were the only means preventing her from drifting away into space. The dreadnaught's own artificial gravity wouldn't reach outside, and its mass attraction wasn't strong enough to compensate for the takeoff speed an unlucky push could give her.

There was a tradeoff between safety and speed — the faster she advanced, the higher the risk of losing contact forever, but the more time she took, the higher the risk of facing a welcome team.

It felt like ages, although it could've only been a centicycle or two, until she reached the hatch. She found some unfamiliar symbols and a few more obvious ones and followed the latter ones' instructions.

The hatch opened, and she quickly climbed inside. That seemed to trigger an automatic process—the outer hatch closed, lights went on, she was sprayed with some fluid, and then the airlock filled with atmosphere. Breathable, her oxybox advised her, so that she opened her suit and pulled her head free. Next, the inner hatch slid aside.

Obviously, the enemy had been too convinced of his own success to prepare against boarding maneuvers. She didn't face an infantry party. Instead, only one entirely confounded crew member stared at her.

Bipedal, with body, arms, head like hers, with two eyes, nose, ears, and mouth like hers, and male, with a significant bulge in the crotch of his worker suit.

So at least there were no bug-eyed, eight-legged monsters swarming her home planet now, but people like herself. There'd more likely be rape and pilfering than feeding.

The symbol on his suit triggered a memory from her training classes—*Associated Planets*. She had never really cared for politics, as nobody had ever mentioned the option of interstellar war. That kind of consideration was far above her pay grade. But she had at least learned the names and symbols of the Duchy's neighbors, and the *Association* was one of them.

The man now produced a tool from his belt and pushed a knob, so that it made a humming noise and its pointy tip, aimed at her, disappeared in a blur. Electric drill or sonic screwdriver? Whatever it was, she advanced on him, battered it aside and rammed one knee into his supposed groin. He rolled his eyes and collapsed.

As he was lying on the floor, pale and limp, she saw the veins at his throat calling for her. How often had she felt this strange desire before, but never given in to it? You didn't bite a fellow soldier in the Fleet, even if such a rule wasn't mentioned in the Book. And she hadn't known any home, any family but Fleet for all her life. Nobody knew where she had come from, who her parents were. She'd been found in a lone corner of Base Four, had been adopted by an old petty officer, raised as his platoon's mascot until she had grown too old and too obviously female to remain an uncontrollable civilian girl among Fleet personnel. Whereupon she'd been tested, recognized as promising pilot candidate due to her good reflexes, and sent to Fleet Officer School.

Still suffering from the adrenaline rush of battle, from the aftereffects of psyjuice withdrawal, and from the resonance of her fading arousal, she could no longer restrain herself. She went on her knees and bent down to his throat, her fangs bared.

CHAPTER FIVE

Syreen was all excitement. This was so much better than psyjuice. Her senses felt sharpened, her body so much stronger, and — *oh* — her labia and clit so swollen and wet that the slightest touch — *here* — instantly triggered orgasm. *Ah!*

Her tongue casually licked a drop of blood from the tip of her fangs while she watched the four little holes in her victim's throat slowly close.

Realization hit Syreen like a hammer.

Fangs? How can I have fangs? She reached up and felt for her teeth. Indeed, her canines were longer and pointier than she remembered from the last time she had gazed into a mirror. While she still mused about this strange news, she felt her teeth shrink back to normal size. With them, her excitement — arousal — faded, too.

She'd have forgiven herself for being shocked, distracted, frozen in place, but she wasn't. She was fully aware of standing next to a blood-deprived corpse in a remote corridor of a hostile warship, with no weapons but her own hands and teeth, so she'd better leave *now*.

Which she quickly did.

After a few turns of the maze of corridors, all looking the same with their light-gray walls, indirect lighting, and well-concealed air supply, she felt safe enough to slip into a small storage room and pause for SitOps.

Situation — yet undetected aboard an unknown enemy warship, no weapons, no equipment but a now useless oxybox and tac. No

14

clue about the ship's layout, staff, or ordnance. No clue about internal security, although there had been no obvious cameras to spot until now.

Options – surrender to the enemy, with the prospect of interrogations at best, rape, abuse and even torture at worst. Out of the question. Attempt sabotage, cause a little crucial damage here and there until getting caught, outcome as before. Defeat the entire crew and assume command of this dreadnaught? Just kidding. Try to hijack a smaller craft and commence battle? What a glorious way to commit suicide! Try to hijack a smaller craft with hyperdrive and escape from this system? This last idea came with a plethora of *ifs*, but it felt promising, at least way more promising than the other options.

The rhythmical steps of many feet approached her hideout. *Not now.*

While most of the feet continued, one had stopped outside her door. She tried to blend in with the shelves around her, which of course wouldn't help at all. Her evac suit didn't have any camouflage features.

The door slid open, and a young man in full indoor combat gear peeked inside. His gaze seemed to cut right through her, but his face didn't show any sign of surprise or recognition. Only when he glanced down at the small pad at his left wrist and spotted a bright-red symbol there did he look up at her in amazement.

She liked the look of his tousled hair, his large eyes, his small nose, and the dimple at his chin, but he was an enemy, and worse, he acted like an enemy by moving his right arm.

Before he could fully raise his gun, before he could grasp what he was facing, she was over him, and her fangs were in his throat. He fell limp and no longer tried to fend her off.

CHAPTER SIX

Syreen quickly fought down the arousal that had come with another wave of strength. Next, she took the soldier's gun and his wrist tool. The gun operation wasn't difficult to figure out, and the wrist tool turned out to be similarly straightforward — it offered a pale-yellow map, showing his fellow soldiers' positions in blue and her own in red, plus it allowed her to zoom in and out and change levels.

It also showed a dark-green symbol for its former owner.

She tapped her own symbol, just out of curiosity, and a small hexagon with six colored areas appeared. Her finger moved over the blue area, hesitated, then she touched it.

The hexagon vanished, her own symbol turned blue, and the dark-green symbol disappeared, too. Should it be so easy?

While the other blue symbols continued on their way, she took the time to quickly skim through the dreadnaught map and record the images with her own tac as well as memorize them, until she had identified several areas near the outer hull that could be hangars.

Finally she dropped the tool. The risk it could give her own location away was too high to take.

Before she opened the door of her storage room, she listened for noises outside, but heard none. So she dared to leave and walk on.

The Association dreadnaught's crew still seemed to take the case of an intruder lightly, although meanwhile they should have found her first victim. There were no sealed hatches, no scores of infantrymen swarming all corridors, and she still hadn't found any hint of internal surveillance.

Were her enemies too arrogant to consider her a serious threat? Were they too arrogant to consider a boarding of their ships feasible? In any case, she was glad about it until she met another crew member whom she hadn't heard coming.

She turned around one corner, he around another, twenty legs away, and they were facing each other. The boy was definitely too young to become her third victim.

That shouldn't have happened, she thought, and then, *I'm not even here. I don't exist.*

A stupid idea, yes, and she prepared herself for what was to come. But the boy seemed to look right through her, came toward her and seemed to be determined to run into her as if she wasn't there. She had to step back around the corner where she came from to avoid collision, and the boy didn't even acknowledge it.

She remembered the soldier's initial reaction to her presence — none. Back in the storage room, she had tried to blend in, be unnoticed, and hadn't been noticed at first. She looked at her hands and saw a little blood stain. No, she wasn't invisible. Most importantly, she wasn't invisible to technical devices, only to people. And yet, her first victim had instantly spotted her. What was the difference? That she hadn't *thought* herself to be unnoticed?

Chapter Seven

The next crew member she came across was a female dressed in whites and with a med kit—despite the otherwise unfamiliar symbols, the marking on this kit seemed to be universal.

Ignore me and hurry up, Syreen thought.

The female accelerated her steps and hurried past Syreen, who watched her until she had passed the next corner.

This is convenient.

Now Syreen could walk up to the hangar area, claim a ship and leave, as easy as that. No, she knew that wouldn't work. Even if she could cheat a bit, her new tricks wouldn't get her past the hangar door. She couldn't control computers, and she wouldn't bet on her mind control working over distance. She needed a better plan. *Aw, in the first place, I need a plan at all. Any plan, but preferably a workable one.*

Number one—I need a cover story for my escape. My ship—the ship I yet have to acquire—needs a reason to depart. Some secret order nobody's allowed to ask about would be nice. Where do I get those orders? From the top.

Number two—to make sure my cover isn't blown, I need a distraction. If the dreadnaught suffers some distress just during my departure, so that they're unable to answer any inquiries regarding me . . . perhaps I should have another look around and find out where the main power station is?

Number three—once I have my ship, how can I fly it? Do I hijack the pilot, too? No. I don't know how long I could keep up mind control—surely not for tencycles. I must sleep now and then. Moreover,

I'm a pilot myself. I've been trained for small and large ships, including interstellar navigation. I don't need to burden myself with a hostage, I only need to learn their symbols and controls. But where and how do I start?

CHAPTER EIGHT

The more time Syreen spent on the Association dread-naught, the more familiar the different symbols looked. Actually, once she had a first clue about the basic system, they appeared quite logical. Anything blue was connected to security, damage and fire control, hull integrity, shield generators. Dark red indicated ordnance — missile launchers, close-range defense lasers, heavy medium-range pulse cannons. White was used for medevac, yellow for power supply, green for life support.

For a while, she followed the yellow symbols, trying to avoid contact with crew members as far as possible, using her mind control if she met anyone.

Here and there, she eavesdropped on crew conversations. While she initially didn't understand a single word of their foreign language, she by and by heard words that sounded at least somewhat familiar to her own vocabulary, and then she realized that in fact the Association people spoke a very distant dialect of the Common she knew.

Or perhaps it was just the reverse — the Common spoken in the Duchy included a lot of local slang words, abbreviations, insinuations, words deliberately used wrongly in a sarcastic way, terms that weren't defined in the Book, and so on. Stripped of all that local flavor, the Common she heard here was understandable to a certain extent. Of course, the Association had their own slang, abbreviations, and redefined vocabulary.

She followed a sudden impulse and left the corridor to

enter a crew quarters section. She checked a few doors —
locked, of course — and then found one that opened in front of
her to let a young, smart man out. He was about her size, and
wore a light-gray uniform with a single golden stripe and an
unmistakable silver pilot's badge at his chest. He smiled at the
sight of her and said something Syreen didn't understand, but
which was accompanied by a rocking motion of his pelvis that
she understood well. She smiled back, pressed a button at her
suit that let the entire front of it open from throat to crotch,
and pushed him back into his room.

Syreen could tell that seeing her so invitingly naked
switched his brain effectively off even without her mind control, as he voluntarily shed his uniform, offered her a not very
large but nicely hard cock, and helped her out of her own evac
suit.

He seemed to be the kind of male who considered foreplay
unnecessary, or perhaps he took her offer as a sign of recipro-
cal preparation, as he reached straight between her legs. In
any case, she felt her own arousal grow together with her clit-
oris and labia, felt the first wet drips trickle down her thighs,
then pushed him back on his bunk and mounted him for the
ride to climax.

With loud moans, he announced his upcoming orgasm,
and with a strange fascination, Syreen watched the pulse in
the veins at his throat. When she leaned down to him, his eyes
grew wide in joyful expectation, his trembling lips opened —
and then she sank her fangs into him. His semen and his blood
shot into her, and she sensed his last orgasm together with her
own — *oh!*

Never before, not even in the psyjuice-inebriated group
fuck after flight training, had she felt such intense ecstasy. In
this moment, she felt as if her senses were flooded with his
thoughts, his emotions, the ship around her, the Duchy's

central star, the universe, and in some way, it seemed to call for her.

Nonsense, gal. You just killed an enemy with his hard cock sticking inside you. You're as hot as a used pulse cannon muzzle and dare to enjoy it, bitch! You're high from drinking his blood and fantasizing. Come down and gather your senses.

Yes ma'am, she acknowledged her own command and rose. A gush of cum soaked his cock when it slipped out of her.

Calm and determined, she stuffed her evac suit into a drawer, put on his underpants — *used, yeah, so what? I just had his male parts inside me, that's way closer* — his socks, and his uniform, and then tried his shoes. Too large. She found another pair of socks, put them over the first, and tried again. This time, the shoes fit.

Next, she scanned his gear and belongings and — *Yakka!* — found his Pilot's Handbook, together with his Associated Planets Officer's Commission, issued to a Lieutenant Merigo Luquin.

Syreen glanced at Merigo's dead body and felt a little pang of regret. Yes, he was an enemy, part of a raid to her own system without any previous declaration of war, as far as she knew. This equaled an act of piracy by all standards she had learned about.

At least he had died a joyous death.

CHAPTER NINE

The handbook contained all the clues Syreen needed to understand commanding an Association's starship. There were fewer differences than expected — the main controls were based on Common and seemed to have the same origins as the Duchy's.

Especially the basics around the hyperdrive were the same, only the color codes derived from the hyperflight calculation differed. As long as she relied on the numbers, she'd be fine.

Again, she gave her latest lover's corpse a glance. The holes in his neck had closed — or shrunk? The riddle of his death — deprived of almost all his blood with no visible wound — would keep the physicians busy for a lifetime.

It was almost time to leave him. There was only one more task to do — she had to remove the Association's symbol from her uniform.

The stripes didn't matter, nor did the pilot's badge, but it was illegal to wear enemy insignia, and as the Duchy's Fleet Commander in Charge, she was supposed to be a role model and observe such rules, even if there was nothing left of Fleet but her.

On second thought, she went back to the drawer and retrieved the Fleet symbol from her evac suit. She had to hold it in place for a while before it stuck to her chest, as if it would refuse contact to the enemy uniform, but in the end, it stayed in place as it was supposed to.

The uniform was a bit tight around Syreen's chest — where

Merigo had been clearly less well-endowed than her—and a bit loose in the crotch, but should suffice for her purposes. She picked up her tac and the gun and turned to the cabin door. It opened for her, she stepped outside, and it closed behind her. She shrugged and continued her way to one of the ship's main power plants.

The only mental command she now had to issue was to ignore her Fleet symbol. Otherwise, no noncom or enlisted crew member questioned her way. She only had to return salutes.

The situation changed when she reached the plant access. A senior noncommissioned officer was unimpressed by her stripes and frankly asked for her business with his plant.

"Why, I'll sabotage it, of course," she advised him calmly and nudged his mind to play along.

The noncom laughed out loud and pointed at his dashboard. "Sabotage it? Hah, you can't foul up a Soltech plant—it's foolproof. You'd have to shut every single safety down to cause trouble—and the automatic repair will instantly start the next safety up again. No way."

"Why would you shut down a safety anyway?" Syreen asked innocently.

"For maintenance, of course. Every ten-thousand cycles you should check them, and every third check you should replace them. All done automatically, you know. You can't fool that system."

"Bet I could?"

The noncom frowned. "I'd hold that bet—only I may not let you try. You know that."

"I know. You will stand aside and watch." Syreen added a mental command to her statement.

She stepped before the dashboard, where the noncom gave way, and started to push symbols.

Safety shutdown. Start extended maintenance, replace this safety. Estimated downtime—ten cycles or one full duty-rest interval.

She repeated the same with the next safeties, and saw realization in her victim's face. Once the safety was down for extended maintenance, it could no longer be restarted, whether automatically or manually.

"You'll have us all toasted," the noncom complained. "Stop that."

Syreen repeated her mental order and continued her sabotage work. One after another, the safeties went down, and the estimated downtime grew—obviously, the automatic systems couldn't handle them all together. This kind of deliberate mishandling wasn't what the builders had had in mind when designing the system to be *foolproof*. This kind of mishandling wasn't in the Books, but Syreen again didn't play by the Books.

She sensed the rising panic in her victim and the slippage of her mental control over him. He jumped forward toward the dashboard—for the alarm button, no doubt—and she intercepted him.

They wrestled for a moment. She surprised him, first with her physical strength, and then by biting his throat.

CHAPTER TEN

Without the safeties, the power plant could operate for a few more decacycles without trouble — unless there was a demand for higher output, which would cause it to heat up. With locked safety ducts, the excess heat couldn't escape, and the reactor would melt.

She'd better be somewhere else when this happened, so she briskly walked outward again, following the symbols for the main corvette hangar. For one, that was the class of ship Merigo had been trained for and about which his handbook had contained the most notes, and two, it could be handled by a single person, and three, it was the smallest class capable of hyperflight — not counting unmanned scout and messenger ships.

Nobody questioned her way, not even the few higher-ranking officers she came across. As long as she saluted them appropriately, they automatically assumed she had some urgent duty to tend to, so she expected to reach the hangar within a few centicycles.

No, stop. I still need my cover order.

At the next crossing, she turned toward command central, knowing she was entering a dangerous path. The density of higher-ranking officers would increase, and thus the risk of blowing her cover.

No risk, no fun. Nobody aboard expects a spy.

After all, her plan required a higher-ranking officer, so she had to go where her victims were, and the second-most likely

26

place was near the bridge or command central.

The most likely place would be inside either of those, but she knew she couldn't go there. She was brave, but not that foolish—well, after attacking a dreadnaught with just one skirmisher, perhaps she was, but not suicidal. So she tried to avoid the main route and used secondary corridors wherever possible.

She felt confident enough that she'd withstand the heat. Continuing her drill of hurrying and saluting, she passed several more officers and noncoms.

When a man with silver-gray hair and a star on his shoulder boards stopped before a door only twenty legs ahead of her, she accelerated her stride. *This might even be the ship's commandant.*

The flag officer paused and looked at her.

She covered the remaining distance, stopped, and saluted.

"One moment of your time, Sir!" *You're curious.*

"Come in." His gaze focused on her chest, and he frowned. *Ignore that symbol.*

She entered his room—a surprisingly spacious apartment with a large conference table, a smaller table with couch and seats, a pantry with crystal glasses, and two doors leading further in—and mentally ordered him to follow.

"I need your signed order for a top-secret mission for which I require the next available hyperflight-capable vessel. You will issue that order now to a Lieutenant Syreen."

The flag officer frowned again, but fetched a pad from his pocket and began to type.

Syreen focused on her request. When the Association admiral looked up and nodded, she gave him a little mental leeway.

"Who are you?" he asked, and he didn't mean her name and rank.

"That's top secret," she said. *Well, in a way it is, as I can no longer be sure myself who I am. If nobody knows, it is a very well-*

kept secret indeed. "What's your mission in this system?"

The admiral's face froze. "I may not tell that to anyone."

Oops.

That was another new experience—her victim could resist her mental command?

Whatever the reason, this wasn't the time for experiments with unpredictable results. There had to be a different way.

"You won't tell me. You'll just look your orders up once again." *You're alone. It's safe to recheck your orders now.*

Syreen held her breath until the admiral held up his pad and retrieved a document marked *Top Secret.*

The admiral diligently read the entire document again. It started with a lot of details on how to assemble his crew—secretly—comb out less reliable members, acquire provisions and ordnance, attain mission-readiness, and then report to Vice Admiral Cornelius Ravenport aboard *APS Illustrious.*

Syreen felt initially tempted to let him skip that part, but then refrained from messing with her mental control. It might even be useful to learn how this foreign navy worked.

The next part of orders appeared confusing even disregarding the fact that it included some words she had never read before—were those Common at all? In any case, the gist of it was that the Associated Planets had gained intel on an item called the *relic* that would give its owner superior power. Such power must not get into the wrong hands—that was, hands other than the Association's. Intel indicated that this *relic* originated from a group called the *Forgotten People,* and might be located in one of the systems colonized first in this sector of the galaxy, among which the Duchy was the oldest. The Association's fleet was supposed to strike quickly and firmly, secure access to this *relic,* or, if necessary, by all means prevent the Duchy from deploying it.

Details on the latter part were rather unsettling. As far as Syreen knew, kinetic bombardment was considered a major war crime, as it would indiscriminately kill military and civil population together and could render the affected planet un-inhabitable.

How dangerous would this *relic* be if the threat of its existence alone could justify such ultimate measures in the Association's eyes?

The remainders of the mission orders did not cover any details on how to proceed with the Duchy if the item could not be located. The issuer or issuers seemingly hadn't taken this possibility into account.

So if we can't prove we don't have it, the only way to get rid of you is to kick you out, right, bastards?

She felt anger rising within herself.

"Listen, Admiral. You're found guilty of commanding an unprovoked attack on a peaceful nation without issuing a declaration of war first. This behavior is considered piracy among civilized nations."

Why did she bother to tell him? Was it only to soothe her conscience? She didn't give him time to reply before she sank her fangs into his throat.

Chapter Eleven

The corridor ended at a hatchway. A screen at the right-hand side showed most of the hangar.

Her heart jumped when she spotted the slender silhouette of a corvette on the center launch pad. Obviously, it had arrived only recently, as the pad was still turning.

A small unit of marine infantry in full gear was waiting near the pad. This didn't match her plans.

She turned left and followed the symbol to the hangar master's office. His door was open, and she walked in and saluted.

The only inhabitant, an older officer with the three stripes of a captain, gave her a brief glance and returned her salute with a casual gesture. "Later."

Syreen focused on her next words. "My order is to relieve the corvette's pilot of his duties and ship his cargo back to the Association. This mission is top secret."

"I must check . . ."

Again, Syreen had to underline her statements with a mental command. "This order is already checked with the admiral. It's in your system. The cargo must not be unloaded. The infantry will not enter the vessel, but leave the hangar immediately. The vessel is released for launch in ten centicycles."

His gaze seemed to focus on some spot far behind her.

"Launch in ten. Yes."

When Syreen left his office, she already heard him issuing commands to the infantry and the hangar crew. She gained a little more distance before she took a deep breath. Would her mental command last? Would he check the dead admiral's

30

last order? And if so, would he be satisfied with what he found?

The hatches put her patience to the test, first the large inner hatch, then the armored double outer hatch. At first glance, the hangar seemed clear — the marine infantrymen had disappeared through another hatch, hopefully together with the last pilot, and the corvette waited on its launch pad, facing outward, its own hatch invitingly open to her.

Raydancer, she read on the hull next to the open airlock.

She placed one hand over her Fleet symbol before striding forward. No way she'd cheat the cameras. Observers should guess she'd just run into an obstacle and was holding her shoulder for the bruise — a few more legs, the steps up to the pad, the ramp to the hatch — once the corvette's outer hatch had closed behind her, she let out a long breath and took her hand down.

There wasn't much time left. She went to the cockpit, dropped into the pilot seat — missed the familiar stimulator and syringe for a brief moment — adjusted armrests, headrest and belts, and flicked the main switch.

Her dashboard came to life. There were no alarming symbols, so she quickly checked the unfamiliar controls. Stick, throttles, shields — she might need them soon — and hyperdrive console.

"*Raydancer,* you have clearance for launch in two."

Where — ah, here — she activated her radio. "Roger. *Raydancer* is ready to launch in two. Initiating automatic sequence."

"Good journey, *Raydancer.*"

Syreen leaned back in her seat and watched the countdown. Automatic sequence, as if! It only had to look that way . . .

As the countdown reached zero, Syreen flipped the switch for the landing gear, at the same time pulled at the stick to lift the small spaceship a few legs above the launch pad, and pushed the throttle forward.

This was something every pilot was taught not to do—full throttle inside confined space. The engines' energy wreaked havoc on the equipment stored along the hangar's inner walls, melted the armored hatches in place and probably evaporated every camera and similar installations.

There was a loud curse on her radio, but Syreen was focusing on her trajectory—a tight curve toward the next dreadnaught and then between it and her own, which would prevent their automatic systems from targeting her, and then she directed her small craft system-outward. If she could pull off this stunt, she'd leave the Duchy for the first time in her life.

Inquiries from both ships followed soon. She sent a typed message—*Raydancer departing on top secret mission*—and otherwise ignored them. She only needed to buy some more time while the crews of the Association's ships made up their minds whether to shoot a supposed colleague, then gain further distance. Once she was out of reach of the large pulse cannons, her odds for escape weren't bad.

Meanwhile, one power plant of the dreadnaught she'd just departed from overheated. Alarm signals reached the bridge, and urgent inquiries to the tech on duty remained unanswered. Further inquiries to tech personnel resulted in reports of a dead noncom officer and the embarrassing confession that it wasn't possible to revoke any of the maintenance orders, not even for safeties not yet retrieved. Someone asked for programmers who'd dare to fiddle with Soltech coding, but too late. The plant was already overheating, and the excess heat also strained the adjacent plants. All plants together went into emergency shutdown, and thus deprived the mighty dreadnaught of almost all of its power. Due to a minor design flaw, this also affected the secondary safety systems which otherwise could have discharged most of the excess heat — which soon reached the numerous missile warheads in their magazines.

The command crews of the other Association warships watched with horror as one of their dreadnaughts simply melted away, accompanied by the fireworks of overheated heavy ordnance. Few of the unlucky ship's crew had reached their emergency pods in time.

Nobody cared for one little corvette with secret orders which had been lucky enough to escape this inferno.

CHAPTER TWELVE

In theory, Syreen knew how to compute a hyperflight. In theory, she had successfully calculated several jumps before. Her instructors had been happy with her results, but as skirmisher pilot, she'd never had the opportunity to do a real jump.

Now she had the opportunity, and she'd better take it before the enemy overcame his surprise, found out there were no secret orders for the little corvette, and sent some missiles or even stingships after her.

Usually, you looked up your points of departure and destination from the ship's library, created a first hypervector, and then ran the entire trajectory through the computer again for known obstacles. If the results were acceptable, you computed the precise vector and impulse, transferred it to the hyperdrive, and once you had reached the calculated jump velocity, the computer executed the jump. Good navigators — as her instructors had credited her — could do this in less than a quartercycle.

Merigo's Pilot's Handbook had given her all the clues to tame the unfamiliar Association computer, but finding all necessary data would have taken way more time than she could grant herself.

However, she had memorized some of the jumps in and out of the Duchy. Her instructors had approved of that — hyperjump data didn't change every other tencycle, so saving time by using known data could be the difference between life and death. Of course, you had to be very sure of the data you memorized. Duchy computers would test against a check-sum. As long as the checksum matched, you could trust your memory. Whatever Association computers did, Syreen would take her chances anyway.

The hyperdrive control panel didn't give her any riddles to solve—similar problems should result in similar solutions, shouldn't they? She only had to ignore the unfamiliar colors. The calculation results looked promising, so she approved and transferred them.

Meanwhile, *Raydancer* had reached the fifty percent light speed needed for a safe jump, so the computer could instantly trigger the engine.

The last impression she had was that there were indeed no pursuers coming after her.

CHAPTER THIRTEEN

Syreen spent one cycle scanning the destination system for bogeys before she triggered *Raydancer's* collectors to unfold. An experienced warship skipper used every opportunity to recharge his hyperdrive, even though the capacitors could hold enough power for six to eight jumps, depending on distance, entry speed and interstellar obstacles. Only merchants would optimize for travel time and leave recharging to systems where they stopped and shopped anyway.

The Carix Alpha system was empty, as expected. This system was no destination for enemies and had zero advantage for pirates, not even a hideout. There were no planets, only a sufficiently powerful sun for hyperdrive recharges, which had made it the preferred training destination for all Duchy pilots and navigators.

Syreen congratulated herself for her first live jump before she allowed herself to realize what she had just done. There were so many new impressions to process!

She didn't really credit herself for being Fleet's only survivor. That was due to her obstinacy of disobeying the Book and thus no real surprise. Anyone with a little imagination and skill could have done the same—her comrades had only lacked the balls to do it. Where she had no balls . . . *well, so much for proverbs.*

Shooting some stingships was no big feat either.

Approaching the dreadnaught without being shot—that was an entirely different animal. Boarding it, blowing it up and escaping with a hijacked corvette was certainly without precedent. Only — to what strange new skills did she owe her success?

There had to be some clue in her past, but without returning to the Duchy, she couldn't do anything about it. What she could do was to check the *cargo* the marine infantry should have welcomed aboard the dreadnaught. She prepared herself for welcoming some Very Important People who'd hopefully relieve her of the heavy burden of responsibility.

Syreen walked down the short corridor and checked the doors on both sides one by one. Right behind the cockpit lay the airlock, and opposite, a room for evac gear.

Next came a galley with many lockers, appliances and a table with two benches, a bathroom, a small passenger compartment with six empty seats in three rows of two, and a cabin with one bunk and a tiny desk, with all walls and furniture designed in at least fifty shades of gray. According to the symbol at the door, the cabin was the pilot's private room. Hers, for now.

She considered taking a comfort stop, but decided to check the cargo compartment at the end of the corridor first. Whoever accompanied her on this crazy journey probably had more urgent needs, and it wouldn't be good to anger her future superiors.

She made a point of checking her uniform. Skirmisher pilots were used to nudity on duty, so she had to recall the drill step by step, just to be sure.

When she felt ready, she took a deep breath, then pushed the door release.

PART TWO—COMING DOWN

CHAPTER FOURTEEN

Earlier that same day, down on the planet . . .

Herman's morning was brutally interrupted threefold—by a priority message in the platoon's commset, by the sudden wail of the barracks alarm, and by the orange-red light trails at the horizon that were soon followed by angry roars.

Those were not quite as angry as the sergeant's calls as he drove his unit forward to its mounts, even though his unit didn't really need his orders. Battle gear, power pack, combat bag, helmet, combocharger, check your partner, all green.

"Mount!"

Yes, sure, that had been practiced often enough, everyone knew his place. Nevertheless, Herman's skimmer was the last to depart. Stephan had taken the opposite seat, between Elmo and Andrea, and grinned at Herman.

Their captain was grinning, too, sitting on the forward hood. The fanned-out spark fountains behind him had become regular forked patterns—occasionally, the anti-air tracers tore gaps into the deadly symmetry above the city.

The captain now cocked his head, placed one hand over his commset and closed his eyes. He nodded several times, accompanied by short verbal acknowledgments, and finally gazed at his team again. This time, there was no grin. The officer looked dead serious.

"Okay, folks. You already found out that this is no drill. The Duchy is under attack by a hostile fleet. While the Fleet jockeys will defend us in space, it's our job to defeat the forces deployed planetside. Here's what we're gonna do . . ."

Herman didn't need Stephan's rolling eyes to understand they were fucked. The enemy had already passed Fleet's defenses and was dropping his forces more or less unmolested — which meant that there was no Fleet worth mentioning anymore. If their enemy was strong enough to catch the Duchy's fleet with their pants down — even though Herman had heard Fleet pilots didn't wear pants anyway — the little resistance their own planetary forces could offer would be wiped away as well.

Herman didn't mind losing a war, although he had felt pride in being a soldier so far — the girls liked his pretty dark-green uniform that went so nicely with his dark hair, with the awards for marksmanship, good conduct and brown-nosing — but he'd mind losing his life for such impossible odds. He knew Stephan felt the same. He didn't often agree with his senior comrade Stephan, but in this regard, they knew what to expect from each other.

" . . . so once the skimmer stops, ya get out, find cover an' giv'em bugs a hot welcome, do ya?"

"Ooh-yay!" the team roared.

Chapter Fifteen

The following cycle was a nightmare. In the beginning, Herman's infantry unit quickly advanced toward the skyport, shattering the enemy's advance party by sheer numbers, but with the first hostile reinforcements, the tables turned. Meanwhile they knew they weren't facing bug-eyed monsters but humans. Not that it mattered.

Only due to their better knowledge of the area — of sewer ducts, maintenance backdoors, and fire escape tunnels — could they survive and withdraw, now commanded by a green lieutenant and an older sergeant who at least managed to keep their shrinking team together. Still, they scored a few hits and added to the enemy's death toll, but they'd soon reach what their instructors had called the *critical number* — the headcount from which they'd no longer be able to give each other cover while continuing their withdrawal.

Stephan gave Herman a nudge when they passed a large flat commercial center, then mouthed *energy bypass* soundlessly.

Herman nodded. Of course, entering an energy duct was definite suicide while it was hot — but as the skyport's power plant was a black ruin now, the energy bypass held no more power. The duct could offer their team a safe escape.

While Herman considered drawing the sergeant's attention to Stephan's idea and Stephan was already fiddling with the maintenance door lock, the sergeant lost his head.

Or, put differently, his head evaporated in a strong pulse beam.

The next few pulses made quick work of Herman's unit, and when Stephan disappeared through the door into a dark shaft, Herman didn't hesitate to jump after him as fast as he could. The ground he had kneeled on a moment before melted away in another beam from a stingship's pulse cannon.

He stumbled across a ledge and barely managed to get hold of the topmost rung of a very primitive ladder. His knee gear bumped against lower rungs, and the clang of metal against metal echoed down a deep shaft.

"Herman?" That was Stephan's voice, echoing from below.

"Yep."

"Come down. Not long and they'll dig everything up around here."

"On my way." Herman wouldn't discuss priorities now, not even his first — getting a safe hold for all four limbs. He could do that without Stephan's snarky comments.

Soon he reached the bottom of the ladder.

"No light?" he asked.

"No." Instead, Stephan reached for Herman's visor and activated night-vision mode. "Okay?"

"Okay." Herman felt a bit foolish.

They walked on and soon reached another door. Herman's visor only unveiled the contours of some signs, but he could imagine all sorts of warnings imprinted on them. He didn't really care.

"What do you think, Stephan? What will happen when we reach the exit?"

"We'll be shot," his comrade dryly replied. "No, honestly, I have no clue. I only know that we won't change the outcome of this war. It's only about dying now — or later. I prefer later, and you?"

"The same," Herman said. "That's why I'm dropping my gear now. There's no point in carrying all that stuff around if you don't want to fight, or what do you think?"

"You may have a point there."

Herman watched Stephan's silhouette dropping the heavy battle gear, and then he copied his comrade.

CHAPTER SIXTEEN

A constant itch in his neck accompanied Herman's progress through the energy bypass. Should anyone activate the duct for any reason, they'd be instantly electrocuted. They'd probably not even have time to notice, but that thought didn't help him.

Stephan didn't appear to be worried. He ambled on as if he'd shed his entire old life together with their gear — of which they'd only kept their visors and the combat bag with their personal belongings — and would look forward to a bright future, at least as bright as Stephan's blond hair.

"Don't think I'm reckless," Stephan said, as if he'd guessed Herman's thoughts. "Technically, we're deserters since we left our guns behind. One might claim it a safety precaution — you never know what happens if you bring guns or power packs to this place — but I wouldn't expect our superiors to be open to such subtleties. Our only hope is to remain out of sight until the invaders have settled in."

"And thereafter?"

"We're just two more civilians trying to adapt to the new situation. Maybe the invaders will eventually hire locals for garrison duty."

Herman felt a bit irritated about the ease with which Stephan was willing to shift his loyalty, but had to admit that his own loyalty belonged to survival, too.

Act honestly, fight bravely, die in honor — that wasn't what he had joined army for. Oh, perhaps the first part, nothing wrong with honesty as long as it wouldn't imply marriage. He had never explicitly promised it, and no one could blame him for unvoiced expectations, right? Whereas that little ginger girl, back when he was a freshman . . .

"What are you dreaming of?" Stephan's voice interrupted him. "Gimme a hand with that hatch. It's stuck somehow."

Indeed they had reached another maintenance door. Stephan crouched on his knees and leaned forward. Herman reached over his teammate and put his hands on the door, strangely aware of the fact that his crotch now was quite close to Stephan's head.

"On three. One, two, three."

They pushed together. The door gave way a little, then something clattered on the other side, and then they could push it open far enough to slip through.

Cleaning equipment was scattered across the floor. A cart prevented the door from opening fully. Herman didn't care, but then his gaze followed Stephan's toward the tools. Would those provide a better cover story?

The opposite door opened with ease. Herman first saw the muzzle of an enemy rifle, then the uniform, and with raising his arms he gave Stephan a nudge.

CHAPTER SEVENTEEN

There was no way to pretend innocence, not with their visors still covering their faces. They were motioned outside with unmistakable gestures, where someone took their visors and combat bags away. Next, another soldier applied manacles, exchanged few words with someone of seemingly higher rank, and then pointed at the open door to the empty cargo compartment of some kind of light-armored skimmer.

Stephan shrugged and climbed inside, where he then dropped into a corner and leaned against the hull. Herman followed, but just then, he saw someone handing their combat bags to the driver.

Stephan drew one finger across his lips. *No talking.*

Herman nodded, leaned back and closed his eyes. He tried to remember the little redhead — where not only her head had been ginger — and smiled absently.

He sensed the skimmer moving for a while, then for another while, then slowly advancing with many twists and turns, and the next stop seemed to last for more than a quartercycle.

The opening cargo door was no big surprise. Had they reached their destination, some kind of makeshift headquarters?

The first glance outside unveiled some kind of makeshift chaos — skimmers, grav-lifters, cargo containers, cargo sleds, troops in different stages of disorganization, and in the background the bulky shapes of freight shuttles. Next, he spotted the familiar shape of the skyport portmaster's tower, and then the muzzles of two rifles signaling them to exit the skimmer.

When he followed the order and turned left as indicated, the slender, spindle-like hull of a small spaceship with an open door was the only obvious destination, so he headed for the ramp.

One of their guards said something, and the other laughed. For one moment, Herman considered escape. Or perhaps, if he distracted their guards, Stephan could make something of the situation? Before he could make up his mind, he had reached the spaceship's hatch. A brisk young officer with a handgun pointed to a door at the end of a very short corridor. When he passed through, he found himself in another cargo compartment, only dimly lit and stuffed with small boxes. There was little room to sit down, and with Stephan following him, they had to shuffle around before they both found a somewhat acceptable position.

Herman only briefly glanced at his comrade. Stephan shook his head. This was still no place to talk.

His throat felt dry and sore anyway, but perhaps he should be happy not to have anything to drink, as the enemy didn't seem inclined to offer them the luxury of a bathroom soon. Perhaps this was part of some insidious torture?

One of the boxes he was leaning to felt rather light. He took it and shook it. Empty?

There was a lock, a bolt and a lid. He opened it and found his suspicion proven right—empty.

Herman rose, turned away from Stephan and opened his fly. He quickly relieved himself, and then arranged his clothes again, before holding the container out to Stephan.

Stephan nodded, rose, and then took the box. While Herman sat down again, Stephan took his own cock out. He didn't bother to turn away or hide his erection, but smiled at Herman encouragingly.

Herman only shrugged and closed his eyes to return to a more pleasant dreamscape.

Chapter Eighteen

"Ah!"

When Herman looked up, the first thing he saw was Stephan's hard-on, and the second was the big white load that shot into the small box. Stephan squeezed his shaft twice to bring more of his semen out, and then closed the box and put it down.

He made a point of very slowly packing his manhood away.

Herman didn't care. In his current situation, he had worse things to worry about than the advances of a gay fellow prisoner, and he didn't want to worry.

He only wanted . . . in fact, he didn't know what he wanted, only that being imprisoned wasn't it. A tight pussy, perhaps, or some meaningful task—heck, even fighting and risking his own life for some esoteric target was better than this! Wasting his life away in prison with no prospect of ever seeing his home planet again wasn't what he had envisaged for himself when following Stephan's initial idea.

Well, he didn't blame Stephan for it—being hit by a pulse cannon would not have been the better option.

Next, he felt the small ship move.

Stephan quickly sat down. Motion compensators were good but never perfect, so if you couldn't buckle up, you'd better find some other stable position.

Their ride turned out rather smooth, but they had to find another box eventually. Herman again turned away for his own relief, but this time did not close his eyes when Stephan once more masturbated.

Who knows how long we have to stay together? I better stay on his good side before I find his cock in my ass some night.

"Are you ashamed of your dong?" Stephan asked. "I won't bite it off, you know?"

Herman didn't know what to say. What about keeping quiet? But their cocks probably were no matter of secrecy.

Stephan went on, "Too small?"

"Certainly not as big as yours."

"I've heard that before."

"You like to show it around, do you?"

"Yeah, you could say I'm quite proud of it. Showing off turns me on."

"Even with — uh, well . . ."

"With straight people around? Sure. What about you? Like to parade your boner for the girls?"

"Parade? Uh."

"Come on. You're not the type of guy who switches the lights off first, slips under the sheets and then unpacks your tool, are you? Give 'em girls something to look at, do you?"

Herman felt his cheeks warming up.

"Every wet pussy wants to see a proud hard-on, I tell you. Do you know how often I had to disappoint the girls? Not interested, I told them where they had already spread for me."

"But you let them spread first?"

"Yeah, sure. Not for me — to show them what sluts they are. Army sluts, that's what I'm talking about, not nice civil girls. Army. Always hot, always willing, always eager for cock — any cock, but hard to stop once they see a tool like mine."

"Though you turned them all down."

"Yes — oh, I made an exception once."

"How that?"

"Oh, it was a week before the final camp, you know? And

someone had given me a hint that the Colonel's daughter was among the recruits. Well, we had gone through the usual routine — her dropping her clothes, watching my boner, spreading her legs, trembling in anticipation, her wetness already soaking the maintenance hall floor, when I told her I was gay. She only smiled and said, *I know, but if you don't fuck me right here and now, my dad will have your balls for breakfast. I can't,* I said, and she said, *bet you can.* She turned around on the container — it was a high-protection box for tactical nuclear warheads, only empty at that time, I had checked that — and showed me her ass. *I know you can fuck ass,* she said, *mine's not that different. You only need lube, she said, and the maintenance shaft for that is right below, so you just get your tool sufficiently lubed and then you can fuck my ass.* I already had an idea what she meant but I asked anyway, *what's sufficiently lubed?* And she said, *that's when I stop making noises.* Okay, and that was the first time I put my cock inside a pussy."

"How did it feel for you?" Herman felt a strange fascination for Stephan's story.

"Awkward. Oh, okay, I couldn't ignore the fact that this part of her anatomy was made to receive a tool like mine, especially the way she leaned forward. Combined with the way she pinched her muscles down there, and the noises she made each time I pushed forward, and all the time only looking at her ass and imagining entering it, I somehow managed to maintain my erection and get her off — no embarrassing sloppy moment, you know?"

"And then you collected your reward?"

"I must admit I had considered turning away and leaving anyway, but she must have guessed my thoughts. *Don't you dare,* she said, *and now put it in before it's dried, and don't you pull it out before you shot your load. I want my ass filled with your juice, she said, and I'll come again when you do* — which she did in the end. Not many of my friends do, so yeah, I think you can call it a reward." Stephan waved at Herman's fly. "Did my story turn you on? Come, show me what you've got. Now that I proverbially let my pants down for you, I deserve a reward, don't you think?"

Herman didn't think of it as a reward, but the story had indeed aroused him, and now his cock demanded room to grow.

CHAPTER NINETEEN

Herman was torn out of his musings by a harrumph. "We're there," Stephan noticed, "wherever that is."

Indeed, their ship's movements had stopped and the distant humming ceased. He checked his fly—closed—and the position of the abused boxes—locked and safely stowed away—and flexed his muscles, so that they wouldn't fail him when he had to get up.

Which didn't happen.

They were silently waiting for nearly a quartercycle for anybody to collect them or at least ask about their needs, but instead, the humming recommenced.

Next, they sensed a lift, and then, before the motion compensators could kick in, a powerful shift forward.

"Whoa!" Stephan cried out. "What's that bastard doing now?"

The humming became a howling—the pilot seemed to be squeezing every erg from the plants and funneling them into the engines, where both had to be located right behind the aft bulkhead.

"Whatever he's doing, he's in a hurry," Herman observed. "Which means he won't come to look after us soon."

"Yeah. So what?"

"I need another empty container."

"Oh." Stephan reached behind. "Take this one."

"Thanks." Herman rose, made sure he could rest his back against a pile of containers, and opened both box and fly. This time, he didn't bother to turn away for peeing.

The howling faded and gave way to a different kind of vibration that made the hairs on Herman's neck stand up.

"We're doing a hyperjump," he told Stephan. "Get ready."

"Ready? Hyperjump? How?"

"Just make sure you don't have to cough within the next few centicycles, and you'll be fine."

Herman's vision blurred, twisted, and then he could focus on his teammate again. "You're okay?"

"Ugh, yes, that was it?"

"That was it. A smooth one, by the way. We're in a different system now."

"Which?"

Herman rolled his eyes and waved his arms. "Have a look for yourself. What does it look like? We're in the box system, approaching box city on box planet. Welcome to the box folk."

"Ah. I see. Yes, I should have recognized that myself."

They smiled at each other, then burst into laughter. After a while they calmed down.

"How come you recognize a hyperjump? Have you done one before?" Stephan asked.

"Several. Two out, three back in. My parents took me along to Kyris once when I was twelve."

"Rich parents?"

"Merchants."

"Interstellar merchants?"

"Yup."

"So you're a rich brat. Why army?"

"I'm the third son. Da wouldn't allow the company to be split up, so Angus will get it all. Myron doesn't mind playing the second voice, as long as he can spend some time for his music. I was the little one. *You must learn the business from the bottom,* they told me—which Angus never had to do. *You're family, you must be an example, you must work harder,* they told me. I must work hardest, that was—two cycles for sleep, eight cycles for the business, and always the ugliest, dirtiest, nastiest jobs. I tried my best—and a few tencycles later, I eavesdropped on Da talking to Angus, saying I'd never make it. Not worth the ransom if a pirate once gets him, he said. That tencycle, I decided I'd rather learn how to handle a gun than how to clean the pulse cannon barrels."

"Which you did anyway."

"Yeah, literally. I didn't know that you can indeed clean pulse cannon barrels—I mean, they can't get dirty, can they?"

"If you ask me, no. If you ask a drill sergeant, they're created dirty and will always be dirty except for the few millicycles after a thorough cleaning—such a one as only the sarge's favorite brown-nose can achieve eventually."

"Yes, probably."

"But you said you did five jumps—on one journey?"

"Yes. Two out, three back in. It's how jumps work—you rarely can reach the destination in one. You can't jump across black stars and neutron stars, you know? So you make a detour—jump to a star you can see, and from where you can see the destination, and then you're fine. Two jumps are the standard—for longer journeys, you might need more. Sometimes, when the next system is close, you can do it in one. That's what we did on the return leg—from Kyris to Stratholme, and from there back to the Duchy."

"But you didn't stop at Stratholme, I reckon?"

"Nah. That's a mining colony. Nothing worth going there, unless you're a miner. However, it's even less worth going just there. If you can do it en route to another destination, you only need one extra jump."

"I understand." Stephan nodded at the pile of boxes. "Give me another. If we're doing another jump soon, I'd rather be prepared."

"Oh, I don't think we'll jump again soon. We'll probably

recharge first."

"Which means we'll probably die of thirst before we reach our destination?"

"You could put it that way, yes."

That was the moment the door hissed. Herman jerked aside, and then they watched the door slide away. Behind it, they saw a pretty female face, black hair, green eyes, and an unmistakably female body wrapped in the gray of an enemy uniform—with a Duchy Fleet badge on her nicely curved chest.

PART THREE—COMING TOGETHER

CHAPTER TWENTY

Syreen found two startled faces staring at her from inside the cargo compartment. One belonged to a pretty, somewhat boyish young male with black stubbly hair, the other to a handsome blond guy with tempting wrinkles around his eyes. Both wore green Duchy uniforms.

The blond prisoner overcame their mutual surprise first.

"Atten-hut!" he called out, jumped up and saluted—no easy feat with manacled hands.

The other, more boyish one, automatically went into attention and tried to salute, too.

The first one continued, "Private First Class Stephan Smith and Private First Class Herman Doeken, Fourth Battalion, Second Company, at your service, Sir!"

Dirtbugs.

Syreen cursed her fate. She had expected officers, at least of captain's rank, but more likely flag officers, to be the Association's oh-so-important prisoners. Hadn't they been able to capture officers yet? Or were these two hiding their officer's ranks to fool the enemy?

Syreen wasn't the enemy, and the way these two were looking at her, they had already recognized that. Especially the boy—Herman—who was making puppy eyes at her. *Well, there are formalities to observe.*

She returned the salute. "Lieutenant Syreen, Duchy Fleet, Skirmisher Silver Wing, *Raydancer's* pilot and Fleet Commander in Charge. At ease, guys."

Both took their arms down.

Herman found his tongue first. "Fleet Commander in Charge? That means, you're . . ."

"I'm the highest-ranking survivor, yes."

"Pardon, Sir. I didn't want to doubt your legitimation."

"Or qualification?" She smirked. "Nobody asked me if I wanted that job. But Fleet won't give up, right? And I wanted to survive, so I had to do something."

"Which was . . . Pardon, Sir."

"Oh, I think I should fill you in, as I guess we'll be spending some more time together. But maybe I'll give you a chance to visit the bathroom and the galley first, okay?"

She could watch the conflict between need and curiosity in their faces while she undid their manacles—a key token had conveniently been placed right next to the cargo hatch, so that any replacement crew wouldn't have to search for it.

"We'll be charging for a few cycles anyway, and I need refreshments now, too. It's been a hot ride. Come along."

When she turned away, the two soldiers followed her.

"Where are we right now?" the second one—Stephan, he'd called himself—asked. "Herman said something about a jump."

"He's right, we jumped once. The system's called Carix Alpha. No planets, only a powerful sun. Good place to recharge . . . well, at least that's what the Books say."

She opened the bathroom door and ambled on to the galley. "Hot forwine, anyone?"

To her surprise, both men ignored the bathroom and followed her into the small room. Both smelled like sweat, and on Stephan she also noticed the aroma of sperm—had he jerked off on the trip?

She took their silence as approval and poured three of the hot, red drinks with the right amount of alcohol to be allowed on duty.

"Here. Excuse me for a brief moment, and then we'll exchange our stories."

CHAPTER TWENTY-ONE

Herman watched the lieutenant disappear to the bathroom and smiled at Stephan over the rim of his mug. "Hot."

"Indeed," his teammate agreed. "Good looking by all standards. But as our commanding officer, she's off limits for you."

"Oh, I know. Not in my dreams, though."

"I don't think she's the dreamer type. Somehow she managed to steal this enemy ship—from what little we noticed, it must have happened off-planet, which can only mean inside a hangar, and that means a very big starship. She then escaped that very big starship without being shot, and I have no clue how one could do that."

"It blew up," the lieutenant explained, as she returned from the bathroom and reached for her own mug.

"And why would such a ship blow up?"

"'Cause someone sabotaged the dreadnaught's main power plant?" The officer's smile wasn't reassuring at all.

Stephan gave Herman a warning glance. "You had help, then? Someone who stayed behind and gave his life for our escape?"

"No, I was all alone. I told you, I'm a skirmisher pilot—the last of Fleet. There's no second seat in a skirmisher."

Stephan frowned. "You mean you reached the dreadnaught in a skirmisher?"

"Actually, I left the skirmisher before reaching the enemy. I approached it in my evac suit while my spacecraft was shot."

60

Syreen saw the disbelief in the men's eyes. No wonder. It was still hard to believe even for herself.

"Let me start from scratch. There were no warning signs of this. We had been warned to prepare for a potential pirate raid, and our superiors didn't tell us about the reasons behind it, but there's been no declaration of war as far as I know, no ultimatum—we were alarmed, got our birds and went off, and were at battle, just like that. We skirmishers had to clear the way for Fleet's destroyers, and we managed to get them one clean shot on an enemy dreadnaught."

"Dreadnaughts are the real big ships, right?" Herman asked.

"Right. Dreadnaughts and battle cruisers are largest, next come cruisers, then destroyers and frigates and corvettes—like this one—and last the single-crew ships, skirmishers and stingships. The enemy came with five dreadnaughts, a score of cruisers, plus stingships and a few corvettes. Well, the outcome was mostly clear—we lost all our ships and bases and the enemy lost a few stingships and two dreadnaughts."

"And a stolen corvette," Herman added, earning a smile from his superior.

"Indeed. But that came later. Once our destroyers were gone, the enemy stingships left their menace—that is, our skirmishers—behind as cruiser exercise targets and retreated down into the planetary atmosphere, where we couldn't follow. Only I managed to get away, and as there were no bases left, I knew I had to board an enemy ship."

"Skirmishers can't jump?" Stephan interrupted.

"No. That's why I headed for a dreadnaught. Initially I planned to hide aboard and travel with them once they'd left, but that didn't feel promising. So if I wanted to leave, I needed a ship that I could fly alone. Like this."

"And how did you achieve that?"

"Well, let's say I cheated a bit." Syreen wouldn't tell them about herself. "Which you can't give away if you don't know about it."

"Oh."

"Now tell me how you managed to be the only prisoners the enemy considered worth taking skyward?"

Chapter Twenty-two

"Frankly, we have no clue what they wanted from us," Stephan concluded his carefully edited report. "They didn't talk much, and the little we heard wasn't understandable."

"They speak a different kind of Common," Syreen advised him. "After a while, you recognize some words—however, that would require more talking than you were granted. So we can only guess—perhaps by using secret passageways, you appeared like spies? Perhaps they wanted to learn more about similar ducts? But it doesn't matter, as they haven't told us yet why they came to the Duchy in the first place. Or did you find a clue on that?"

"No." Stephan shook his head. "What are your plans—if I may ask?"

"You may." Syreen shrugged. "We're in this together, after all. I have no plans. I had an idea of gathering reinforcements—well, allies—and then taking up the fight again."

"Really?"

"Don't assume I don't know how bad our odds are against a hostile force of that strength. But Fleet doesn't give up, and I'm what's left of Fleet. I simply refuse to give up myself."

Stephan paused and watched the young officer's face. "If you put it that way—you don't look suicidal. Pardon, Sir. I'm in."

"You're welcome."

"Don't get me wrong—you're our commanding officer aboard, and I don't expect to see any army brass soon. I will follow your orders. By saying *I'm in*, I mean I support your cause any way I can."

"Thank you. You're right, I'm your commanding officer and I will not accept any insubordination or neglecting of duties—but I'm well aware of the fact that I'm also responsible for you. Saying that, I spotted two combat bags in the passenger compartment. Yours?"

"Probably. Thank you."

Her glance seemed to nail him down. "You two may adjust the furniture there to your liking. Once you've finished your forwine, I propose you both take a shower and a shave. I'll prepare dinner—or what *Raydancer* has to offer in exchange—and then we can continue our conversation."

He eyed his mug hopefully—empty—and felt dismissed by her. So he placed the mug down on the cleaner and left. Herman followed him.

Herman had left most of the talking to his teammate for two reasons. Firstly, Stephan was the mastermind behind their adventure—he no longer regarded it as desertion—and secondly, he had only had eyes for their host. *What a woman! And what an attitude—fighting a dreadnaught single-handedly. This is a woman worth following.*

Herman hadn't voiced it, as Stephan had, but he was in, too.

He felt so happy that he didn't care when Stephan watched him undressing and thereafter squeezed into the small bathroom with him. The refresher could handle both their uniforms together, and while Stephan took a shower, Herman started shaving before the mirror.

Both men sported a hard-on for different reasons, but they smiled at each other when they swapped positions.

When Herman finished his shower, Stephan had already returned to their passenger compartment. Herman put his uniform on, grabbed his bag and Stephan's uniform, and followed his teammate.

CHAPTER TWENTY-THREE

Syreen pretended not to notice the remarkable cock Stephan paraded across the corridor from bathroom to passenger compartment. On a ship as small as this, there was limited room for privacy, and as skirmisher pilot she was used to nudity anyway. *It's your problem to get that tool stowed away in your uniform.*

What a strange couple she had picked up there—she wasn't entirely sure what to make of them, but at least Stephan's commitment had felt sincere.

She couldn't figure out Herman yet. He seemed to follow in Stephan's wake but he was not attached—in contrast to the occasional glances Stephan gave him. Instead, he reacted to her presence like most males she had met so far, only he didn't seem as ready to show off as Stephan.

In any case, both men were off limits for her. She had no experience as *commanding* officer at all, and she'd need some respect to guide them. Considering that, was it okay to prepare their meals instead of letting them do the routine work?

This time, she decided. This time, it was a compensation for the hardships they'd had to endure before she could release them. From now on, she'd do what an officer was supposed to do in a situation like this—only a situation like this wasn't covered by the Books. *I mustn't let them get away with disrespect. But I won't gain their respect by insisting on formalities. How do I find a balance? Well—as long as they behave, I don't have to act. We're in this together, and I need a team, not brainless followers.*

While the two were getting dressed, she had to check her

instruments. It wasn't advisable to leave the bridge alone for too long and thus neglect her own primary duties.

Herman was the first to show up in the galley. He had only tossed Stephan the uniform and dropped his bag, and now he was alone and their meal almost ready.

The lieutenant hadn't set the table yet. He briefly rummaged in the lockers and found all he needed—placemats, cutlery, water jug and glasses, condiments. When Stephan and Syreen entered and their faces both lit up, he felt rewarded.

"Thank you, Herman," the officer said and waited until they had all taken a seat. "Once we're settled in here, I wanted to talk about sharing the chores, but it seems that's not necessary."

"You must do the flying, and we can't help you there," he observed. "That leaves the housekeeping for us, doesn't it?"

"Indeed, I wanted to propose something along that line. However, I'll take care of my own stuff. You're soldiers, not servants."

"You're the boss," Herman summarized.

After that statement, they enjoyed their frugal meal in silence.

When they had finished, Stephan started to clean the table.

Herman and Syreen watched each other. Finally he asked, "You said you're looking for support—reinforcements or allies. Where?"

She shrugged. "Frankly, I have no clue. When I saw the marine soldiers marching up to welcome this ship, I expected to find some officers or politicians—superiors who'd tell me what to do, where to go. Instead, I got you."

"Sorry for that."

"Aw, not your problem. The fact remains that I've never

been anywhere outside the Duchy. So I don't know where to go."

Her gloomy gaze hurt Herman. He felt the urge to take her hand, but fought it back. "I've been out once, with my parents. I'm from a family of interstellar merchants. My family has an outpost on Kyris, and if I remember right, the Duchy has an ambassador there. I don't know much about that place, but it's no pirate's nest and probably not the worst cesspool for scum on this side of the galaxy, otherwise we wouldn't do business there. It's only two jumps from the Duchy."

Syreen's face lit up, but not for long.

"It can be any number of jumps from this place, and I won't go back to the Duchy. The names and codes in the Association's database differ from ours. I don't know if we'll find a *Kyris* there."

"If not, we can look for Stratholme. It's a mining colony and only one jump from Kyris."

"That would give us a clue. One-jump routes are rare. I will have a look in the library."

"Do you have any specific instructions for us?"

"Yes. Get acquainted with the ship, provide me with an inventory, and then try to make sense of *Raydancer's* records."

Herman felt scrutinized.

"I guess you might have noticed that inventory records don't always match reality in the Duchy's army — I can assure you Fleet is no different. That's why I don't expect any better from the Association. Meanwhile, I must familiarize myself with the ship's controls. However, both tasks are essential — our lives may depend on them. Understood?"

"Yes, Sir!"

"Thank you, Herman."

CHAPTER TWENTY-FOUR

The library wasn't difficult to understand. Syreen needed a little more than two cycles to find Kyris — under a similar name, only in Common — and an unnamed nearby system marked as *potentially suitable for mining*. Data on this star had to be at least a megacycle old.

The computer had already identified Carix Alpha, but only as a number. Now that Syreen had starting and ending points, she only needed a viable course. The direct route wouldn't work, her guts told her when she examined the three-dimensional display in the small navsphere, and the computer agreed. Too many obstacles too close to the jump vector.

Computers could eventually find a solution — by trying almost every combination of two, three or more jumps across stars within the smallest possible sphere around the direct vector. There were a few optimizations to this brute-force approach, but as her navigation instructor had put it, no pile of silicon could outsmart a human brain.

A quick look into the navsphere showed her three easy-to-navigate corridors from Carix Alpha in the general direction of Kyris. She quickly discarded two of them and zoomed in on the third. The pivot system was obvious, with a strong star and no planets. *Looks like a highway.*

The computer confirmed her choice — two easy jumps across an infrequently used stopover system.

Back to school. She had to learn every symbol and every function before she'd jump as much as a finger out of this system, and she had yet to change the identification to Fleet.

Stephan looked up when the young officer entered the galley and paused his counting. "Sir?"

"I know where to go, and recharging is done. How far did you get?"

"Herman's checking the cargo. I'm almost through with the galley provisions — for the three of us, sufficient for a few weeks, I'd say."

"Okay. I'll take a nap now. Once you're done with the galley, you and Herman should get some rest, too. We should be fit when we're doing the jump."

"You're expecting trouble, Sir?"

"We've only just left some unexpected trouble behind."

"That's a good point."

The woman smiled. "Our skirmisher wings had been training to fight pirate raids. I doubt any pirate will dare to raid the Duchy right now. They'll be somewhere else. I won't make assumptions on where that is, but be prepared."

"What if we encounter a pirate?"

"Depends, but any pirate would be well advised to steer clear of a corvette. A commercial vehicle with a few poorly adjusted laser guns is no match for us."

"If you say so — sorry, Sir. I didn't want to imply — "

"Yes, you did." She smirked. "You're right. I'm nothing but a young lieutenant who never flew anything larger than a skirmisher, now handling an entirely unfamiliar enemy prize, and worse, such a small one. But a pirate wouldn't know that I'm unfamiliar with this vessel yet, and I can assure you that I feel quite able to apply my skirmisher practice — with more than twenty recorded kills in the last battle alone — to this very agile corvette, which in fact was built for escort purposes."

"So it is armed?"

"Of course. Shields and lasers and a medium pulse cannon.

I can always enforce the respect we deserve."

He grinned. "Okay. You made me feel much better about it. Thank you, Sir."

"You're welcome. Please don't stop asking—unless we're engaged in battle—as I might indeed overlook something. I'll take any assistance I can get."

"As long as you have the last say. Sir."

"Exactly."

Stephan nodded, and she left.

CHAPTER TWENTY-FIVE

Syreen checked her programming for the third time. She could see no flaw, and the computer had confirmed the same. *Raydancer* had already reached the necessary 0.5 c, so what was she waiting for?

On her first jump, she had been in a hurry, with little time to think. She had jumped to a known target, at least known to her instructors. She had jumped along a known route. She had been sure that her calculations were correct because her instructors had told her so. She had trusted herself.

For the upcoming jump, she had benefited from all the time in the world to prepare and check it. She'd jump to a known target, at least known to the navigation library. She could be sure her calculations were correct because the computer had told her so three times. She could trust herself. However, she'd jump along a route that probably had never been tested before.

Which wouldn't change, regardless of how much time she spent stalling.

She focused on the intercom symbol.

"Crew, prepare for jump in five."

Next, she initiated the jump sequence. Now she could only lean back and wait for the characteristic vibration of the ship erecting its jump field.

The counter changed to zero, and her vision blurred.

Stephan shook his head. "I don't know if I ever get used to

that."

"It's just a minor inconvenience," Herman objected. "After we did our first jump, our skipper told us that in the past, travelers felt like they'd been turned inside out—and it was common to eat backward."

"Okay, but that doesn't mean I must love it."

"No . . ."

"Leave it. I feel inconvenienced, and I'll get over it soon. Next time, I'll complain again, and that will be another inconvenience to you, nothing more. Okay?"

His teammate shrugged. "Okay. In any case, she took us through this jump nicely."

Stephan leaned over. With three rows of two seats, they had turned the second row around to form two comfortable bunks and left the first row as seats, where they had stayed through the jump. "She's the only survivor of a fierce battle in space, and not because she chickened out. She survived because she's good. So I expected nothing less."

"You're a fan."

Herman's remark sounded a little bit biting, but Stephan only grinned. "Yes, I am. I acknowledge good performance where I find it. This is a different brand of officer than the jerks we had. This is the kind you can follow, because she uses her own head before making decisions. That's why she's still alive—and why we're still alive and free."

"You're not about to change your—alignment?"

He shrugged. "She'd be worth considering, eh? But no—it just doesn't feel right for me. I'd like to call her my friend, though, not just my commanding officer." Stephan focused on his teammate's face. "I'd like to call *you* friend, my brother-in-arms."

Herman smiled, leaned forward and held out his hand. "That's okay with me, mate."

Stephan was a bit surprised about the ease with which

Herman accepted, but he took the offered hand and shook it. Should he leave it at that? No, better speak it out loud.

"You're all fine with me being gay?"

Herman didn't release his grip. "Yes, I'm fine. You're not pushy, so I don't care."

The screen mounted to the forward bulkhead came to life. At the same moment, they heard Syreen's voice.

"Folks, we got trouble ahead. I'll show you."

CHAPTER TWENTY-SIX

Syreen's screen showed the large bodies of two commercial ships close to each other — too close for her taste. Of course, in the unlikely case of distress, linking two ships offered easy access for the helpers, but the two ships' transponder signals didn't indicate any damage. They identified themselves as *Light of Mandalay* and *Hardigan's Hauler*.

While she had been able to pick up their signals upon reentry, her own lightspeed emissions would need some more centicycles to reach the cargo ships. Time she wouldn't waste.

Firstly, she needed a different angle for her approach, so she changed *Raydancer's* course. Next, she estimated the earliest time for a first call in either case, and then the best moment to change her vector again. If the supposed merchants took a little more time . . .

They did, and when the call came, Syreen was prepared. The merchant's Common was unfamiliar again, but she'd become used to understanding other dialects.

"Raydancer, *this is Captain Rutloff speaking. Whatever your business in this system is, I advise you to discharge your batteries and surrender your ship. In case you don't comply, the* Light of Mandalay's *crew will die a slow and instructional death. I expect your answer within five centicycles after receipt of my message.*"

Pirates. Syreen wasn't surprised, not even by the cynical proposal to surrender herself to the same mercy as the unlucky second ship's crew.

Taking hostages, blackmailing, cruelty, those were

powerful weapons in their hands, way more powerful than the laser cannons they deployed on their ships, even though those could cut dangerous holes into a merchant ship's hull.

Pirates were universally despised. Even the Association's Books contained strict rules on how to deal with them. Any merchant caught with unregistered laser cannons would face instant arrest and trial.

If you intercepted a pirate before he could capture his victim, everything was easy. If he didn't surrender or tried to shoot the victim, you just blew him away. But in a situation like this, the best you could do for the victims was to jump away before the pirate's blackmail arrived, leaving the pirate in fear, uncertainty and doubt about what would happen next. If he was unsettled enough, he might leave quickly, with or without the hostages, which either meant a merciful quick death or a minor chance for ransom later.

She had skipped her chance for jumping out. For one, because she wouldn't do that next jump without proper preparation. For two, because she indeed despised pirates and was in no mood to play by their rules.

So she rechecked her aim, sent a prayer to her Lady Luck and triggered her already heated and adjusted pulse cannon once, twice, a third time without even waiting for the result.

Hardigan's Hauler was hit midships, straight through its main power plant, then at the bridge close to the bow, and in the aft hyperdrive section. Her shots penetrated hull and bulkheads, aggregates and equipment, and any unlucky crew member in their path. This wreck would never again be a threat to anyone. Whether there might be survivors aboard didn't concern her.

"*Light of Mandalay*, this is *Raydancer*, Lieutenant Syreen of the Duchy Fleet speaking. The Duchy's standing policy is to eliminate the threat of piracy wherever it's encountered and protect the ships we escort. Please identify yourself again—

are you a merchant ship which requires our escort, with its original crew in charge and any pirates aboard under arrest? Or are you a pirate ship under pirate control, in which case you will share *Hardigan's Hauler's* fate? My pulse cannon is ready. I give you five centicycles after receipt of my message."

Herman and Stephan glanced at each other, then again stared at the image of the wrecked ship. Okay, their skipper didn't play by the Books, but they both hadn't expected such an outcome.

"That message couldn't be mistaken," Herman commented.

"Very straightforward," Stephan agreed. "What if the pirates had already taken prisoners?"

"They're probably dead now. That's what I meant. The message is clear. *We're here to shoot pirates, and anyone getting in our way is collateral damage we don't care about.* You see, they could still have threatened to kill the crew—but they never had the time for that *slow and instructional death.* That's what the lieutenant took out of the equation."

"Oh, okay. I didn't think that far yet." Stephan looked down. "Young as she is, she has her ways to gain respect, doesn't she?"

Herman didn't comment, as the sign of an incoming message flashed on their screen again.

The answer came earlier than Syreen expected.

"Raydancer, *this is Captain Kasai of the* Light of Mandalay. *The pirates aboard surrendered their weapons to my crew and are currently being escorted to a safe place. I'm very glad that you're here and I'm willing to negotiate the terms of escorting. Please advise on how to proceed—first of all, how we can transfer the prisoners.*"

"Captain Kasai, *Raydancer* is a corvette-class ship. I don't have the space for prisoners aboard. I must leave them to you to deal with. I will adapt my vector to yours and monitor your neighbor for any traces of power while you gain safe distance."

While she had to wait for the transmission delay, she programmed her deceleration and vector adaption maneuver.

"Captain Syreen, I do not understand. It was your ultimatum to the pirates that caused them to surrender. I assumed that you'd take care of them after promising them quarter."

Syreen didn't correct him about her rank.

"I did not promise the pirates quarter. I only promised not to blow up your ship if it's not pirate-seized. Common procedure in the Duchy is to put them to trial — which any licensed skipper may do — tell them what crimes they're accused of, hear witnesses — I'll gladly bear witness for their threat of killing hostages — present evidence and eventually announce their sentence, all diligently recorded for later reference. And then, of course depending on the sentence, space them without suit."

Again, she had to wait for the captain's response. The delay shrank with their distance.

"Captain Syreen, I thank you for this warning with regard to our forthcoming negotiations. I will very carefully observe your wording. For the records, I accept you leaving jurisdiction over the pirates to the damaged party. I will proceed as you proposed — and I don't doubt the outcome either. Evidence is overwhelming. By the way, I congratulate you on your precise shooting. I didn't know a pulse cannon could be reliably used over such distance."

Syreen smiled in relief. *In fact, neither did I.* The Books strongly advised against a use across more than a light second — the Duchy's Books as well as the Association's. However, Syreen's maneuvers upon reentry had given her a little data to work on — different positions for triangulation and calibration — and the time the pirates had needed to address her had given her time to stabilize her trajectory. *If you have enough time for aiming, you can hit almost anything,* her instructor once had told her. He had also told her that she'd face a court-martial if her shot went wrong, and that the Books would sentence her.

"Your ships were sitting ducks, Captain Kasai, and yet those were no easy shots. So I gladly accept your congratulations. In one regard, I must correct you though. My official rank is still lieutenant."

Pause.

"*Lieutenant Syreen, my apologies. I automatically assumed a higher rank with someone of your experience. This surely wasn't the first pirate you shot.*"

She raised her eyebrows. *That's a way to elicit information I won't fall for, even if I'm willing to feed you a few bits.*

"Again I must correct you, Captain Kasai. This was my first pirate, but I can assure you that this wasn't my first kill. Until now, I fought moving, heavily armed targets—targets that shot back."

Pause.

"*You faced open combat? I haven't heard of any incident for decades. So you could score before?*"

"All detailed information is strictly classified, but yes, I did."

Pause.

"*Well, thank you again, Lieutenant Syreen. You showed up in time. I have to prepare a trial now. We will negotiate later, if your time allows.*"

"I agree, Captain Kasai. I will use the time for recharging, as I had originally planned."

CHAPTER TWENTY-SEVEN

The *Light of Mandalay's* captain and crew only needed half a cycle for trying and sentencing the pirates—after that time, there was a sudden spill of bodies into the vacuum. Some were still waving their arms and writhing for moments, before the cold of space and the lack of air led to the expected result.

Syreen swallowed hard. She had never actually observed such an execution and now had to fight her nausea. She knew the rules on piracy, she knew this was common procedure across most spacefaring nations, and she had made that proposal herself, but that didn't make it any better. Now she knew what happened to a pilot whose ship was shot into a wreck and whose evac suit failed—what could easily happen to her, too, as they didn't wear evac suits aboard *Raydancer*—and she was sure she wouldn't be able to forget these images soon.

There was a knock at the cockpit door.

"Come in," she said.

Stephan entered and pointed at her screen. "Darn ugly sight, ain't it? But those bastards deserved it."

"Yes."

"I had an idea, Sir."

"Go ahead."

"Sir—let me start like this. I'm no choirboy. Since I joined the army, I've always struggled with regulations in some way. Nothing serious, nothing to get me kicked out or worse, but all kinds of stuff from not saluting a senior officer fast enough or brisk enough, untidy gear, misdemeanor of all flavors, to violations of rules during leave, mistreatment of civilians—who didn't complain, but their statements didn't count. There's one lesson I really learned. Those regulations are a truly nasty bastard. And if they are to me, what pitfalls must you, as Fleet Commander in Charge, face? You know, I was curious what rules we must observe with regard to you, to not get on your wrong side just by accident."

"Oh, don't worry. I wouldn't blame you for not knowing."

"Thank you, Sir. I checked, anyway, and found out that you, as Fleet officer, can indeed command army enlisted staff temporarily—as long as it takes—but army officers could never command any Fleet member. It's the same with Fleet marine infantry. When I spotted that part, I thought I should ask you whether you already checked your new privileges and authority, as well as duties and responsibilities, or overlooked that part so far? It might become a necessity before entering negotiations with this merchant, not to mention arriving at a foreign port."

Syreen looked at him. He seemed to be truly concerned, and he was right. She should already have checked what it meant to be Fleet Commander in Charge beyond running this little spaceship.

"Indeed, I missed that. Thank you, Stephan."

"Glad to help, Sir."

She smiled. "You just want to not be regarded as a pirate only because I fail, don't you? Don't worry. I will revisit the Books' respective sections and make sure I don't put my foot in mouth anytime soon."

The private understood that he was dismissed and left. Syreen produced her tac. What had she already done wrong? Was a Fleet Commander in Charge allowed to leave the system, even as a tactical withdrawal? Or should she have fought until death?

The most interesting part was the one he had quoted — did her temporary role indeed outrank all other Fleet and non-Fleet staff? And what were the *dos and don'ts* with regard to escorting a foreign merchant?

CHAPTER TWENTY-EIGHT

Syreen felt mentally worn out after reading the regulations, but at the same time much more confident in her current role. There were only few rules in the Books she had to worry about, as most others could be changed or paused by Fleet command, and those were rules she already knew. However, as guidance on how to act in her role or what others would expect from her, the Books were helpful. At least now she could consciously violate the rules.

The thought made her smile. This was a field she could really excel in.

Captain Kasai's call thus found her in good mood.

"Raydancer, *this is Captain Kasai of the* Light of Mandalay *again. May I bother you?"*

"*Light of Mandalay,* this is Lieutenant Syreen of the *Raydancer.* What can I do for you?"

"*Lieutenant, we will soon be ready to continue our journey, so I'd like to enter negotiations with you.*"

She grinned. *Kasai doesn't take long to get to the point. Ah, he probably lost quite some time here.*

"Sure, Captain. I'll gladly negotiate with you whatever you'd like to negotiate."

"*Great. Lieutenant, we need to settle the terms for your escort services.*"

It's much easier to talk without these delays. Syreen sat upright, even though her partner couldn't see her. "If you like, Captain. Before we start, let me clarify one topic, just for the records. You're not obliged to anything with regard to escort services. Should you decide to continue your journey without me, you're entirely free to do so. Should you decide to tag along and incidentally travel the same direction, you're free to do so. It is not the Duchy's policy to collect mandatory security fees. The only thing I need from you is a copy of your incident report and of the pirate trial's recording for my own log, and I would expect to receive that copy free of charge, in exchange for my previous assistance."

"You are very generous, Lieutenant. Of course I will see that you receive the requested reports and recordings immediately. Now — my company would be delighted to see me continuing on my route without additional expenses and without further delay. Out of responsibility for my crew, I'd prefer to take the opportunity and hire your service as a mitigation against further risks, as I don't know where the pirate's home base is. Moreover, you insinuated there are hostile activities in this part of the galaxy, so we can't be sure what to expect at our destination."

Yes, that's what I more or less expected, she mused. "Captain Kasai, I cannot grant you unconditional safe passage. I'm not entitled to enter hostilities with other space nations to protect trade foreign to the Duchy. Nor can I neglect my current mission to become your escort. What I can offer you is my assistance against further pirate attacks on my next leg to Kyris, including reasonable protection in case the pirates made that system their base." *Where the latter would mean a tough fight — but I wouldn't let any pirates get away with their crimes. Not with a pirate fleet raiding my home.*

After a pause, the captain replied, *"Kyris is my next destination, too. I understand your reservations. I accept the assistance you offer. What would be your fee?"*

"My fee? Oh — I'll get back to you in a moment."

She muted the external line and focused on the intercom symbol. "Herman, I need your advice in the cockpit. Can you spare a moment?"

Syreen stared at her screen, but it didn't come up with any useful information. She had to rely on her crew.

The private arrived only a centicycle later, knocked and opened the door at the same time, and leaned inside.

"Sir, how can I help you?"

"Herman, do you perchance have any clue what fees to charge for escort services?"

"What, escort services?" He stared at her chest.

She suppressed a grin. "If I offer our protection to this merchant on our way to Kyris."

"Oh." His face reddened. "Escort services, of course. The usual fee is calculated from cargo value and freight charges, which again depend on distance and risk assessment. Let me remember — we calculate twenty per cent of freight charges for risk mitigation, that is, either an escort or — uh — loss coverage."

"What does the latter mean?"

"That we could afford losing on average every fifth shipment, where escorts aren't available or not feasible."

Syreen wouldn't believe what she just heard and squinted. "So you accept that every fifth ship and crew are lost to pirates?"

"No, no — just the cargo. Not every pirate takes the crew, as far as I've heard. It's just — sometimes you can't get an escort, for whatever reasons. None available, wrong route, docked, whatever. The freight schedule is merciless, though."

"Okay — you mentioned cargo value, too?"

"I did. Well, basically every cargo has some value, otherwise it wouldn't be shipped offworld. However, most of those goods are valuable only because of specialization — basic nutrients, pharmaceutics, rare ores, machinery. Then there are the truly rare and exclusive goods. There's a surcharge on them, which is needed to cover taxes, customs and, of course, escort fees."

"And how much is that?"

"Sadly, that depends on the individual tax and customs regulations, and the escort fee is negotiated individually, too. It can be a multiple of the standard fee. For you, the only important detail is that those goods must be declared. The carrier must be able to present a valid export declaration upon request. You can ask for it."

"Thank you. This is indeed helpful — only I still don't even know the original freight charges and don't know how to calculate the share for the last leg to Kyris."

"All the information you need should be in the export declarations, route, freight charges, as well as cargo value and classification. If you're supposed to escort them, you're entitled to ask. He may be reluctant, though, as some merchants don't like to share this kind of information with strangers."

Syreen made a mental note of that. "Do you have any clue of the usual amounts?"

Herman didn't reply at once. "If I remember rightly, a few years ago the minimal freight charge from the Duchy to Kyris was around one point eight million credits. That's for a full cargo on a norm-sized freighter."

"There's a norm?"

"Yes, for practical purposes. Standard cargo compartment sizes, standard docking space, standard spare parts — it simply doesn't pay to be exotic unless you must haul oversize cargo, but I've never seen an oversized commercial vessel. Okay, there are smaller ones, specializing in exotic cargo with special needs or optimized for speed, but this one — " he waved at the display — "pretty much looks like standard size."

"Okay." Syreen briefly closed her eyes. "So, let's say, it's one-eighth for two jumps, half of that for one jump, and twenty percent of that half makes one-hundred and eighty thousand credits as a baseline, before I ask for exotic goods."

Herman nodded. "You could ask for more. After all, you already proved your skills, and with those shots you're clearly above average."

"I will keep that in mind."

"Anything else I can do for you, Sir?"

"Not right now. Thank you, Herman."

She turned to her panel and sorted her thoughts. How should she proceed? Probably the way she knew best — ignoring the Books, and at full attack speed.

Captain Kasai answered Syreen's call without delay.

"Lieutenant Syreen. Did you reach a decision?"

"Of course, Captain. However, I should first ask for your export declaration."

"Oh, well, Lieutenant Syreen, uh, yes . . ."

"Or I could calculate a flat charge, no questions asked."

"That would be convenient."

"In which case I would arrive at five-hundred and forty-thousand credits, payable within one cycle after safe arrival in the Kyris system — in case of trouble, one cycle after we cleared obvious obstacles. Is that acceptable?"

There was a very brief pause. *"This is very generous of you, Lieutenant Syreen."*

Which means too cheap. Well, okay, I'm still learning. She added a brief note to her log.

"Do you need any kind of warrant, Lieutenant?"

"I assume the recording of our negotiation will do, Captain." *Moreover, I'm the one with the guns.*

"Oh, sure. It's a pleasure to negotiate with you, Lieutenant. Would there be anything else we could do for you? My crew asks for some way we can compensate you for your help — something more personal, and more tangible."

"That's very kind of you."

"You might think so, but you haven't been at the pirates' point

for cycles, with no prospect of ever seeing your beloved again. We feel obliged to do something, and it would be a huge relief if we knew we could help you somehow."

Syreen had never collected many personal belongings, the same as she had never really belonged anywhere. Fleet was her home, Fleet took care of her needs, and her needs were listed in the Books — first of all her tac, hygiene articles, a tidy uniform or two, where skirmisher pilots didn't even need one, except on formal occasions.

She'd face more formal occasions in the future, and the Association's gray wouldn't be appropriate.

"There's one thing I might appreciate, Captain, but I don't know whether you're equipped to help me."

"Just tell me."

"Okay. Captain, could you provide me with a new uniform?"

"A uniform? That's not very personal."

"I can assure you, for me it is. Do you have any green cloth?"

"If this is what you want most, we will have green, Lieutenant. My chief is quite skilled at tailoring. She will need some measurements, though, and some details on cut, insignia, and decorations."

"The Duchy's uniforms are quite plain, but I'll check our regulations and send you the specs, okay?"

"Of course. There's the little difficulty of how to pass it on to you. Would it be okay after docking at Kyris Orbital Base?"

"Sure."

"Which would give me an opportunity to meet you in person. I'm looking forward to it."

"I am, too, Captain."

PART FOUR—COMING IN

CHAPTER TWENTY-NINE

Syreen's vision returned to normal. She checked her board — no symbols that required her immediate attention. A moment later, she spotted the *Light of Mandalay*. So her jump had gone without trouble, too.

The two ships had exchanged their calculation results beforehand, and Captain Kasai had quickly adapted his own jump data to Syreen's. In a continuum of valid solutions, hers had been confirmed as more efficient by both ships' computers.

Kasai's only comment had been, "If you ever retire from active duty and need a job, I'd hire you as pilot. Just call me."

Indeed the four-dimensional math needed for jumps had never caused Syreen headaches, unlike many of her fellow cadets at pilot school.

She triggered her intercom. "Guys, we're fine. No trouble lurking for us so far. Herman, do you have any advice on how to introduce us to the local authorities?"

Herman appeared at her door again.

"Sir, our beacon should do until we're called. After all, we arrived together with a merchant, so unless he sends a distress signal, we're considered his escort, and that makes our arrival legit."

"Thanks, Herman."

"You're planning to dock, Sir?"

"Yes, why?"

"Don't be surprised about the fee. You will soon find out why merchants rarely spend more than two or three tencycles at any port."

"Hum. I thought I could take some time to gather intel and talk to allies."

"You can always undock. There will be shuttle services."

"Expensive, too?"

"Oh, no, shuttles are affordable—as far as I know. Only docks are rare."

"I see. Okay. Make me a list of provisions we should buy. If you can, stock this baby up to the max. Nothing truly exotic, but not just dry rations, either. If Stephan and you need something—within reasonable limits—put it on the list, too." Syreen didn't mention their pay.

"What about you, Sir?"

"Oh, I'll be fine with some forwine. But if I understood you right before, it would be wise to buy local produce. So check out what Kyris can offer. I'll do a systems check and make another list for maintenance." Another thought caught Syreen's attention. "You'll check that with Stephan anyway, but you might as well tell him now that he'll be the one to receive those goods, as we're probably the ones going out."

"We, Sir?"

"You're the one who's been here before. You have family business here. Plus I assume—sorry—that Stephan might be a bit smarter spotting any mischief during delivery."

"Oh, he is, I'm sure. If I know the rules, he knows the cheats."

"That's settled, then. Okay, I expect Captain Kasai calling any moment now. You know what to do."

"Yes, Sir. Within the cycle. After the port authorities have established contact, you can place your orders and expect the first offerings."

"Oh—you mean, there's a bid process?"

"Unless you go for something exotic, yes. Of course, you can address any local trader directly, if you know one."

"Or if I don't want to give away what I need."

"No way." Herman shook his head. "That kind of information travels faster than light."

Syreen laughed, and then pointed at a flashing symbol. "There he is."

Herman left. Syreen checked her data panel again before answering the call.

"Raydancer, Lieutenant Syreen here. Captain Kasai?"

"Light of Mandalay, Captain Kasai speaking. Raydancer, *Lieutenant, my congratulations for your jump again. To me, this system looks clean. What are your insights?"*

"Aside from two other merchants, my panel shows me six old-fashioned customs vessels which *Raydancer* would outclass, outmaneuver and outspeed. So far, I can't detect any immediate threats or evidence of pirate infestation."

"I agree. I will authorize the transfer of the agreed fee now. You wouldn't perchance be available for our trip out?"

"Ask me again before you leave, but right now I wouldn't count on that."

"Too bad. Well, once we're docked, we'll have something for you."

"I'll be pleased to invite you to my ship. Due to the limited space available, I can only extend this invitation to a total of three persons."

"Three – oh, that's very generous of you. Yes, my crew will be delighted. We'll be with you once the port authorities clear our ship."

"And mine."

"Yours – oh, you're joking, Lieutenant. Of course, you don't need clearance. Or did you bring any cargo?"

"No, of course not, Captain. We'll meet."

The Kyris port authorities took their time. When the call symbol finally flashed, Syreen had her short maintenance list ready, had already approved Herman's, and had made a preliminary schedule for the first tencycle of her stay.

"Warship Raydancer *for Kyris port authority. Please identify yourself and state your business here."* They spoke their Common very slowly and well-pronounced. Syreen had no trouble understanding, and that was surely how it was meant.

She tried to speak as clearly. "Kyris port authority for *Raydancer*, Lieutenant Syreen on behalf of the Duchy Fleet. I'm here as escort for the *Light of Mandalay* and with diplomatic messages for the Duchy ambassador at Kyris. Moreover, I will resupply here, your permission assumed."

There was the usual pause, while *Raydancer* continued system inward.

"Raydancer, a Duchy ship is always welcome at Kyris, including resupply. Do you require docking, and if so, for what time?"

It was nice to learn that previous Duchy skippers hadn't left burned ground behind.

"Kyris, if it's no inconvenience to you, I would like to dock close to my protégé, the *Light of Mandalay,* as that would ease our farewell come-together. I currently envisage extending my docking stay to two full tencycles following arrival in order to pick up provisions. I have no plans or orders yet beyond that time."

Again she had to wait for her message to arrive, and the answer to return.

"Raydancer, you are assigned to docking bay Gamma Two, next to the Light of Mandalay, *for two tencycles following arrival, with the complimentary option for another two tencycles extension. Your fee for the first two tencycles is twenty-five thousand credits, payable before attempting to dock."*

Syreen congratulated herself for having studied all of *Raydancer's* controls and not just the ones related to navigation and ordnance. She knew how to access the accounts kept in the ship computer, and found her escort fee there. She'd be able to transfer the docking fee anytime—however, she wouldn't do it yet. She suspected that would give her away as a greenhorn.

CHAPTER THIRTY

The docking maneuver went smoothly. *Raydancer* behaved well, so Syreen had no trouble steering her into position. She had always compared docking her skirmisher to a male penetration—of course you could do it either gently or roughly, depending on the occasion. She wasn't a pilot who'd earn frowns from the hangar chief for making dents in his equipment.

When the little ship had used up its speed, the docking clamps could simply close. There was no adjustment necessary, no shaking or trembling to pull the ship into place.

She let her stick go and switched most controls to *port*.

"Guys, we're there. Prepare the galley for our visitors and check your uniforms."

A moment later, Herman and Stephan poked their heads in.

"You opted against docking?" Herman asked.

"No, why?" Syreen grinned. "We're safely docked."

"The one journey I made before, there was quite a rumble each time we docked anywhere, both shuttles and freighters."

"I don't rumble if I don't want to."

Stephan poked Herman with his elbow. "Of course not. Our skipper knows her stuff. Sir, you mentioned the galley. It's a bit tight there, so we prepared the passenger compartment—arranged the seats to both sides—and put our stuff in the lockers. Is that okay?"

Syreen nodded. "Of course. Thank you both. That was very considerate."

"No big deal, Sir. What are our next steps, after the visit?"

"Let me see—I've paid the docking fee, placed our shopping list, announced my arrival to the Duchy embassy—that's where I should go next. I'll take Herman along so that we can talk with his family business representatives later—before I make any decisions on our next steps."

The two privates nodded and left. Syreen rose from her pilot's chair and left the cockpit, too. She needed a comfort stop before receiving guests. As the *Light of Mandalay* had been placed second in the docking queue, their visitors couldn't arrive yet.

Stephan pouted. "I can understand her reasoning, but I'd really like to get out of this can soon."

Herman placed a hand on his shoulder. "We'll take turns, okay? One of us must stay behind—this is the only ship we have, and if we lose it, we'll never get back home."

"But . . ."

"No buts, mate. We can't afford the passage—if there'd be any commercial travel in the near future anyway. We'd never be able to gather the money with the work we might get—our skipper's the only one who'd be hired for work on a starship."

"But your family could afford it, too. Are they so rich?"

"That's different. We could accompany our own shipment—that's affordable. Merchant captains sometimes take traders or their representatives along, but they are very reluctant to admit strangers—you never know if you've just let a pirate accomplice in."

"And that's different for traders?"

"Yes, because it's their own cargo. Why would a trader deliver his own cargo to a pirate? Doesn't make sense. So that's a rather safe bet."

"How do other people travel, then?"

"Not at all, or as crew, but captains are very picky about new crew, for the same reasons. Oh, and there are passenger ships. No cargo, so pirates wouldn't try to get on them for easily sellable goods, just people."

"No pirates?"

"As far as I've heard, rarely. Pirates could capture a passenger ship to get a ransom—but there are three issues with that, as my father once told me. Firstly, the pirates must keep their loot alive. Secondly, they must become visible to collect the ransom. Thirdly, they must fear that their hostages might remember faces or other details. And if the family or company won't or can't pay the ransom, they've wasted time and effort."

"No other way to make money out of the passengers?"

Herman frowned. "Slavery comes second after piracy—any honorable nation disapproves of it. So, yes, you could take strong men and pretty women to one of the lost colonies or to a pirate lair, but that won't cover the cost to maintain a starship. Not worth the effort."

Stephan shrugged. "Okay. So we must keep the ship. Do you really think someone would steal it?"

"Sure. Think of it—it's the most powerful ship in this system, perhaps beyond. If you could use it for piracy, you might even be able to challenge another escort."

"Oh." Stephan scratched his chin. "Yeah, that makes sense. Okay, I'll be very careful. I'd better not let anyone inside while I'm alone."

Herman smiled. "They'll offer to take the deliveries to the cargo compartment. That's common procedure. It's not advisable to leave them outside at the dock."

"No. Into the airlock, and I'll take over from there."

"Yes, that'll be better."

"Okay." Stephan felt his chin again. "I reckon I need a shave now."

CHAPTER THIRTY-ONE

Syreen's screen showed her the dock area outside of her airlock, and the three new arrivals, one man, one older and one younger woman waiting there. Their brisk white uniforms with golden sleeve stripes, with white berets and black boots, stood out against the pale dock floor. Huge smiles on their faces accompanied the even bigger package under the older woman's left arm.

The captain looked ageless despite his wrinkles and chiseled features. His black hair was cut short around his beret. The older woman had bound her blond hair into a ponytail. Her weathered face reminded Syreen of her first drill sergeant, but this impression was softened by the cheerful attitude, shared also by the second woman. The younger — perhaps the same age as Syreen herself, no more than twenty-three winters — was slightly taller than the other two, with short black hair, bright brown eyes and a chest that almost triggered envy in Syreen.

The three people saluted toward the dock camera, and then the captain waved his right hand.

"Captain Kasai, Chief Engineer Robertson, Junior Assistant Mendoza of the *Light of Mandalay*. May we kindly ask for admission?"

Syreen jumped up and went to the airlock. She impatiently waited for the inner hatch to close and the outer one to open, and then she stepped outside and saluted back.

"I'm Lieutenant Syreen. Welcome to the *Raydancer*, Captain Kasai, Chief Engineer Robertson, Junior Assistant Mendoza.

Would you please follow me inside?"

The captain cleared his throat and pointed at the package his crew member held up toward her. "Lieutenant, we brought your new uniform. Perhaps you would feel more comfortable if you wore it during our visit?"

Syreen wasn't sure if a different uniform would contribute to her comfort, but she understood that wearing it would contribute to her guests' comfort, so she agreed. "In that case, I will change before rejoining you. Would you please follow me anyway? My crew will meanwhile tend to your wishes."

Kasai didn't argue with that. Syreen took the package, and together they squeezed into *Raydancer's* airlock.

Inside, Herman was already waiting to guide their guests to the passenger compartment. "This way, please."

Syreen stopped at the door to her cabin. "I'll be with you in three, okay?"

Now that she placed the bulky package on her bunk, she felt excited. She couldn't even remember the last time she had received a gift—surely not since entering Fleet.

She had to restrain herself to not rip the wrapping apart but open and unfold it carefully. She spotted green, silver and burgundy. Why? She hadn't told . . . oh, yes, Kasai had said something about an encyclopedia of stars, planets, nations and their military. If the Duchy's regulations hadn't changed during the last megacycle—which she had confirmed—they could work with their own data. He had also asked for a contact card from her tac. What had her own gear unveiled about her?

Obviously, a bit more than she had planned to publish.

No time, guests are waiting.

She quickly dropped her current garment and started to put the new uniform on. Green pants, tight fit. Soft black boots, adjusting to her feet. A green top, tight as well. So far, everything would conveniently fit inside an evac suit.

The jacket wouldn't, which didn't matter, as it wasn't supposed to be worn in combat situations. She quickly slipped inside, closed the magnetic zipper and the black belt, and then checked the insignia and decorations — *decorations?*

The sleeves showed the single silver stripe for a lieutenant, and on her left chest she found the expected Duchy Fleet badge, but there also were the ribbons for scoring first in her final pilot test, for precision shooting, for exemplary conduct — which she almost had lost on several occasions — the five-ray silver star with halo for a hyperflight command, the four-ray silver star for a warfare command — both awarded on the first occasion, never multiplied — followed by a long parade of small four-ray stars for acknowledged kills, and finally the silver spiral-galaxy symbol for the Fleet Commander in Charge.

On top came — literally — the burgundy beret of an acting starship skipper, again with the galaxy symbol at its side.

Syreen scrutinized her mirror image for flaws. She couldn't find any, except for the person wearing all this fruit. That was the only issue she couldn't fix yet.

Finally, she clipped her tac to the belt, turned on her heel and walked out.

Stephan picked up his full-laden tray, stepped out of the galley — and held his breath upon sight of the woman who had just exited the room at the other end of the corridor.

"Wow!" he uttered a moment later. "Uh — Sir, I mean . . ."

His commanding officer smiled and made a slight curtsy, which somehow spoiled the impression she had made on him. "Thank you, Stephan. I appreciate your compliment."

"Oh — Sir, yes, these colors suit you so much better."

"Indeed. Okay, we shouldn't let our guests wait any longer, should we? Please go ahead."

Stephan entered the room first and placed his tray down before Syreen followed.

Two gasps acknowledged her entrance—Herman and Captain Kasai were the source. Chief Engineer Robertson's face showed a broad smile, and the young Junior Assistant stared at her open-mouthed.

Stephan made sure to not block their field of vision. His superior deserved the attention. But why was the merchant captain surprised?

"Niki, you didn't tell me," Kasai accused his chief.

The older woman grinned. "Wouldn't spoil the surprise for you, Skip—'twas too tempting when I got the specs. 'Tis not every tencycle I tailor admiral's gear, ay?"

The merchant captain focused on Syreen. "Well, Lieutenant, Fleet Commanders usually don't deal with pirates and escorts either. That and the impressive number of stars on your uniform tell an interesting story by themselves. Not to mention that you arrived here with a borrowed uniform and ship—*Raydancer* was previously registered for Associated Planets, correct? Oh, I won't inquire, that's not my business, but surely I won't be the only one to notice the striking facts."

Stephan began to distribute the drinks he had brought. Without asking, he had provided Syreen with a mug of hot forwine, which she took with a nod.

"I can't deny the obvious, Captain Kasai."

"Please—you can call me Noriaki. If I may be so bold."

"Sure. Just Syreen, then."

"Oh—I thought that's your family name?"

"I don't have a family name."

"I thought everyone has. And your parents?"

"I don't know my parents."

There was a brief, embarrassed silence. Stephan felt compelled to ease the situation. "I'm Stephan. This is Herman. We were prisoners on this ship when the Lieutenant, um, *borrowed* it."

"I'm Niki, and this is Teresa," the chief engineer added.

Syreen leaned forward and folded her hands. "It's true. I captured this corvette—I needed a new ship after the Association shot my skirmisher down."

"You boarded it—alone?"

Stephan listened attentively. He anticipated new information for him, too.

"I just walked in when it was parked in a dreadnaught hangar."

"And flew away with it?" Kasai shook his head. "And nobody stopped you?"

"No, they were busy with their own problems." Syreen smiled. Stephan didn't like that kind of smile, though.

She went on, "I had sabotaged their power plant. The dreadnaught is no longer. You could say I killed it single-handedly."

CHAPTER THIRTY-TWO

The silence that followed Syreen's admission felt awkward. Should she have withheld that information?

"That takes *daring* to a new level," Niki commented.

"A story to tell my grandchildren." The captain shook his head, and then glanced at his crew. "For now, this news will not leave this room. Clear? Not a word to our crew, and no chatting about it even if you think you're alone. I assume the Lieutenant will decide if and when this information becomes public knowledge."

Syreen nodded. "Thank you, Noriaki. I guess the word will eventually spread anyway, but a little head start might help my cause."

"We're privileged to know about it, and we will not spoil it." Again, the captain looked around, and Niki and Teresa agreed.

"Now," he went on, "you might ask yourself how I chose the two of my crew to come along. It was easy—Niki and Teresa are the two who had to fear the pirates most, as they're the only women in my crew. You can imagine what that means."

Syreen couldn't entirely imagine, but she nodded anyway. Yes, she knew that pirates sometimes would take women for their entertainment, but Noriaki's voice seemed to insinuate worse.

"Well, when the pirates showed up, we told Teresa to hide in a maintenance duct with a knife and stay there, and if none of us came to get her out, better kill herself quietly with that knife than trying anything foolish, like an escape."

Syreen watched the poor girl's expression. *Commit suicide with a knife? How awful.*

Teresa only shrugged and whispered, "Didn't need it, thanks to you."

"We couldn't do anything about Niki. A ship without a chief engineer would have caused suspicions—we didn't want them searching all the ducts and shafts." Noriaki watched his chief with a frown. "That was no easy decision."

"'Twas," Niki disagreed. "Couldn't let them get the girl. Skip, you know what'd happen."

"Yes, but—well."

Niki leaned forward to Syreen. "Didn't need to argue with him long. He's good-hearted. Wouldn't want to lose his chief, okay, but wanted even less to sacrifice our pet, would he?"

Syreen shook her head. She didn't understand entirely yet.

Teresa helped out. "D'you know what Junior Assistants are needed for, Lieutenant?"

"Uh—no."

"Nothing. Oh, gofer work, sure."

"Gofer?"

"Go for this, go for that. Gofer."

"Ah."

The young woman shrugged again. "You don't hire another hungry mouth only for preparing meals and forwine. When I signed up, I didn't know 'bout cargo, steering and all. Just two skilled hands and a wet pussy, y'know? Pressure relief on long hauls. Understand?"

Yes, Syreen understood now. The ship whore. But she didn't voice it.

"I need the money. Have my own bunk, get regular food, learn about ship work, and the guys aren't bad. Once you know them, they can be kind. Little gifts from each port, y'know?"

"And pirate bait, if it gets to the worst," Niki added. "To

spare the older women, the ones who do the real work. Those girls never come back. It's an evil game, but that's how it's played. Not Noriaki, though. Too soft, he is."

"You insisted," the captain argued.

"Yes, I did. See my old flesh. Not very attractive—not much in danger from pirates. No need to waste such a nice girl for nothing."

Syreen shuddered. "I wasn't aware of such customs."

"What—never heard of the ship's cat?" Niki asked.

"I did," Herman chimed in. "I thought those were needed to hunt rats and mice."

"And that's what they do," Niki agreed. "Big hairy rats and little mice. The real challenge is to catch the latter—and not tell anybody aboard who's who."

Herman blushed, while Teresa smiled.

"But you saved us—them—from that fate," Noriaki stressed again. "And now that I have at least an idea what you went through before, what worries you already must have, it's worth even more."

"She's our lucky angel," Teresa said.

The captain stared at her. "Yes. Yes . . . why haven't I thought of that before?"

"Of what?" Syreen asked.

"It's old spacefarer's lore, of angels who mean luck to every ship they travel on. Superstition, sure, but there's a real part to it—*star angels,* as we merchants call them, will get a free ride on any ship, to any destination. Some skippers will only offer air and water, and you must bring your own food, while some will give their own bunk away. In any case, yes, I think Teresa's right—you deserve that honor. I will do the necessary."

"Which means?"

"I will register your name in the merchants' rolls."

"What's that?"

"The rolls? They are the merchant guild's collective brain. That's where all commercial ships and their captains must be registered, where all export declarations are logged, and where we keep track of violations of any kind—like tampering with declarations, failing to pay escort fees, and such. That's where we record pirate encounters, and that's also the place to record commendations and recommendations. As any other kind of changes, the information on you will be propagated by every ship leaving Kyris, through every port they visit and beyond, and probably travel faster than you."

Syreen felt touched—and then the emotions of the three guests overwhelmed her and she could no longer hold her tears back.

CHAPTER THIRTY-THREE

The meeting turned into a convoluted group hug, as everyone tried to comfort Syreen. The physical contact didn't help her to block out their emotions—she had to give in and let them come, and after the first round of hugs she could bear them.

After this emotional interlude, they shared the urge to talk about less moving topics, chitchat about life in the army, in the Fleet, or on a merchant ship. Eventually, they arrived at Kyris Orbital Base.

"I've never been dirtside," Kasai admitted. "Everything is done on the base. The local people seem reluctant to let strangers come down. Instead, they've made sure that there's no need for a planetary visit. Maintenance, administrative stuff, business, amenities—the base provides it all."

"It's huge," Syreen said. It had been impressive during their approach. "I felt like I'd never reach it. It grew and grew and grew. It surely dwarfs every dreadnaught."

"If *you* say so." Kasai winked. "However, it's quite well-arranged inside, mostly well-lit, and with their guidance system, you can't get lost—as long as you stay in the main corridors."

"Did I hear a warning in your last words?" Stephan inquired.

"Yes. In general, ports are dangerous territory. Every port gets its share of pickpockets, cheaters, gamblers, broke people, lost people, desperate people."

"People like me," Teresa chimed in. "People who'd do anything to get away, to find a better place."

"Only to find out that there's no paradise waiting at the other end of the jump." Niki shrugged. "Only more of the same dirt, despair, and desolation."

"I'm lucky," Teresa said. "I found a ship, a job, education. Maybe I'll eventually become an engineer, or a cargo master."

"I encourage that," Kasai said. "Teresa's very diligent."

"In addition to your . . . job?" Herman asked.

Teresa smiled at him. "Yes. What's the difference? Everyone else is doing his duties, too, when he's not with me."

It was not such a big difference to her own Fleet experience, Syreen mused. Of course, one pretty female pilot in an otherwise male team attracted not just professional interest. Worse, if every training flight meant unsatisfied sexual stimulation, a whole gang returning to their base with boners. She hadn't been obliged to do anything about it—that was the major difference—and had been supposed to not distract the others from their duties or neglect her own, but there had been an implied expectation anyway. Skirmisher wings had to build a team, had to learn to get along with each other, had to learn to be one head and one ass . . . so if they were just one body anyway, they might as well plug in.

"You'd better go out in teams," Kasai picked up the previous topic. "Anyone going solo may find trouble either with thugs or with the police. May be considered a mutineer or strayer or alley cat."

"In uniform?" Stephan asked.

"Yes. Those are the worst. Trying to complement their pay." The captain shrugged. "Police won't check all your insignia first. They see your lieutenant stripe, a pretty face, and their judgment is settled."

"I had planned to take Herman along on my first trip anyway," Syreen said. "I will heed your advice. There's enough trouble already, I don't need to enter the local authorities' shit list. Well—anyone want another drink?"

CHAPTER THIRTY-FOUR

Syreen walked down the spacious corridor from docking area Gamma to the *ringwalk* — the circular hallway that ran once around the station's center on all twelve main levels. The walls were ivory colored with ornaments in lavender and thistle purple, which were nicely complemented by the slowly varying indirect lighting. The air carried hints of dust, grease, sweat and fruit. She was aware of Herman tailing her and also of his emotions — curiosity, affection and a spoonful of lewdness.

Her attention was directed at her environment, though. She watched for the dangers Kasai had mentioned — pickpockets, alley cats, policemen — and considered the chances she might encounter any Associated Planets' citizen who might enlighten her with regard to their politics and motivations.

Here and there, she involuntarily focused on prominent veins in other people's throats, and imagined sinking her fangs inside. Would they taste as juicy as they looked? Would it feel as arousing as before? Or should she take some guy to a deserted side corridor to ride his cock during the feeding?

"Sir?"

"Huh?" She turned to Herman.

"Pardon, Sir. I said we should turn left to the embassy."

Now she consciously noticed the increase in traffic, and that they indeed had already reached the ringwalk. The slightly curved corridor was wide enough and the levels high enough to fly a skirmisher through.

"Sorry, Herman. I was lost in my thoughts. Lead the way, please."

He did. A ramp led them down three levels, and soon he turned to another wide corridor leading further toward the center. A series of large emblems along each side indicated either the embassies of different star nations or offices of larger merchant houses.

Syreen felt relieved when the Duchy's green symbol came into view. She'd no longer be alone with her problems.

The private waved at a spot at the wall, and the adjacent door opened. They looked and walked into a large anteroom, where two armed soldiers in Duchy green watched them from the rear end.

"What's your business here, Private?" the right one asked. "The ambassador is busy today. We weren't told of any appointments."

Herman looked at Syreen helplessly.

She stepped forward. "I announced my visit in advance. I have urgent news for the ambassador."

"Sorry, Lieutenant, not today. No exceptions."

"The ambassador will have to make an exception for me."

"I told you. No exceptions." He placed one hand on the gun at his belt. "Please leave now."

"I must talk to the officer on duty, Sergeant."

"He's busy, too. No appointments today, as I said."

"I must insist, Sergeant. Get the officer on duty. That's an order."

"You may be Fleet, but no mere lieutenant will order our captain around. Do you really want trouble?"

"There will indeed be trouble around if the orders of the *Fleet Commander in Charge* are ignored, Sergeant."

He paused. She pointed at the silver galaxy symbol on her chest.

"But — a lieutenant?"

"The reasons are above your pay grade, Sergeant. Now move your ass before I consider a court-martial."

CHAPTER THIRTY-FIVE

Had it been Syreen's command voice or the little mental push she had added, or both? In any case, the sergeant had left through the inner door.

Two centicyles later, he reappeared with a man wearing the stripes of a captain.

The officer's gaze touched her galaxy, lingered on her small stars, and then focused on her face. "Lieutenant? I'm Captain Jones. Please follow me inside. Whatever you've got to tell, it's surely not meant for the general public."

He led them inside and into a room with a table and a few chairs and waited until they had taken a seat.

"Lieutenant . . ."

"Syreen. This is Private Herman Doeken. He's one of the two men who were aboard when I left the Duchy system."

"Yes — well . . . I can hardly imagine a sequence of events leading to a lieutenant becoming Fleet Commander in Charge. No disrespect meant, Sir."

"I'm all that's left of Fleet, Captain. We're at war."

He leaned back and stared at Syreen. After a while, he licked his lips. "War."

Syreen nodded.

"Well," he went on. "We didn't receive any messages about this yet."

"Nor did we." Syreen focused on him. "There was no declaration of war before the attack. They came, blasted everything out of space and dropped their troops to the planet."

"After bombarding the planetary defenses," Herman

added.

"What does that mean—blasted everything away?"

"They came with five dreadnaughts, Captain," Syreen replied. "Our destroyers could destroy one, flanked by the skirmishers, before they were wiped out. We could prevent some of their stingships entering the atmosphere, but in the end, they eliminated our skirmishers, too."

"And you?"

"And me. My skirmisher was destroyed during its approach to another enemy dreadnaught."

"But you survived. How?"

"I had abandoned it before they hit it. My evac suit held until I reached the dreadnaught. I boarded it, sabotaged its power plant, and escaped in a corvette from its hangar before it blew up."

"So you killed a dreadnaught. All alone. Unbelievable."

"You can check my tac recordings, or *Raydancer's* log."

"Oh, no, sorry. I'm sure you wouldn't make up such a story, only—it's still hard to swallow."

Syreen smiled. "Indeed."

"Okay, and because you're the only survivor, you're in charge now?"

"That's what my tac told me even before I engaged the dreadnaught—which means any staff dirtside must have been wiped out, too."

The captain frowned. "What are you going to do? What are your orders, Sir?"

"The Duchy's standing policy is to eliminate the threat of piracy wherever it's encountered, plus Fleet will never give up. As there hasn't been any declaration of war, I cannot even consider surrender. However, I can't take out the entire enemy fleet all alone. I don't know what to do now. So, Captain Jones, I can't give you any orders. You know better how to proceed with regard to this embassy."

"Okay." He nodded slowly. "So your orders are to protect this embassy and the Duchy's people to our best abilities, as before, only now with knowing we're potentially under a pirate or terrorist threat?"

"If those were your orders before, Captain, yes." Syreen mused. "I wouldn't expect any imminent danger — yet. The enemy was looking for some artifact within the Duchy's boundaries, not for our people."

"How did you learn about that?"

"Oh, I eavesdropped on the dreadnaught's commandant before leaving his ship. The opportunity was there — too tempting to pass up."

The captain leaned forward. "You boarded an enemy dreadnaught in your evac suit, sabotaged the power plant, escaped with a captured corvette — and in between, you dared to spy on their commandant?"

"Exactly. It would have been much harder to return after I left it — even without the sabotage. It was necessary to get at least some intel on our enemy."

"Sure. Oh — you didn't mention yet who it was."

"Associated Planets."

"Bastards."

"Yes." Syreen shrugged. "May I talk with the ambassador now?"

"Sure — you don't have an appointment?"

"I announced my arrival. He didn't bother to reply."

"No. He doesn't check his messages when he's not in the office. If you insist . . ."

"I do. Oh, that reminds me — as Fleet Commander in Charge, I declare martial law for all Duchy soldiers and citizens."

"I was about to ask." He rose. "If you excuse me, Sir. I will remind the ambassador of his duties in time of war."

Chapter Thirty-six

Syreen watched the captain leave.

"He was impressed," Herman commented. "If you allow, Sir."

"Oh, sure. Yes, he was. I'm still quite impressed myself. When the enemy attack started, I was sure I'd die within the cycle. The longer I survived — and scored — the stranger it felt. In a way, it's still surreal." *Like my fangs. No, first of all my fangs.*

"You are good, Sir."

"I know I'm a good pilot, Herman. I know I'm no fool, too. I know it's not just luck that I'm here now. I know I owe that to my own doing, and I know I may be proud of that stunt. Damn, I *am* proud — if I had a cock, I'd be walking on it now." She paused. "Uh, sorry."

Herman seemed tempted to laugh, but her gaze stopped him.

She shook her head. "I won't be able to live up to the expectations I've created there. I can't go back and eliminate the other dreadnaughts with a snap of my fingers."

"You don't have to. I mean, what others expect is their problem, isn't it?"

"I won't be able to live up to the expectations I've created for myself, Herman. I won't be able to do what a fleet commander is supposed to do. I don't see *anything* I can do now."

He sat up. "Yes, you can. There's one thing you can do, and that's what we came for. Talk with the ambassador."

"And then?"

"Doesn't matter. You needn't do all this alone. Talk to

114

people. If there's nothing else we can do, we travel to another system and talk to more people. Eventually, someone might come up with an idea. Until then, keep spreading the news."

Syreen considered that.

"What does the Association fear most?" Herman went on. "Maybe we can find a lever. What about this artifact you mentioned? Perhaps if we find it first . . ."

The relic. A device so powerful that the Association ignored all rules on civilized warfare to find it.

"Thanks, Herman. That idea might be worth consideration. You don't perchance know a location for starting the search?"

He shook his head. "Nope. But we haven't really started asking around yet."

"And we shouldn't. What if someone with even worse intent — if such exists — finds it first?"

He frowned. "I didn't think of that."

"I could travel there and check their libraries. If I can find out what pointed them to our door . . ."

She felt strong emotions building, and rose.

CHAPTER THIRTY-SEVEN

Syreen glanced at her uniform once again. No, everything was in place. Now she could hear hurried steps.

The door opened, and an older man entered, followed by the captain. "Your Lordship, the Fleet Commander in Charge, Lieutenant Syreen — uh."

"Just Syreen," she helped out. "No family name."

"Oh. Lieutenant, the Duchy ambassador to Kyris, Lord Hakon Persson."

"Milord," she said, saluted, and then reached out her hand.

"Lieutenant." The ambassador took her hand, bowed and brushed it with a kiss.

She returned a curtsy.

Both rose and briefly examined each other. She saw a friendly face with wrinkles, framed by short gray hair, alert blue eyes, and a large nose. He wore a green robe. She sensed friendly curiosity together with a slight alarm. He didn't appear overly excited.

"Please have a seat, Lieutenant. I've already called for refreshments. I hear you're the bringer of grave news."

"Sadly I am, Milord. The Duchy is facing undeclared war, and Fleet is no more."

"My old eyes see proof of the opposite, young lady. Fleet is strong and energetic, even though low in numbers. But let's not get ahead of ourselves — tell me about you first, and of your company, and then we'll revisit the events that led you here."

Syreen decided to like the old man. About being called

energetic—she analyzed her feelings. Indeed, Herman's idea already had sunk its fangs into her mind and was triggering her imagination, to an extent that she already longed for finishing the conversation that had only just begun.

She forced herself to refocus on her host and began with her resumé. Lord Hakon listened patiently. When their refreshments arrived, he indicated for her to pause, allowing the young steward to place his tray down on the table before them, and after he left, his nod motioned her to continue with her report. She diligently went through the sequence of events in every detail, but deliberately left out any mention of her fangs or mind tricks. She briefly mentioned her discovery of two prisoners during her stay at Carix Alpha, and went into detail again about the pirate encounter.

"Finally, we arrived at Kyris. *Raydancer* is currently docked for resupply, but of course, the fees must come from somewhere."

If she had hoped he would volunteer to pay, he disappointed her.

"Lieutenant, thank you for your concise report. You must understand that these are difficult times for all of us. You see, we're financially dependent on our home system. With that either under siege or defeated, the flow of funds is interrupted. Without funds, I cannot compensate you for your harbor fees or even your pay. I fear that your prize—the corvette—and the escort fees you can earn with it must support you and your crew, unless you plan to issue yourself a letter of marque, which I would be glad to countersign for you."

"A letter of marque? But—the Duchy's rules on piracy . . ."

"Do not apply in this case, young lady. As the Duchy and the Associated Planets are at war with each other, it's a legitimate measure of warfare to interrupt their own trade in return. You would only capture ships traveling from or to their systems or registered in the Association."

"Oh. Is that advisable? Wouldn't it make them angry?"

The ambassador smiled. "They would doubtlessly try to kill you. However, as you are in command, I must point out the options available to us as well as those currently out of reach. Having said that, I will try to assist you in any way I can. What are your plans?"

"I came to Kyris hoping for support—reinforcements, allies, anything that helps me defeat the invaders and reconstitute order in the Duchy."

Her host reached for his mug and waited. She took the cue and her mug, and raised it.

"Duke's health," they both said. The captain and Herman followed.

"Well." The ambassador took a sip. "You're the expert in space warfare here. You've doubtlessly checked the forces guarding this system upon your arrival. What's your professional assessment on their odds against an enemy fleet like the one that attacked the Duchy?"

"These customs boats? A snowball in hell. A few stingships would suffice to wipe them out."

"So what would you expect of the Kyris government if you applied for an alliance here?"

"Uh." His question caught Syreen off guard. "I might hope for their moral support."

"That would be a brave thing to do—but not a wise move. They would be well advised to kick you out of their system, or even arrest you and turn you in to the Association."

"Turn me in? Why? I didn't commit any crime here."

The ambassador put his cup down and shrugged. "Believe an old man, young lady, who has watched the machinations of politics for most of his life. If the Association doesn't need a court to attack the Duchy, why should Kyris care about law?"

"Because they might be the next ones?"

"And why would you think that assisting your cause would prevent the Association from coming here, after you've seen what this system can muster?"

Syreen couldn't answer that. She slowly nodded. "I see."

"Believe me, young lady, fate is never fair. Don't rely on fairness unless you have no other choice. However, don't worry about arrest now. Governments need time to make up their mind, and before they do, you'll probably be long gone. At least that's what I'd recommend—that you don't stay in one place long enough for the enemy to corner you. If you'll allow a civilian to advise you in matters of strategy, Lieutenant."

She waved with her mug. "Milord, I'm not in a position to turn down anything, whether it's advice or something else. I'm grateful for any insight you can give me. Moreover, I'm sure I can profit from your experience with regard to Kyris."

He spread his hands. "Despite your undeniable youth, you've already collected a treasure of patience and wisdom. So let me tell you about Kyris. You may have noticed this rather large station—it's designed to keep all foreigners away from the surface. Kyris prefers to be left alone. They try to play nice with everyone and avoid trouble. The best they can do, and surely will try, is not to attract the Association's attention. As long as they're unaware of the current quarrel in the Duchy, they won't have to act on it. Which means—as long as we don't tell them about it formally, they can pretend they haven't heard about it, even if some rumor should spread."

"So I'd better keep my mouth shut."

"With regard to formal announcements, yes. Let me be frank. The little you could gain here isn't worth the trouble you could attract."

Syreen frowned.

"You're not happy with that," he noted.

"No. There's still the issue of the Association not having declared war. In my eyes, that's piracy and should be opposed by every civilized nation."

"You may have a point there—and yet, I doubt that you'll find anyone willing to accept that challenge. Not here, not anywhere else. Not against dreadnaughts."

She sighed. "That's not right."

"Well, take that as a lesson in politics. If you work on a small scale, you're a pirate, and people will come after you. If you work on a large scale, people will call it war and try not to get involved."

"Milord, you're not just old and wise, but also a cynic."

"The proverb says that wisdom comes with age. You prove that wisdom doesn't need age, and my experience is that cynicism comes with wisdom. You will soon adapt, young lady."

Syreen didn't know what to say, so she raised her mug. "Duke's health."

"Duke's health," the ambassador replied.

CHAPTER THIRTY-EIGHT

Syreen waited, while the old lord stared at his mug.

"I should not ask, and you certainly should not tell me, Lieutenant — but do you already have any plans where to go?"

"Nothing tangible yet. I might pay the Association a visit and ask their leaders what the heck they are doing, and whether they'd eventually consider calling their hounds back before I conquer their system. Single-handedly, of course, that's where I'm best."

Lord Hakon laughed out loud. "That's the spirit! As long as you can come up with such jokes, you'll be fine."

She focused on his eyes. "I'm not joking."

"But . . ."

"I need more intel. Of course, we know about dreadnaughts, so it shouldn't have been a surprise seeing one — but was the Association supposed to operate one, or even five? It must be terribly expensive to keep even one such tank in operation, I mean, why did the Duchy rely on destroyers alone? Because those were sufficient to hunt a pirate down, protect the system against pirate raiders, or make ambitious neighbors with similar equipment consider twice, and cheap enough to afford some bases along with them. I'd never heard of dreadnaughts in our neighborhood — well, okay, it may have been above my pay grade. But now I need to know more. I also need to know who else might run such big tanks. That will require a lot of asking around."

Her host nodded. "Valid questions. I may be able to help you there — I can ask around. Sometimes my colleagues from other nations are willing to share a bit of information with me, and I might be able to pay in kind."

"How?"

"You see, while intel about military power is usually kept secret, merchant captains sometimes do share information about the escorts they used, which nation operates them, which other ships they saw in the systems they visited — the news that some other nation has lost two dreadnaughts within one battle will trigger curiosity and perhaps loosen some tongues."

"Once you share that, people may add up two and two and guess where the battle happened."

"Not necessarily. The fact that one of our skippers arrived at about the same time as this news will certainly trigger imagination — but if the Duchy were under attack, why would we spare one of our valuable warships to come to Kyris in the first place? That is highly unlikely."

Syreen glanced at the marine infantry captain. "Captain Jones. You've been very quiet all this time. Do you have any ideas you'd like to share with us?"

The captain looked up. "I, Sir?"

She didn't reply, only kept her focus on him, and waited.

"Well, now and then my men and I may pick up news when we're off-duty. Under martial law, this will be a bit more difficult, though."

"Just go on — we'll deal with regulations later."

"Okay. Thank you, Sir. I thought we could listen around what other guards are saying — are they alarmed, have they received any notice, did they hear anything about dreadnaughts, and so on. Basically the same as Lord Hakon already proposed, only among a different group of people. Once we put the parts of the puzzle together, we might find some insights."

Syreen glanced at the ambassador, found no disapproval

in his face, and focused back on the local detachment's commandant.

"Captain, there are two major paragraphs I remember with regard to good conduct off-duty under martial law. One requires people going out in groups. Group size depends on the expected risk level and is at the responsible leader's discretion. The second paragraph strictly prohibits the consumption of intoxicating beverages. Correct so far?"

Captain Jones nodded.

She went on, "However, the Books also hold rules about covert operations. Maintaining cover may take precedence over regulations. For example—if we don't want to tell the world that we've declared martial law internally, we may grant our people the right to a drink or two. If anyone asks why they can't do as before, it's because there's new brass in town. They might expect unannounced inspections any time, so they'd better be careful for a while."

He nodded again. "I understand."

"As I said before, you're the boss here. You're granted the freedom to act at your own discretion and maintain the pretense of peace and innocence, while protecting your people from danger."

The captain folded his hands. "Okay. Thank you, Sir. That brings me to one more question I must ask. What if the situation deteriorates?"

"What do you mean?"

"What if I can no longer ensure the safety of our people here?"

Syreen watched Lord Hakon from the corner of her eye when she answered. "If you have to leave, do it. Only I cannot provide you with the funds to do so."

Next, she turned to the ambassador again. "And about my plans again—I'll have a look and listen around the base myself. Do the Associated Planets have an embassy here,

Milord?"

"No, they don't," the lord replied. "Luckily, so I needn't advise you not to go there."

"Well, I wouldn't tell them that I'm the one they're searching for. But I get your point—if I want to remain one step ahead of them, I must not go back to them. Instead, I'll try to evade them for now."

CHAPTER THIRTY-NINE

Herman felt his commanding officer's presence at his side, and also the heavy burden she carried. He had never aspired to a commission. He hadn't wanted such responsibility. The better pay would have been nice, but the price had always appeared too high, even in times of peace. Now — well, war had its own rules.

Still, Stephan, Syreen and he could consider themselves lucky, as they had survived the initial attack — and hadn't become prisoners. He tried to suppress the thought of all the kinds of torture the Association could have applied to get information they couldn't give.

He'd better focus on the task at hand — trying to get support for their cause from his family's business. The entrance to their Kyris office wasn't far from the embassy, and the entrance was guarded, too. The Doeken family employed well-trained private guards, equipped with protective overalls and batons.

He stepped forward to the door and addressed the single man. "I'm Herman Doeken. I must talk with the executive secretary on urgent and secret matters."

The guard examined him for a moment, and then briefly glanced at the lieutenant at his side, before he stepped aside. "Come in, please. I will report your arrival."

He entered, followed by Syreen, and found himself in a spacious room with several chairs around low tables.

"Have a seat, please. The secretary will be with you in a centicycle." The guard disappeared through another door, and they both dropped into neighboring chairs.

When he returned to his post a moment later, an older man in trousers, shirt and vest followed him.

"Welcome, Mister . . ."

Herman rose. "Doeken. Herman Doeken."

"Of the Doeken family? Oh, yes, now I recognize you. The third son, right? You know you've got no business here. I'm expressly instructed to ask you to leave, should you ever appear in this office."

"Mister Secretary, I have news—"

"Which I don't care about. You will leave. Now." The man clapped his hands once. "With your pretty friend. You won't get a single credit here."

Two more brawny guards appeared from the rear. One approached Herman, the other tapped the lieutenant's shoulder with his baton and barked, "You—get up and out."

The woman rose swiftly and faced her opponent. "You dare to touch a Fleet officer on duty once more, and I will break your neck. I will leave as asked for, but untouched."

The guard made one step back. Herman didn't like the anger in his leader's voice either. Nor did he like the baton in his own opponent's hands or the grim face.

He headed for the door, again followed by the lieutenant, who didn't say another word. A moment later they stood in the public hallway again.

Syreen felt the anger rising in herself and fought it down. She waved Herman along and headed back toward the embassy.

"Bastards," he said.

She wouldn't object. "Your family ousted you?"

"Yes. I knew they'd kick me out formally—Da once said I'd not be worth the ransom should a pirate ever get me—but I hadn't expected them to go that far."

She nodded. "They will bear the consequences—if you have no objections."

He shook his head. "You've heard him. This is no longer my family, my business. Do as you deem appropriate."

"Oh, I will." She strode toward the embassy and the guard sergeant, who instantly gave way. Herman shrugged and followed.

Captain Jones and Lord Hakon interrupted their discussion when she entered.

"Yes, young lady?" the latter asked her.

"I only came back to tell you that Fleet will no longer protect the Doeken company."

"Which Fleet couldn't do anyway," the ambassador observed.

"No, but I want to ask you to spread the news over your diplomatic channels, and I will also record that fact with the local merchant's rolls."

"Oh." Lord Hakon raised his eyebrows. "Would you mind telling me what happened?"

"We were kicked out. Herman is *persona non grata* at his own family's office—which doesn't bother me—and we were both forced to leave. We had no chance to get a word in about the current danger for trade with the Duchy, and if they won't hear me, I won't protect them."

"What do you mean—*forced to leave?* Did they apply physical violence?"

"Almost. No, not really."

Captain Jones chimed in. "Please, Sir—did anyone touch you?"

"Nothing serious. One guard tapped my shoulder with his baton. I'm not hurt." *Only pissed off, but that doesn't count.*

The two men frowned at each other.

Lord Hakon picked up the topic again, making a grim face. "Young lady, there's more behind it. It is—so to speak—a constant struggle between Captain Jones' people and the Doeken guards. Put plainly, they are bullying his men and insist on being the ones who pay for our presence — with their taxes. Without them, we wouldn't need a diplomatic representative here, is what they claim. On several occasions, they overstepped the limits of civilized behavior — not only on formal occasions, but also off-duty, so we felt compelled to establish a red line — their guards may not touch our military. Doing the same to the Fleet Commander in Charge is unacceptable. We must enforce their respect, or the situation will become worse."

"To be frank — I don't think they even noticed my current role. I'm a mere lieutenant, so they didn't look any further."

"They might have considered her being my girlfriend," Herman now added from the back.

"Which is no excuse for disregarding the rules. Young lady, if you allow, I will consider sanctions."

An idea was poking Syreen's mind, and she grabbed hold of it. "Milord, you said before that they claim to pay you?"

"I did, Lieutenant. Why?"

"Due to the current interruption in interstellar travel to the Duchy, their taxes can't be taken there and your pay can't be brought here. What if you collect your pay from them directly?"

"I cannot do that without authorization."

"Could the Fleet Commander in Charge authorize you to do so — under martial law?"

Syreen saw the understanding grow in Lord Hakon — and saw her own evil smile mirrored in both men.

CHAPTER FORTY

There were guards at the entrance to the merchant guild's hall, too, but they stood to attention the same moment they spotted Syreen, and let her and Herman pass. Her gaze lingered on one guard's throat for another moment.

They entered a larger room with marble floor, marble walls and marble pillars with golden bases and capitals, where plushy chairs in ebony and burgundy invited them to rest.

A short man with bald patch, wearing a white robe approached her. "Lieutenant Syreen, I assume? Welcome to the guild. My name is Jacomo, and I'm the guild secretary at Kyris. We're honored by your visit. May I offer you refreshment? Or can I do something else for you?"

Do they use first names only? Not that I'd care.

Syreen sensed friendliness, curiosity, and reluctance, while his eyes rested on her chest — on the place where she wore the spiral galaxy. This man wanted to talk with her, but didn't dare to ask for it.

"Herman and I'd be glad to share a mug of forwine with you, Jacomo, where we can discuss what I came for. I have news for the rolls."

"For the rolls? Oh, of course! Please come with me — this way please."

Syreen walked toward the indicated door, followed by Herman and Jacomo. The secretary directed them down a short corridor, with plain ivory-painted walls and light-gray doors, to a small conference room — as Syreen assumed when she saw the oval table and the eight chairs around. This room was decorated with pale wooden furniture, light-green tapestry and upholstery and smelled like vegetables to her.

"Please take a seat. I'll be with you in no time." Jacomo walked up to a wall, waved, and then fetched a tray from an opening that had been concealed before. Syreen smelled the intense aroma of fresh, hot forwine and dropped into a chair.

The secretary placed the tray down on the table and passed the mugs around.

"Cheers — or how do you say? Duke's health."

"Duke's health," Syreen and Herman echoed.

She took a cautious sip, but the beverage was perfectly tempered. The aroma was more intense than she had experienced ever before.

"Very good," she praised it.

"Isn't it? Emperor's Reserve, from Adamant III. An exceptional forwine for exceptional occasions."

"Exceptional? How did I earn this honor?"

"By your assistance to the *Light of Mandalay,* of course."

"I'm sure you don't consider every successful escort skipper's visit an exceptional occasion."

"You can't be fooled, Lieutenant, which doesn't surprise me after all I've heard — and all the rest that I can only guess, as Captain Kasai was unusually tight-lipped with regard to you. However, never before was an escort skipper registered as star angel in the rolls. That is an exceptional occasion." He waved at her chest. "The decorations and insignia you bear are exceptional, too. We've never before received a fleet commandant at Kyris, and we've never before seen any warship skipper with such a kill count."

"I told Captain Kasai before that I can't deny the obvious. Your observations are correct, of course."

"If I may say so, you are very young for so many kills, Lieutenant."

"Sadly, my enemies didn't consider my age before attacking, so I decided to ignore this fact, too."

The secretary squinted. "You also appear quite young for a fleet command."

"My success makes up for that. My tac can confirm the status, if you want to check it . . ."

Which would be very impolite. Accessing a foreign tac, even with consent, is the closest anyone could get to espionage without actually hacking anything.

So Jacomo quickly refused. "No, no, I won't challenge your rank. I'm only puzzled by the fact itself."

"I can understand that. Let me put it this way — my promotion is overdue, but I can't currently file a complaint."

"Why not?"

"Because it would be forwarded to the Fleet Commander in Charge. Pretty pointless."

She felt Herman's amusement and Jacomo's consternation.

"You won't tell me there aren't any more senior officers?"

"No, I won't," she replied. "I can only tell you that there's currently no senior *Fleet* officer available, otherwise he'd be in charge instead of me. They could be retired, sick, or suspended, or simply incommunicado. A peculiarity of the Duchy is that no army officers can command Fleet, not even generals."

"And yet — Lieutenant, pardon me, but I might still conclude that something serious happened to all your seniors, where I don't even count in the fact that you arrived in a ship that had been registered to a different star nation before."

He was coming closer and closer to the conclusion which Syreen shouldn't unveil officially — that the Duchy had to be at war. She had to offer a different solution.

"Yes. That's why I must ask you to record the fact that the Duchy currently is not safe for interstellar trade of any kind, as we suffered from a severe pirate attack — which killed many brave men."

"A pirate attack?" Jacomo took a deep breath, and then relaxed, while tapping his fingers on the table. "Oh, I see. I feared war. So you borrowed the corvette?"

"I procured a secret order from the Association admiralty for assuming command of the *Raydancer,*" Syreen replied with a poker face. Taken literally, it was the plain truth. Only the way she had procured this secret order was objectionable.

"Oh." She placed one hand over her mouth. "I shouldn't have told you."

Herman was close to laughing out loud. *Don't,* she thought, and he calmed a bit down.

Jacomo nodded and smiled. "What's said in this room, remains in this room, unless explicitly agreed otherwise. I will record your warning. Is there anything else?"

"Yes. Duchy Fleet explicitly revokes protection for shipments of the Doeken family."

The secretary paused and stared at her. "Revoke protection? But—do you know what that means?"

Syreen leaned forward. "I assume they will have difficulties finding an escort, and not just mine."

"Indeed. If you don't deem them worth an escort, nobody will dare to escort them, which means there won't be any interstellar transport. What did they do to deserve such a verdict?"

"The charge—to be recorded with the revocation—is inappropriate behavior toward the Fleet Commander in Charge, including the threat of physical violence and the application of physical insult, thereby overstepping rules of conduct established by the Duchy's representative on Kyris."

"Oh." Jacomo diligently checked the transcript shown on the table before him. "Were you hurt?"

"No. In that case, I'd have charged them with malicious injury of an officer on active duty. Which I wouldn't put past them."

"Oh. Okay. I've recorded that. Would you please have a look at the two transcripts?"

CHAPTER FORTY-ONE

Herman waited patiently until the lieutenant had approved the transcripts and the secretary had filed them away.

"Is there anything else I can do for you?" Jacomo asked.

Before his superior could deny, he chimed in. "May I file a charge, please?"

The secretary seemed to take notice of him for the first time. "Yes, uh — Private . . ."

"Herman Doeken, third son of the Doeken family. Mr. Secretary, while I currently assume no formal role within the Doeken company, I still feel entitled, if not obliged, to act in the family's interest. I just became aware of the fact that an employee of my family's business has committed an act of misconduct that caused severe damage to the family's reputation and business. Insofar he acted against the company's best interests and against his explicit orders — *to protect and foster our business and maintain the highest standards of business conduct.* That's our family motto, too."

The secretary glanced at Syreen, who nodded, and said, "Well, it seems they've picked the worst moment to anger some people, if you allow the observation. Too bad they didn't make the connection."

Herman watched his lieutenant smiling her predatory smile at the secretary.

"They seem to have built a reputation of pissing people off, if you allow the observation," she said. "We were only the last in a long line, and not the ones to mess around with."

Jacomo nodded slowly. "The way you dealt with the pirates, and now with your firm and quick decision, that message cannot be missed." He waited to see if she'd add anything, and when she didn't, he turned to Herman. "You know that your charge must be reconciled with the company owners, which may take some time?"

"I know," Herman said. To his own amazement, he remembered a lot more of the lessons he'd been taught than he'd expected of himself a few cycles ago. "I also know that such a charge limits the actions the culprit can perform on behalf of the company, if the applicant can provide proof for his charge. I can provide proof. First, there's the undeniable fact that the Duchy's own Fleet Commander in Charge revoked protection. Would you agree with that, Mr. Secretary?"

"I do."

"Second, I can prove my identity as member of the Doeken family. The necessary information is in the rolls. Moreover, I've been to Kyris some years ago, and my previous arrival as well as my genetic fingerprint are recorded in the rolls, too."

Jacomo looked alert now. "Let me check that."

He began to wave at and tap on the table. A moment later he nodded. "Herman Doeken. Oh, you were still a boy back then? Nice. Your father took you around. That's a great opportunity for a young merchant — but you chose soldiery instead? Oh, no, not my business, just a rhetorical question."

"Yes. In my class, the girls were more fascinated by uniforms back then. That was a fact to consider, and I made my decision."

The secretary's gaze went through him. "Yes. Sometimes such considerations can change the world." Then he focused back on Herman's face. "Sorry. The rolls confirm your identity. They also contain a warning that you're not entitled to spend company money for any purpose but immediate medical care. That tells a different story, but matches your career decision—again, not my business. In any case, it doesn't deny you the right to *protect* your family funds. I will present your charge to the guild's board tonight. If it's approved, your company office will receive a preliminary limitation note together with the message on their revocation."

"Sounds fair enough. Thank you." *Immediate medical care.* So his family wasn't as merciless as he had thought all the time?

"You're welcome. That's what we're here for. Anything else the guild can do for you?"

Herman glanced back at his superior, who shook her head. "No, thank you."

"In that case, I'd like to leave you now. Take your time to enjoy the forwine. If you need any assistance, just tap the table."

"I guess we'll find our way out," the lieutenant said. "Later. Thank you for your hospitality, Jacomo."

"You're welcome." The secretary rose and left.

Syreen waited until the door had closed behind the guild secretary. She focused on Herman while raising her mug. Its aromatic smell mixed with the feel of his relief.

"Well done," she praised him.

"Thank you. I wouldn't have thought that my family would even grant me medical care. That came as a surprise."

"They will be surprised, too, that you took care of their business."

Herman nodded. "Your bluff was really nice, too."

"What bluff?"

"About the secret order."

"That was no bluff. I do have such an order. It's on *Ray-dancer's* files. It took some persuasion skills to get it, though."

The private stared at her, aghast. "You *have* such an order?"

"Signed by the admiral commanding that dreadnaught, yes. I needed an order for the hangar master so that he'd let me access *Raydancer*."

"Of course."

Syreen could sense that his mind was working hard to digest this news. She probably could have eased him with little effort, but refrained from doing so. Preventing his outburst earlier had been bad enough — she shouldn't make meddling with other people's minds a habit.

Instead, she took another sip of the warm forwine.

"This is really good."

"Yes." The private drank, too. "Too good for me. I fear I'm already feeling its effect. Sir, if you allow, I'd like to withdraw to our ship soon."

"That's okay. I'll take you there."

It's funny to sense his intoxication without being dizzy myself, she mused. It seems to have less effect on me, though.

CHAPTER FORTY-TWO

Syreen delivered Herman to *Raydancer* and Stephan. The latter was busy browsing and comparing the incoming offers. She briefly considered taking him along, then pondered about going out alone to deal with whatever would come along, and then she made up her mind and called Kyris' port authority.

"Kyris Port Authority for *Raydancer*, Lieutenant Syreen speaking."

"Kyris PA here. What can we do for you, Lieutenant?"

"I'm planning a visit to the local bars to listen around for further escort contracts. Do I need to observe any formalities? I've heard it's not advisable to go out alone in some ports. What about Kyris? So far, it seems to be a rather safe place."

"Of course Kyris is safe, Lieutenant. You might want to avoid dark corridors — where the lights are gone, our security measures might be temporarily out of operation, too. Such a large station needs continuous maintenance, you know?"

"Naturally. Thank you, Kyris PA. I feel reassured now. I will instruct my crew accordingly."

"Accordingly?"

"Sure. Should anybody call them and claim I'd be taken in by your police for vagrancy or hustling, they know it's a fake and what to do about it. In that case I'm quite sure your real police would find and free me in no time — after all, such calls can be traced, yes?" She grinned to herself. "Moreover, should I be addressed in such a way in your corridors, I know I'm facing bogus police. While I don't want to cause any trouble while being your guest, I'd ensure that they can't bring me to a dark corridor where your security and surveillance equipment could no longer protect me. Hypothetically speaking, of course."

"Of course, Lieutenant. Hypothetically speaking, should a true policeman overstep his authority . . ."

Syreen put some ice in her voice. "You might have heard the rumors of how I deal with real pirates. No nonsense. Police should know better than to cross me."

"You wouldn't want to cause a diplomatic incident . . ."

"Nor would your police, I'm sure. Trying to arrest a Duchy Fleet officer and warship commandant under the pretense of false accusations would be quite undiplomatic, don't you agree? Hypothetically speaking, of course."

Syreen was aware of the fact that she currently owned the only warship in the Kyris system, and that a single blast of her pulse cannon could severely damage their orbital base. Were they aware, too?

"Of course."

"So, let me ask my initial question again—do I need to observe any formalities? Like announcing my single-person visit to your place to the local head of police?"

"No, that won't be necessary. Enjoy your stay."

"Thank you, PA. That's all for now."

Syreen disconnected. *I bet they'll call the police now.*

Chapter Forty-Three

The corridors from docks to ringwalk hadn't changed in the last few cycles. Same colors, same fragrances, only the faces Syreen passed were different.

And their throats. How would they taste? Syreen called herself to order. *If I were horny, I should look at their crotches. If I were hungry, I should eat something. Where's the next eatery?*

It had to be the novelty factor, Syreen decided, and pushed the thoughts of her strange physical traits aside. Instead, she watched for police uniforms, but couldn't see any.

Venues of all kind were indicated on the bottom level. Syreen could choose between walking down nine ramps or taking an elevator, and opted for walking.

Each ramp offered her new sights, new smells, and new faces, and a little insight on the station's layout.

She started from level ten with the Gamma docks, dedicated to interstellar freighters and their cargo, and offering convenience stores for crew members. Most of this and the next two levels down were reserved for cargo turnover, though, offering ample storage for the usual container sizes. Some corridors branching off the ringwalk held the characteristic smell of starships — recycled air, stale sweat, grease, and heated dust — but gave her no clue about the stored goods.

Level seven already appeared familiar to her with all the signs of embassies, merchant offices, the guild hall, and with mediators and maintenance contractors offering their services.

She continued her way down to level six. Corridors

branched outward from the ringwalk to the beta docks for intrasystem cargo, and inward to the marketplace, where visitors could buy local or newly imported goods while the major deals took place at the produce exchange.

Aggregates and shop storage occupied the space between levels six and three. When Syreen walked down the ramp to level three, smells, noises and the bustle of countless people announced a change. This level was dedicated to shopping malls for interstellar travelers as well as local visitors with too much money. Her home, Duchy Base Four, had offered the same temptations, and she had often seen fellow Fleet people going broke—she occasionally had funded fellow pilots from her own pay, knowing they wouldn't be able to give it back, so that they could at least afford laundry or uniform repair. She wouldn't leave a single credit here, though.

She had to share the ramp to level two with cheerful shoppers as well as crying brats who hadn't been given their umpteenth toy, and here and there she also spotted sneakier persons following their prospective prey—to what end, she couldn't tell.

The air felt sticky. Too many emotions threatened to overwhelm Syreen. She had to stop, step aside, and take several deep breaths before she could even try to regain her composure.

The people around her gave her the occasional curious glance but otherwise left her alone.

After a while, she was able to suppress her highly tuned reception, took another deep breath, and focused on a sneaky young man approaching her. When he noticed her attention, he quickly turned away and disappeared in the crowd.

This isn't the right place or the right moment to become inattentive, gal. Now get going before you attract even more undesired attention.

She quickly passed the next level with its branches to hotel corridors and to the alpha docks for star liners and passenger shuttles, and continued down the last ramp, still surrounded by many people.

Signs along the sides of the wide main corridors tried to attract guests—but she knew the drill from Base Four on restaurants, too. There were the truly expensive temples of artistic cooking, the high-price blenders, the supposedly affordable venues with their hidden extra charges and fees, often offering rather mediocre quality for too much money, and the typical family restaurants—*Kid traps* they had often called them.

Syreen felt a sting of grief when she remembered her fellow pilots joking about cheap toys and junk food. They'd never return. Their tacs were lost in space or shot to fragments. All that was left of them was her own memory, and she didn't even have anyone to report their achievements to.

Yes, I do. She made a mental note to report their scores and their last brave fight to the embassy, later, when she had done what she had come for.

CHAPTER FORTY-FOUR

She'd find neither potential sponsors nor valuable inform-
ants in any of the tourist traps or in-crowd venues. She had
to go where the crews and their captains went — to the bargain
eateries and bars, and the more crowded those were, the better their prices, and sometimes even their food.

I should have asked for recommendations.

The shiniest places were facing the ringwalk or one of the
three large avenues that crossed through the level center like
spokes of a wheel, where the hub seemed to attract the truly
rich. To find the cheaper places, she had to take one of the side
corridors that were less frequented and less well maintained.

Again, she noticed young men following her or ambling
along the corridors without any obvious destination, but they
all kept their distance when Syreen gave them a look.

There was a distant hum. One turn and another, and she
had found the source — a place that emanated funny smells
and even funnier sounds, as if someone were rubbing oxygen
tubes with a wrench while at the same time kicking the bulkhead with heavy boots. People lingered on both sides of the
entrance for whatever reasons, but Syreen didn't care as long
as she could enter.

Inside, she found a crowd of people, glasses in hands, all
facing a stage where three people indeed were operating instruments that distantly resembled oxygen tubes and boots.
The counter to the right was besieged by people waving
empty glasses, while a smaller door to the left led her to another room.

To her surprise, the side room was far less frequented. A young girl with short brown hair and a green-and-yellow-checkered dress approached her.

"A table for two?"

"I'm solo."

"Oh—okay, no matter. Follow me, please." She led Syreen to a small table with three seats at the left wall. "Have a seat. Tap the table here for the menu and your orders. If you have any trouble, call Charlie, that's me."

"Thank you, Charlie." Syreen chose a seat facing the bar.

"You're welcome—oh, by the way, what kind of uniform is that? Are you a captain? I've heard a freighter arrived to-day."

Syreen could sense friendly curiosity and something else — attraction?

"I'm a lieutenant, and I command a ship, too. If you'd like a chat, why don't you take the other seat—if your duties allow."

"Lieutenant—you mean, military?"

"Yes. Duchy Fleet."

"But we don't—oh! You're the escort?"

"Yes."

"Oh, I'd like to—" There was a beep at her wrist. "Sorry, I must leave you for now. Hope you get along with the menu."

"No worries. 'Til later, Charlie."

The checkered girl left toward the bar.

Syreen tapped the table, and a globe of semi-transparent images appeared above it. A wave with her hand, and the globe began to spin. She pointed at a cup of soup that looked tasty, and it grew toward her. With two fingers, she could pluck it out. However, the illusion wasn't perfect—her fingers moved through the cup, and then it moved to the side without further interaction.

Syreen shrugged. She had sought a cheap venue, and an

outdated user interface—without eye tracking—was acceptable, as long as it accepted her order.

She added strange items only by their looks and hoped that they'd taste at least as good.

Forwine was missing on the drinks menu. The locals seemed to fancy *beer*. Syreen had never heard of that kind of drink and took the first item on the menu—not because it was the cheapest, but because she expected it to be the least exotic.

When she confirmed her order, the globe disappeared and left her alone with her ideas, her worries, and her appetite.

Situation – I have a ship that needs maintenance and provisions, I have some funds that will be used up soon enough, and I have two guys in my crew to feed – not to mention their pay. Okay, they may have to wait for the latter.

We're alive and free.

Options – I can sell escort services. I know my dealing with pirates wasn't pure luck. I'm skilled and I can apply those skills. This can work. Only, that's not what Fleet's supposed to do.

I can return to the Duchy, pick up the fight from where I've left, and try to score once or twice before they get me. Fleet spirit, but pointless.

I can continue my search for allies. Considering the ambassador's words, smaller star nations will be anything but eager to help my cause. Larger ones, if I find any, won't care about the Duchy.

I can try to search for this relic. *Only, this requires returning to the Duchy. Unseen. No way right now. Perhaps if they give up their search a few years from now, and regular space travel commences, I can sneak in on a freighter. Until then, I must follow other options.*

I could explore my newfound skills. I could walk the dark corridors – those without surveillance – and bite the would-be predators that follow me in search for easy money.

The idea alone caused a welcome tingle in Syreen's crotch, and she almost felt her canines grow. *No!*

She accepted the necessity of killing enemies. She could also accept this strange way of profiting from their death, of gaining power from it. But actively searching for innocent prey without any urgent need wasn't how she pictured herself. *That's not me.*

CHAPTER FORTY-FIVE

Syreen's fine ears picked up a conversation at the room's far end together with strong emotions of curiosity directed at her.

"Is that the escort skipper who arrived today?" a man with bearded, weathered face asked.

His bald companion opposite wore dice as earrings. "Seems so. Her uniform is military—see those decorations? That fits. A woman, an officer, and low-ranking, with such a small ship."

"Small but deadly."

"Oh, sure. Warship against pirates, that's a safe bet."

"I heard she made a lucky shot."

"Hush—I think she heard us."

"So what? She can't bring her pulse cannons here, what?"

Syreen gave them each a piercing glance. The bald man hesitated, then rose, and walked over to her table.

"Excuse me. I'm Bruce, and I think I've heard of you. Are you the escort captain?"

The bearded man followed a moment later and listened.

"Yes and no. I'm the escort skipper. I'm Lieutenant Syreen of Duchy Fleet, and I can assure you, my three precise hits on the pirate had nothing to do with luck."

"Three hits? But—I heard you were still far away!"

"Message delay was still about a centicycle. Nevertheless, I had aimed at the power plant, the bridge at the bow, and the aft hyperdrive, and that's exactly where my shots arrived."

Bruce only gaped at her.

His mate leaned forward. "You can't reliably address a target across, what, fifty light seconds? That's not possible."

"I know the Books, too. I proved them wrong. Of course, it requires a bit more than point and shoot."

When the bearded man opened his mouth to object, Bruce gave him a poke in the arm. "The shots are a fact that can't be denied. We just don't know how it's done, and I bet the lieutenant won't tell us all her tricks."

Syreen smiled at him. "No, I won't. I can only tell you that it requires some precise calculation, and the formulas are not in the Books." She pointed at the free seats. "Why don't you tell me what the two of you are doing here all tencycle?"

Syreen didn't expect to learn anything useful for her mission, but she'd learn about everyday life on this station, places to go or to avoid, people to meet, unwritten rules. Information like that could be useful.

CHAPTER FORTY-SIX

Satiated in one way and yet hungry in another, Syreen ambled down the corridor. The food had been tasty, ample, and cheap, the cold *beer* had been refreshing but not to her taste, her company had told her a lot about the station and the regular traffic from and to the surface, and yet — she felt a different yearning inside, as if some beast had woken inside her and raised its demands now.

Was it this beast that made her walk a rather poorly lit corridor, or just the fact that it was the straightest way to the bar Bruce had told her about?

Two men blocking her way with their greedy, slimy emotions didn't care about her motivation, they only saw easy prey.

Syreen didn't regard herself as prey, just the opposite, but she wasn't in the mood for a brawl, nor was she willing to submit to her subliminal urge to kill. Blood would only spoil the aftertaste of her recent meal now.

A brawl wouldn't make her feel any better either. There had to be another way.

The two men slowly approached with a mischievous grin. They radiated lust now, and this lust made her beast stir again.

You don't know what you're awakening. If you knew, you'd wet your pants. You should feel fear. Yes, fear. You feel fear. You want to run.

There was a hint of wet fabric, then of urine in the air. That was all the two left behind when they dashed away.

Syreen had to pause and recollect herself. The urge inside her wasn't satisfied yet—despite the lack of immediate targets, it didn't fade but still grew stronger. *No, I won't give in. I'm the one in charge.*

She felt as if something inside was grinning at her and then turned away, like saying, *this time you get your way. This time.*

She credited that to her own imagination—the entire situation was still too new for her, too strange to easily adapt to it. Perhaps another such *beer* might help her get over it. Her destination was supposed to offer the best, and that was the reason she might find interesting contacts there.

Chapter Forty-seven

On the outside, the venue didn't live up to its reputation. Only after Syreen entered and found the room crowded with people, embedded into a loud mix of smells and a colorful soundscape did she understand what Bruce had wanted to tell her by calling the place *anti-deserted*.

She had to make a choice again—subtly make the people give way through mental command, or get into full body contact to squeeze her way to the counter.

No, I won't wake the beast again. She began to push through between hot, humid bodies, wrapped in cargo or maintenance worker gear, merchant crew uniforms, or rather skimpy dresses leaving little room for imagination. The latter were firmly attached to the former, which partially determined her way.

Occasionally, she had to firmly twist a finger feeling for her tits or buttocks, but otherwise she reached the counter unmolested and examined the long row of functionless tap levers. Bruce had mentioned this nostalgic element. In ancient times, this mechanical device had been used to start and stop the flow of liquids from carbon-dioxide-pressurized containers. Nowadays, it mainly served to present the different brands of liquid offered.

"Yeh?" the barkeeper grunted at her.

Bruce had warned her about this moment, too. She had three millicycles of his attention, after that he'd be gone to the next client. She had no time to study the offerings and make up her mind.

"The *bitch*," she said, following Bruce's recommendation

for her first choice, a pale, opaque wheat beer with a fruity taste—at least that had been his description.

When the glass arrived before her a moment later, she agreed with him. The fruity smell she immediately noticed was promising.

Syreen was granted a first sip before she felt herself being pushed away from the counter. The crowd's continuous movement slowly washed her toward the rear bulkhead, where she found a free seat.

Friendly faces smiled at her, nodded, and returned to their conversations.

Only one man kept his focus on her. "New to Kyris?"

"I arrived today."

"I've never seen the colors of your uniform."

"It's Duchy Fleet."

"The Duchy, eh? I think I've heard of that. Two or three jumps away?"

"Depends on the route, yes."

"What are all the decorations for? If I may ask—oh, by the way, my name's Bertrand."

"Hi Bertrand. I'm Syreen." She raised her glass and drank.

He took another sip from his own, dark beer. "The star with the belt?"

"Belt? Oh—the halo. Indicates a hyperflight command."

"Oh—you command your own ship?"

"I do."

"Wow. I never met a starship captain before."

"I'm no captain. I'm a lieutenant, and in Fleet, commandants are called skippers."

"Skipper. Okay, skipper—what's the larger four-ray star for?"

"Warfare command. It says I've commanded in battle."

"In *battle?* Uh." Bertrand drank again. "You're still young—no offense meant—so that must have been recently."

"No offense taken." Otherwise, she didn't comment.

After a while, he shrugged. "Okay, I won't ask. What about the smaller stars?"

"One for each acknowledged kill."

"Kill?"

"For each enemy starship eliminated."

He stared at her chest and began to count.

"Before you ask," she added. "Only those that can shoot back count."

"But you weren't shot at."

"I was, but I wasn't hit. I dodged in time, each time."

"I almost fear to ask about the stripes."

"Stripes? Oh, the ribbons." She pointed at her own chest. "That's for ranking first in the pilot's exam. This one is for precision shooting, and this one for exemplary conduct."

"You're very proud of your military career," Bertrand observed.

"Yes." She had never thought of herself that way.

"So — you'll surely tell me what this spiral galaxy is about, too. Some extraordinary achievement, I'm sure."

"Sorry, no. It's the one symbol I did nothing for, although I've learned to wear it with pride, too — the sign of the current Fleet Commander in Charge."

Bertrand shrank back. "You're kidding." He watched her, but Syreen only nodded, confirming what she had said. "No, really? But what are you doing here?"

Syreen smiled and raised her glass again. "Drinking beer."

"Oh, yeah — but what did you come here for?"

"The same — the beer was a recommendation, and I'm glad for it."

"Which did you pick?"

"The *bitch*. Suits me best."

Bertrand paused. When the corner of her mouth twitched, they both laughed.

CHAPTER FORTY-EIGHT

When Bertrand left the table to refill his glass, another man took his seat. Syreen was glad for the change. Bertrand had been too impressed by her insignia and decorations—perhaps she shouldn't have told him so much about them? But he was right—she was proud about her achievements, and why shouldn't she be?

She just didn't feel as cheerful about the circumstances that had allowed her to score so many kills. Too many of her Fleet mates had given their lives, and she didn't even want to know what the aggressor did to her people meanwhile.

The newcomer's gaze lingered on Syreen's chest for a while before he addressed her. "Sum navvy, eh?"

"Yeh," she replied tight-lipped. Her latest line of thoughts had put her in no mood for boasting.

"Lookin' fer sum fun?" He leaned closer, and a wave of beer assaulted her sense of smell. "Ya lookin' pretty, gal. Lemme show ya my funner."

"Funner?" she echoed.

He grabbed her hand and pulled it to his thigh, where she could feel an impressively long cock.

"Ma funner, gal. Lemme puddit in all de way, an' I'll make ya scream."

I shouldn't fall for such a primitive pick-up. However, Syreen felt reminded of her stimulator—*Raydancer* definitely lacked such a device. She hadn't had any sex since leaving the Duchy—her crew was out of the question. She also couldn't amble down the corridors of Kyris Orbital Base and try to hook some guy up—the local police might ignore any previous orders if she gave them reason to act.

In this place, at this time, with this crowd, she'd be as anonymous as she could be. She felt her own excitement rise.

A little voice in the back of her head asked how this would help her mission. *Not at all,* she told herself, *but it won't make it any worse either.*

So she leaned forward, too, and stroked his member with her hand. "Where?"

"Round conner," he advised her and pointed to a door in the back she hadn't noticed before. It was marked as emergency exit. "Dis way."

"Lead the way."

He rose, swayed a little, and then pushed through the people.

Syreen followed the emanations of lust she sensed in the man. He was obviously inebriated, and as obviously, it didn't adversely affect his libido.

The emergency exit led into one of the almost-dark corridors she had been warned about, but this part was empty except for herself and her cavalier—who had already opened his fly and presented her a quickly rising boner of most remarkable proportions.

She reached out and caressed it with one hand while tearing at her own pants with the other. She almost regretted letting go of it, but she needed both hands to push her clothes down all the way.

He made a step forward. She stopped him with one arm and felt between her legs—already wet. When she licked her lips, there were pointy obstacles—her canines again. *No.*

There was only one easy way to reduce the risk of accidentally biting him. She turned away from the man and bent forward, resting her beret on the bulkhead. Next, she felt his cock pushing against her buttocks.

Syreen reached behind and guided his tip between her labia. When she felt him in the right spot, she pushed her pelvis back. *Oh, that's sooo good.*

He tried to be considerate, probed her readiness, pulled back, and tested again—too considerate for her impatience. Although . . . it felt good, so good, and he penetrated a little bit deeper each time anyway. He felt so big already, and yet, the next push went deeper again. Again, and again, and still his pelvis hadn't touched her cheeks—how could there be so much cock?

"Ya so tight," he groaned and grabbed her hipbones. Once more, he pulled back until he almost left her, and then he thrust forward and all the way in.

"More," she demanded.

"Oh yeah, babe," he acknowledged and repeated his actions—slowly pulling out and quickly pushing in, then slowly pushing in, and then fast again.

I should take him with me. Oh! Only, once I hire him, he's crew and off limits. Oh! So what? Oh! He'll be hired as a pet. Oh! Worth the trouble? Oh! Yes, yes, yes, that's worth every trouble! Oh! I won't let him go—ever. Oh!

"I told ya."

Oh!

"Yes you did—go on! Oh!"

"Ready fer jumpin'?"

"Yeees!"

He paused deep inside her before pulling out again very slowly, as if taking measure for a shot—and started rocking. In, out, in, out, forth, back, faster and faster—she had to take her head away from the wall—they both moaned, gasped, wheezed, and then he squealed once, twice, a third time—she felt him tensing, tensed herself, and she screamed and came. He came, too—she could tell from the difference in his movements. She didn't care though, she only enjoyed—the relief, the fading tingle, the big hard tool inside her, the wetness slowly running down her thigh and the tickling coming with it, his panting breath, his male smell, the sense of his satisfaction.

Syreen wouldn't let go. *I want to keep this cock right in place, as deep as that, and never out again – except to push right back in.*

Syreen couldn't let go. *If he pulls out now, I bite him – I couldn't stop me if even if I wanted to.*

Syreen shouldn't let go. *We didn't exchange names, but he could easily identify my uniform and thus me. He must not spoil my reputation.* Nor could she let him pay the price for her recklessness. He wasn't to blame.

She took several deep breaths and concentrated on her teeth. *No bite today, my lover must go away . . . leave me in a place dark and lonely – pull out, turn away, forget me, and don't look behind. Now. No bite today . . .*

Keeping her mind focused on her mental commands, she hardly noticed his cock sliding out, and his cum slowly following.

Only when she no longer sensed his mental presence did she dare to move, turn around and rise, rearrange her clothes, and check the corridor.

She was alone. No one had come and spotted her with her pants down. No one had tried to take advantage of her situation – no one had come to submit to her fangs.

CHAPTER FORTY-NINE

Syreen had to follow the maze of dark back corridors around several turns before she reached a populated area again. She knew instinctively where to go to return to the previous place, but she decided against it. Yes, it had been a good recommendation with regard to the beer, but it wouldn't be the best place to negotiate an escort contract or gather more information. She needed a place where the noise level allowed serious talking, and where the crowd still allowed some anonymity.

She might as well enter the next venue she came along—like this one. The red-and-green sign at the entrance—Duchy colors—looked homelike to her, so she opened the door.

It was less crowded than the other bars she had visited. The way to the counter was free, as was the counter itself. Groups of men sat around at small tables, quietly chatting with each other, only occasionally interrupted by a laughter.

The barkeeper ogled her with a frown. "Are you sure you came to the right place?"

"If you serve drinks, yes." She nodded toward the room. "It's less crowded and noisy here. I like that. Moreover, with the colors, I feel like home."

He briefly glanced down her uniform. "Oh, that. Yes. Only, women seldom come here. Not their place, you see?"

She looked over her shoulder. Indeed, she seemed to be the only woman around. Why hadn't she noticed before? Because she sensed an air of affection and romance. This was a good place for lovers—or a good place to come to and calm down after really good sex. Inviting for her, and inviting for the many gay males. Not exactly a place for anonymity—not for her—but she wouldn't withdraw now.

Syreen shrugged. "If nobody takes offense, I don't care. Do you have a wheat beer on tap?"

"I don't have anything on tap, but you can have a wheat beer. Pale or dark?"

"Pale, please."

He went away to fetch her order, and she turned to the room. Her appearance hadn't attracted much attention, but when she scanned the tables, one of the men rose and came toward her. He wore black leather trousers—which seemed the norm here—and a dark-blue shirt made from some soft fabric, matching his soft features. His short black hair stood away in all directions.

He seemed hesitant first, but then found the courage to address her. "Good evening. I'm called Drake."

"Good evening, Drake. I'm Syreen."

His blue eyes focused on her chest. "I don't want to molest you."

"You don't."

"Well. May I invite you for a drink, then?"

"I've already ordered one."

"Oh, Jiggo surely didn't charge it yet. Let me take care of that, please."

"If you insist—Drake."

He smiled and made a sign toward the keeper.

With a *Here you are,* Jiggo placed the glass on the counter before her.

Syreen took it and nodded at Drake, who picked up the cue and led her back to his table, where a baldheaded man in a tight muscle shirt with tattooed biceps guarded two half-full glasses.

"This is Crow," Drake introduced her. "And this is

Syreen."

"Hi, Crow."

Crow grunted something. Drake pointed at an empty chair, and she sat down. She waited until her host had copied her, and then raised her glass. "Cheers, and thank you."

Drake only took a sip and placed his glass down again. He seemed to be searching for the right words, and his embarrassment seemed to condense into a curtain between them.

"Tell me — why did you invite me? It wasn't for my looks, I'm sure."

"No. Uh, sorry. Well . . . you're wearing a navy uniform. Right?"

"Right."

"Not Kyris though."

"No." Such closed questions weren't suitable to make her talk, but for the moment, she just replied and waited to see where it would lead him.

"So — you came with a navy starship?"

"Yes."

"Um — can you tell me whether your commandant would accept escort contracts and such?"

"Yes, I can — I'm the skipper myself, and yes, I accept escort contracts. I came here on such a contract."

"You're the skipper yourself . . . um, yes. It's — I don't have a freighter."

That was odd. But Syreen couldn't sense any hint of malice — it wasn't meant as a trick or trap, of that she was sure.

"Come on, tell me. What's it all about?"

"It's — well, exploration."

"Exploration. That sounds interesting. What do you want to explore?"

"Uninhabited planets — where no regular liner goes. That's why I need a navy ship — a starship with its own shuttle. Otherwise I can't go down to the surface."

Syreen leaned back. "I once heard that some of the old nations send out explorer fleets for such purposes. Wouldn't you be better advised to get in contact with them? They know how to do it."

"No — it would take a megacycle of bureaucratic nightmares before I'd be even allowed to ask my question. I won't live that long. I must find another way, that is, I must find a skipper willing to try a new route."

"A new route?" Syreen tried to remember what her instructor had told her about new routes. You could never know what obstacles you'd be running into. *Reliable suicide,* he had called it. However, every new system had been found by a skipper who had flown a new route, and the early explorers had cherished their lives, too. So where would she find the truth?

She recalled her recent jumps. As far as she knew, nobody had ever jumped from Carix Alpha toward Kyris. The route had been new, only the start and end points known to the computer, but the library had provided the major obstacles around it. That was all a navigator needed — a repository of known obstacles along the route. So as long as the planet in question was anywhere near a known route, she should be able to find a clear path. No — she felt sure she'd be able to find the path.

"Yes," Drake confirmed. "As far as I know, nobody's been there for several megacycles — if ever."

"So how do you know where to go?"

"I have the set of galactic coordinates — only, it's an ancient astronomical system. I tried to translate it, and it should be somewhere in this galactic sector, but I must have made a mistake."

Syreen grinned. That was something her instructor had taught them — he had come up with the strangest sorts of coordinates and a few known stars, and from there they had had to calculate the strange system's root coordinates, and the necessary translation. "I'm good at that. Tell me the numbers, and I'll do the rest—and yes, I'd find a way to jump there, too."

"But would you do it? The actual jump, I mean."

She sensed his tension—she didn't even need her new-found skills for that. "Yes. I would do the jump. I would go there and have a look for whatever you're looking for. Which you didn't tell me yet."

"And would you take us along, and let us take your shuttle?"

Syreen nodded—and shook her head. "I don't have a shuttle."

"But you said you're commanding a navy starship?"

"That's what I said." She reached for her glass. "It's a small one, perfectly suited for this kind of mission. It's a corvette, and it can go dirtside itself, like a shuttle." She saw Drake's face light up. "There's one downside to it, though—it's small inside, too. The passenger room is large enough for six people, and I already have my crew of two—you'd have to get along with each other."

Drake glanced at Crow, shrugged, and nodded.

"There's another question, though," Syreen added.

"Yes?" Drake appeared alert.

She sat up straight. "I don't even know yet how many jumps we'll need to get close to your destination—I will certainly stay on known routes as long as possible. Each jump puts strain on the aggregates. We'll need provisions, spare parts, maintenance and docking fees along the route—you get the picture."

"Sure." Drake was calm again. "Credits. That's the least issue to worry about. When I ventured on my mission, I knew what it would take. I'm willing to pay all maintenance and docking fees along the route—and I trust you to deal fair—

and for flying to our destination and taking two passengers along, I'll offer you a hundred thousand credits per jump. It's your decision how many jumps you need, but as long as you stay on known routes, I may check your choice with the merchant guild. Does that sound fair?"

Should she ask Herman about the deal? No, she had to be able to make that decision herself. She was in charge. She was responsible for making the right choices.

"It does," she said and made a quick mental laundry list. "Five conditions."

"Yes?"

"One—the safety of crew and ship comes first. Should local astrophysical conditions prevent jumping, like a fresh nova close to our destination, I'd cancel the mission."

"Oh. That's not very likely, or is it?"

"No, it isn't likely, and I won't chicken out only because it's difficult. But it's my call as skipper."

"Fair enough. The second?"

"Again, it's safety. I will decide whether I can make a safe landing. If I can't, I won't."

"In which case would you provide us with the hyperjump data for a second attempt, where we could bring better equipment?"

"Of course."

He exchanged a glance with Crow, and Syreen briefly sensed a disapproving emotion. She could understand that, as she wouldn't like to stop before the last step either.

"I agree. What's your third condition?"

"It should go without saying—I'm the skipper, and it's a Fleet vessel. Fleet regulations apply for every person aboard with regard to personal conduct, everyday chores and discipline. I won't make undue demands, but if I order you to shut up, sit down and buckle up, there won't be arguments."

Drake placed one finger on his glass. "Mmm—I

understand the buckle-up part, but why should we be forbidden to speak?"

"Because I might need all my concentration to save your ass from a critical situation and can't have any background babble. Once the crisis is over, you can complain as much as you like."

"Oh—okay, if you put it like this, I understand. Agreed. What else?"

"Fleet regulations again. Should we encounter pirates, I'll deal with them. Should we encounter a merchant in distress, I'll assist in any way necessary, even if that means I must change our route—of course, free of charge for you. Your investment would be extra time spent aboard."

Drake shrugged. "Well—that's just common sense. Standard conditions on any passenger liner. No problem with that."

"Fine. My last condition—before I settle the deal, I must know what I'll be dealing with. Where did you get your coordinates from, and what do you expect to find? I won't blindly jump into a bug-eyed monsters' home system, you know?"

Her prospect glanced around. "Well. I understand your concern, but that is something I'd like to keep secret until we have a contract. After all, I know nothing about you but your name. Moreover, I wouldn't want to discuss it all in public."

Syreen shook her head. "Without any clue what I'm up against, I can't enter such an adventure. But the place—we could continue our discussion aboard *Raydancer,* or we could go to the guild hall."

"*Raydancer*—that's your ship?"

"Yes."

"You're the one who shot the pirates, then? With precise shots over impossible distance?"

"Yes."

"Hmm—you know, that story's going around. On the shots, the deal, and the jump." Again, Drake glanced around, and then at Crow. "I reckon we couldn't find a better skipper in this sector. According to the story, you're skilled and trustworthy." He stared at the table before him. "Okay, what I can tell you is this. I've been investigating ancient history—old records, old lore, old artifacts—on spacefaring races before our time. Now I'm looking for the next piece of the puzzle. A planet that hasn't been colonized by us yet, but has been visited by others before, and that's still as it's been left behind—a so-called *forgotten* planet."

CHAPTER FIFTY

Syreen was glad that they had already negotiated the terms and conditions. She was all excitement and tried not to show it, but instead reached for her beer.

The name might be just a coincidence. But how many ancient, spacefaring races could there be in this galactic sector? What if Drake had access to the same sources as the Association and was following the same, cold trail? Or, even if he wasn't, was there any chance that such a *relic* as the one they were hunting was buried on a secret planet—the reason it hadn't been found yet?

She couldn't pass up that chance, and she couldn't risk Drake getting his hands on such a powerful artifact alone. For her, the mission was settled, whatever he paid.

"Let's say I'm happy with that snippet now. I want the whole story before the last jump, and I need the coordinates before we undock—I must have a chance to check the shops en route, or get more supplies here."

"Mmm—you got a point there. What's your schedule, anyway?"

"I've paid for two tencycles in dock, with an option for two more, and I arrived this morning. If I must extend my stay for preparation of your mission, you'll pay the extension fee."

"How much is that?"

"Twenty-five thousand for the first two tencycles. I don't know what they'll charge for extensions."

He hesitated. Syreen felt concern.

"Trouble?" she asked.

"What? No, no. I tried to estimate the fees on our way. We'll be fine. Okay—do we have a deal?"

His smile was genuine and tempting. Syreen smiled back. This would be a hazardous mission, but she could justify it, not only to herself, but also with regard to Fleet. If she had any chance to get this *relic* first—or at least gain another clue on its whereabouts—it would be for the greater good of the entire Duchy, perhaps even of the entire sector.

She couldn't justify starting recklessly. "We will have a deal once the terms are recorded with the guild. First thing tomorrow morning?"

His smile grew wider, and his eyes flashed with amusement. "First thing tomorrow morning, Captain Syreen."

"Lieutenant, please." She held up her left arm and pointed at the sleeve. "One stripe."

"Oh, okay." Drake nodded and pointed at her chest. "I got distracted by your decorations."

She believed him. Female assets obviously had no effect on him, so it was just her uniform chest and not its content he was referring to.

"However, this brings up another question," he went on. "Can a mere Lieutenant—sorry—decide to enter such a contract without asking her superiors? I assume you already settled that our mission won't interfere with your duties."

"Any Fleet skipper outside the Duchy is entitled to act at his own discretion. I may not enter obligations beyond my command, I may not make contracts against the Duchy's interests, but otherwise I can do anything that I deem favorable. I think that exploring a new route between the stars and discovering a new habitable system fulfills these criteria. Having said that—I might have to claim the planet for the Duchy with regard to political boundaries. As you are funding the expedition, you will have legitimate commercial claims that are not affected by territorial claims."

Drake frowned. "That's not what I had in mind."

"That's how life is. Did you plan to found your own star nation? Or, wait, what was it?" She tried to remember what the Books had told her. "If you have a letter of credence for another star nation, you can claim the system in their name, and I will stand back. That would become part of the contract."

Her own rank as warship commandant included such authority without any separate letter. If there was no other claim, she could just seize it, which was what Fleet regulations said about new territory. Like war without enemies, she had translated the paragraphs for herself.

She'd need a buoy to leave behind when they left, to tell every subsequent arrival of her claim.

"No, I don't have such a letter. You're right, you're entitled to claim it. I only had hoped I'd have some time to explore the planet — undisturbed."

"We will be undisturbed. Only — if I don't claim the system, the very next arrival will, and they will then be entitled to kick us out instantly. In the unlikely case someone followed us."

Now Drake smiled again. "I didn't think of that, either. You're indeed the best skipper I could wish for."

Syreen tried a bow — not easy while sitting, but she managed.

Chapter Fifty-one

Stephan was still awake when Syreen returned to *Raydancer*. He heard the outer hatch, rose, and leaned onto the galley hatchway.

The inner hatch opened and unveiled a cheerful skipper. Stephan was glad for that—they had enough to worry about. They didn't need a sour commandant on top.

"Hey, Sir. All okay?"

"Hi, Stephan. I'm fine. And you?"

"No trouble here. Provisions are coming, Herman's sleeping, all quiet."

She made a sad face. "I should've taken you along. Tomorrow it's your turn, okay?"

"Oh, I'm fine."

"You won't be if I let you rot in this hole for too long. Everyone needs some more space now and then. However, it's okay if you haven't noticed yet. Did Herman tell you anything?"

"Everything, I'd guess. He wouldn't stop talking. About the embassy, about his family's office and the assholes there—sorry, Sir—about the merchant guild and your sweet revenge, and on our order." He focused on her. "Do we really have an order for this ship?"

"Yes, sure. It's secret, so you can't access it without my permission, but I tricked the Association into giving me an order. That way, I could hide the fact that we're at war—the ambassador explicitly warned me that Kyris might not remain neutral if they knew."

"Sounds like we're outcasts."

"Not yet, but close."

She smiled so sweetly that he almost felt compelled to hug her. She wasn't bad for a woman. No, not bad, not at all. And yet—it didn't feel right.

"I don't know yet how to change our situation for the better," she admitted. "But I'm working on it. Until then, we must remain on the move, be alert and earn our living. I've found us a principal tonight."

Stephan frowned. "Herman said something like that—we can't get support here, right?"

"No."

What had she said just before? "A principal, Sir?"

She sighed. "You can call me Syreen, Stephan. The *Sir* sounds so strange. At least when we're not talking military duties, which we probably won't for some time. Yes, I've found us a principal. A paying client. We'll do some exploration."

"Exploration?"

His commanding officer—Syreen, okay—started to give him a summary on her evening and the mission. He registered half of it at best, because his thoughts were racing.

They might never see their home planet again—they'd be lost in space—trapped in a tiny shell of steel . . .

"I know what I'm doing," Syreen said and placed a hand on his shoulder. "I know I can safely bring us there and back. I'm good at navigating. This mission will buy us some time to consider how we can free our planet. I don't plan to run away for the rest of my life, and I won't let them have our planet. Fleet never gives up. Okay?"

Stephan didn't understand how she did it, but he felt calmer. He usually didn't like being touched by women, but her touch was different, reassuring, in a way welcome. *It's not as if she is contagious or something. Or trying to seduce me. She accepts me as I am. A man interested in other men.*

"Okay."

"You should find some sleep now. We'll get up early."

"We?"

"As I said—you'll come along. Herman can handle the deliveries. Oh, before I forget, I must order a buoy. I'll better do it now. Good night."

"Good night." He'd dream of her tonight. Of her, growing a nice, hard cock.

CHAPTER FIFTY-TWO

The next morning, Syreen kept her promise, left Herman behind with clear instructions, and took Stephan along to the merchant guild.

Jacomo didn't appear surprised when they arrived at the door precisely at the appointed time, and Syreen wasn't surprised that he had received the late announcement about her second visit.

He invited them inside and led them to the same room Syreen already knew.

"Refreshments? I assume your contract partners will arrive every centicycle?"

"Yes, a mug of forwine please, and yes, I guess so." She pointed at Stephan. "Private Stephan Smith, my maintenance magician."

Stephan grinned. "Water for me, please. Magician? Nicely put."

"I'm sorry that I'm stirring up things for you," Syreen said to the secretary.

"Oh, don't worry. Docking time is precious, so we're always ready. That's business as usual." He brought their drinks and smiled. "The board decision in Mr. Doeken's favor will cause a stir, though. The message should have arrived now. I'm sure the repercussions will be quite a spectacle to watch."

"You seem to enjoy the idea."

"Oh, I do. While I'm neutral from the professional perspective, I appreciate the entertainment value. It's always the same old, same old, you know — ships coming and leaving, registrations, the usual complaints about late delivery, quality, or fees. This is different. Everything will settle after a while, I'm sure, but in the meantime, we'll watch how everyone deals with the new situation. Frozen funds, rent and fees to be paid, favors to be collected, dispatches to be sent — yes, we'll have a lot to talk about. You know the only three things that are faster than light?"

"Ships in hyperflight, tachyons — what's the third?"

"Rumors."

Syreen could sense Jacomo's amusement and said, "Eventually, someone will exploit that and develop a rumor gun. Faster-than-light weaponry would be decisive in any battle."

The secretary raised his eyebrows. "Young lady, don't underestimate the decisive effects rumors had in past battles."

She nodded. "I still have much to learn with regard to battles and campaigning. I will heed your advice — all the more, as it was offered for free."

When she winked, he laughed out loud. "Got me!"

A chime made him turn away. "Excuse me. Your contract partners."

CHAPTER FIFTY-THREE

Syreen placed her mug down and rose when Jacomo led Drake and Crow into the room. The secretary didn't say anything, but his face was clouded and his emotions signaled disapproval to her.

The two men wore black leather again — whether it was the same as the night before, she couldn't tell.

"Good morning, Drake, Crow," she said and held out her hand.

"Good morning, Lieutenant Syreen," Drake answered and shook her hand.

Crow only nodded and squeezed her hand. She didn't flinch, but paid back in the same manner, and he made a face. She sensed pain, surprise, and then respect.

"Stephan, my maintenance expert. Stephan, this is Mr. Drake —" they shook hands, too — "and Mr. Crow."

Stephan radiated more than a little curiosity, but she had to ignore his feelings for the time being. There was a whole story going on between Drake and Jacomo, while neither said a word.

Drake nodded at the secretary when he addressed her. "Lieutenant, I'd understand if you had changed your mind in the meantime. I'm sure Jacomo already told you about me."

"He didn't."

"No?"

"He didn't know who was coming. I didn't bother to tell him. Now, why don't you tell me why his stories should change my mind?"

Her prospect's smile was thin. "He thinks I'm following an obsession without any substance. A ghost." He shrugged. "The idea of doing an uncharted jump appears plain crazy for most. That's why I thought you might have reconsidered."

Syreen shook her head. "First, I don't think your quest is unreasonable. Second, every jump ever made has been uncharted in the beginning. I agree, it's not a task to be approached without care—but I know I can do it safely."

Jacomo raised both hands in mock despair. "Here meet two of the same mind. What could I say?"

"Just register our contract, Jacomo," she said. "I can reassure you—you're not sentencing us to our doom."

He sighed. "Of course. I will record your names and your terms and conditions now."

On his sign, they sat down around the table. Jacomo tapped the table, and screens appeared before them.

"Contract registration," he began. "Type of contract is charter, for passenger transport?"

"And exploration," Drake added. "No fixed destination."

"Sure. Principal—Mr. Dragutin Petran, as registered to the guild."

"Dragutin?" Syreen echoed.

He smiled at her. "I don't use that name often."

Jacomo waved his hand, and face, iris patterns and finger patterns briefly appeared on their screens. "Contractor—Lieutenant Syreen, no surname, as registered to the guild."

She nodded.

"Contract volume." Jacomo watched her.

Syreen wasn't sure what to say.

Drake helped out. "Payment is on a per-jump basis. As the destination is yet to determine, the number of jumps isn't fixed yet. The minimum number of jumps—and thus the guaranteed minimum volume—is six jumps, three outward and three return, where we can still agree on the return destination. Moreover, I will bear maintenance and docking fees along the way, at least once on our way out and once back."

Jacomo nodded. "Standard guild rates?"

Syreen wasn't surprised to hear that standard rates existed, but she hadn't thought of that when negotiating the price. She had only weighed it against her escort fee and compared cargo to passengers. Now she was curious about what she could have earned.

"For the contract value, standard rates for maintenance and docking, but to be paid as occurred. For the jumps, double rates — one-hundred thousand per jump, as agreed."

"Double? Okay." Jacomo glanced at Syreen. "So you agreed on a high-risk contract, right? Should I classify it as such?"

"What would that mean?" she quickly asked.

"Oh — it's easier for both sides to terminate the contract, should continuation be rendered difficult after a risk materialized. Both sides have the right to demand mitigation in mutual interest, and such. The draft will highlight the respective passages." He waited until she nodded, and went on, "Now, any specific conditions I should record?"

Syreen nodded and quickly went through her bucket list. She didn't mention any forgotten planet, but added shuttle services for planets without orbital base in general to her services and mentioned her reservations with regard to dangerous approaches.

"Yes, that's sensible," Jacomo agreed. "Okay. Drake, anything from your side?"

"One thing that came up tonight — I didn't sleep well, was too stirred up — sorry, Lieutenant — I'd like to have some guarantee that our journey won't end at the next stop because your superiors call you back. I've racked my brain how we could achieve that — of course I can't ask you to break your vows."

Jacomo raised his eyebrows. "You didn't see — she didn't tell you — "

"Tell me what?" Drake asked.

Syreen felt his anger rising.

"What did you hide from me?" Drake called out.

"Hide?" Syreen asked.

"Nothing," Jacomo came to her aid. She sensed his amusement. "She hid nothing, Drake. It's been there in plain sight all the time. You see that galaxy on her chest?"

"Yes," Drake snarled.

"It's identifying her as the Duchy's Fleet Commander in Charge. There is no superior to command her around."

Drake's gaze jumped back and forth between her chest and Jacomo. "Fleet Commander? But — she's a lieutenant."

Syreen smiled. "That's true. I can't help it."

"But how — why?"

"Let's say my promotion is overdue, okay?"

Drake frowned. "Okay. What does that mean for us?"

"Reliability. As I told you, as skipper I'm entitled to enter contracts for the Duchy's benefit. As current Fleet Commander in Charge, I'm entitled to judge what's for the Duchy's benefit without checking back with any superiors, so any decision I make is final. Of course, the Duchy government could appoint a new fleet commander any time — but he or she still would still be obliged to honor any contract settled in good faith." She turned to Jacomo. "Please record that I regard this contract as for the Duchy's benefit."

The secretary eyed her. "Really?"

"Really."

Now he raised his eyebrows again. "It's your court-martial."

"I will duly record my reasoning in my log. Classified."

The secretary tried in vain to raise his eyebrows higher again, but she could sense his curiosity. She could imagine that the information on this judgment alone was a novelty with regard to Drake's reputation on Kyris, but she wasn't willing to explain herself.

Jacomo added Drake's concern together with her decision. When he was done, he let them read the register entry.

CHAPTER FIFTY-FOUR

Syreen had expected at least dozens of paragraphs in complicated legalese, at least as complicated as Fleet regulations, but only found a few very basic, very simple rules plus their negotiated terms and conditions. She asked Jacomo about it.

"Oh, that, yes. Well — the guild operates all over the galaxy, across the star nations. Local laws differ, lawyers differ, judges differ. In the early days of the guild, someone tried to make laser-proof rules, but the lawyers took them apart anyway. Once there was a wise judge. He wrote, *anyone writing such complicated rules deserved nit-picking at court. Only the most simple rules could be considered universal. Only rules understandable to every plain man could be treated as agreements meant to be fair and interpreted as such.* So the guild decided to heed his advice and use simple and fair rules. Since then, most judges dealing with interstellar contracts followed his reasoning and tried to resolve disagreements in a fair way. Rumor has it they dislike the idea of having to read hundreds of paragraphs to find out what could be meant and trying to match those with local law."

"Wise."

"Yes. The universe is full of miracles, and this is certainly one of them."

"In any case, I'm fine with the register."

"Okay. Mr. Petran?"

"Fine for me, too."

"Okay. Would you both please confirm by focusing on the

green spot and tapping the panel?"

They both did as instructed.

Jacomo checked his own display, clapped his hand once, and stated, "settled. You'll receive a copy. The entry will be replicated in the usual way. Anything else I can do for you?"

"Not right now. Thank you, Jacomo," Syreen said.

"You're welcome."

Drake only nodded and rose. Crow copied him, and Syreen and Stephan followed.

Jacomo took a little more time, and then addressed Syreen. "You have an option to extend your docking. Don't use it. There might be trouble ahead."

"Trouble?"

"Remember that I'm supposed to be neutral. I can't tell you more."

"Oh, okay. I will consider that."

"It's your call." It sounded like *It's your hide,* but Syreen had to check their route and other essentials next.

CHAPTER FIFTY-FIVE

After leaving the guild hall, Syreen led her principals—or passengers—straight to dock Gamma Two. They weren't bothered on their way, but Syreen felt the proverbial hairs in her neck stand up more than once. Combined with a distant sense of hate, she reconsidered Jacomo's advice. What else did Kyris Orbital Base have in store for them?

Drake stopped at a window near the dock and peeked outside. "That's a small ship indeed. I thought corvettes were bigger. You feel safe flying that?"

"I'm used to much smaller ships. However, this is the smallest class capable of hyperflight."

He wasn't happy yet.

"If it were bigger, you'd have to deal with a lot more crew—and probably with a way less adventurous skipper." She winked.

Crow laughed. "There, boss!"

Drake managed a smile. "Got me there."

Syreen waved Stephan forward. Drake followed, then Crow, and she entered last.

Stephan stepped aside to let their passengers pass. Herman waited in the galley door and made a curious face.

Syreen introduced them briefly. "Let me give you a very brief overview. Forward—the bridge. When the door's closed, it's off limits for you. You may peek through the door when it's open and talk, but never enter uninvited. Aft—the storage. Nothing goes in or out of there unregistered, so unless you want to deal with accounting, it's not your place. You have two seats in the passenger compartment—quite comfy to sleep, too—and you can go to the bathroom or to the galley anytime. In case I call general quarters or battle stations—your place is your seat, buckled up." She smiled. "Okay—and that's the door to the pilot's cabin. Mine. Again, off limits for you."

"Some skippers would offer their cabin to their paying passengers," Drake objected.

"Well, I don't. I must sleep now and then, too, and when I do, and there's an alarm, I may not have time to return to the bridge. As the designers foresaw that, there are secondary control installations, and that's why I will sleep there."

"Oh—okay. Reasonable." He cocked his head. "At the guild, you said our journey is for your Duchy's benefit. How can you be so sure?"

"Because I have insights that give your story credibility. You're not the only one hunting for the legacy of older space-faring races."

"You meant it," Drake observed. "You want to go there."

"Yes." She pointed at the passenger compartment. "Why don't we have a look where that *there* is. Show me your coordinates."

CHAPTER FIFTY-SIX

Drake watched the lieutenant filling the projection sphere with tiny red dots, indicating the positions of stars.

"See?" she said. "This is your data."

"I've been that far," he said, struggling with his impatience. He should give her a chance. After all, he had needed tencycles to get to that point she had reached within a quartercycle.

"Of course," she replied cheerfully, as if she hadn't noticed his rebuff. "Now let me add our current surroundings at about the same scale."

She tapped on the pad before her, and another cloud of tiny dots appeared, only in green.

"That's a mess," he said. The only thing that matched was the density of both clouds of stars, meaning that there had to be the same number of dots, give or take a few hundred.

"The scale doesn't match." She waved with her fingers, and the cloud of green dots seemed to expand. "Let me see — the orientation is wrong." The red dots twisted and toppled.

"That's still different." The difference in numbers might be less indeed, but otherwise, he couldn't see similarities. Perhaps he should advise her to check his own calculations? By comparing the spectral data of a few dozen stars, he had found close similarities — only the constellations hadn't matched at all.

"Yes, because your data is some megacycles old. Stars don't stay in place. I must move them forward in time."

Drake watched her entering numbers and complicated formulas. A few centicycles later, she let out a happy "Yes" and pointed at the sphere, where the red dots moved into new positions.

He watched with fascination how they melted into the green dots, thus changing to yellow.

"How did you do this?"

She shrugged. "Well, after I had a look at the constellations, it was no deal to turn them around. Didn't you see the patterns?"

"Not before you moved them," he admitted. "To me, it was just a big mess."

"Well, let's say I have an eye for that." Again she shrugged. "Now, let's remove all stars with known planets today."

Some dots changed to blue. Many yellow dots remained.

"And now — those that don't have planets in either library."

All but three dots turned blue.

"Wow," he said. "That was quick."

She gave him a warm smile. "Now, let me highlight Kyris."

One dot close to the center — and relatively close to one of the yellow dots — turned pink.

Only now did he register that her show had three more spectators. They had held their breath and uttered a collective sigh.

"Seems we have our candidate," the lieutenant announced. "Labeled *RAK-11* in your library. According to your data, it has three planets, one in the habitable zone. Now let me see . . ."

The sphere seemed to explode, but all dots reaching its boundary disappeared. A much smaller number of stars remained. Pink and yellow stopped near the edge.

She entered another command, and most green dots darkened. The remaining five formed a crooked line across the sphere. "We have a route."

"Five stops?" he asked.

His charter pilot didn't answer. Instead, she slowly spun the sphere around, back and forth, up and down. Did she even blink? In the end, she marked another star which turned orange.

"This is our destination," she announced. "From there, I can do the jump."

"Why?" he asked.

"There's a free hypercorridor past that red giant." She highlighted another dot, and then pointed at the orange dot again. "This star is cataloged as an auxiliary jump node. The recharge conditions are above average, and there are multiple routes leading in and out. I'd like to make a stopover shortly before we go there." She tapped her pad. "Jakarta is two jumps away." The respective stars lit up.

"Four stops," he summarized. "Two jumps per stop? And then three more jumps, eleven in total. A little more than I thought."

"Is that a problem?" the maintenance guy asked.

"No," he said, not entirely a lie. His remaining budget was two million credits — with eleven jumps one way he wouldn't be able to return to Kyris, not even considering the stopover fees. But he could afford returning to Jakarta, and from there he might be able to travel home by liner — unless he found something valuable on RAK-11.

"Two stops," she corrected, to his surprise. "We can't avoid Brannock, so we might as well stop there. But we can reach it in two, and make another two from Brannock to Jakarta. Seven in total. Sound good?"

"Yes." He stared at the sphere. "All along known routes?"

"Nah. Shortcuts. With the data from both libraries combined, we can take a faster route. That way, we can confuse occasional pursuers, if any, save time and maintenance — and your money. After all, if we can do one uncharted jump, we can do five, can't we?"

"Isn't that risky?"

"Not really. Trust me."

Drake considered the way she had dealt with his ancient navigation library. Was it really so easy? Overlay both maps, have a look at them, turn them around and make them match?

"I still wonder why I've been so far off. Kyris seemed the closest known system to me."

Syreen gazed at the sphere for a while, and then highlighted five stars around Kyris and six more around RAK-11. "These are similar constellations. See—on first glance, the stars could match. Only minor differences in their spectral patterns, but of course significant enough for interstellar navigation."

"Which you see with a glance."

"Nah, the computer tells me. What I see is the constellation. Minor differences in angle and distance could easily be credited to rounding differences or the timeframe. Did you make a full-precision calculation on a navigation computer?"

"No."

"See? Commercial gear crunches natural numbers, sometimes fractions to the third or fourth digit. No need for more detail. But if you're the ten-thousandth part off with a twenty light year jump, you still have a billion kilometers to go. Consider that."

Drake tried to imagine the distance and failed. He shrugged. She seemed to know very well what she was doing—and she had even saved him eight jumps and four stopovers—given they'd return to Kyris indeed—without any need from her side.

His gaze fell at the seat Crow currently occupied, similar to his own. It wasn't the kind of accommodation he preferred, but he'd be able to bear it for a while. What was the minor discomfort compared to the discovery of a new habitable planet and the artifacts of a long-forgotten race?

CHAPTER FIFTY-SEVEN

Stephan sat on a crate opposite his commanding officer and watched her browsing through the inventory. The storage room wasn't the most comfortable place, plus it triggered some more unpleasant memories of having been locked up, but they were alone while Herman had bridge watch. Their guests could enjoy some private time in the passenger room.

"Of course we don't know what our guests prefer, but I don't think we need to restock anything for a two-jump journey, what do you think?" she asked.

"I'm new at this," he said. "So when you asked me to procure supplies, I checked what a fully stocked *Raydancer* should have, subtracted the available stuff and ordered the difference. We're fully stocked for seven persons and a long eight-jump journey, food and drink, spares and fuel. That still left room for payload, so I checked the maintenance intervals for anything due soon and ordered some more stuff for the recyclers. Maybe I overdid it, but I could negotiate good prices — Herman confirmed that — as I didn't know whether we'd dock anywhere else soon."

"Good job."

"Yes." He folded his hands. "I don't know what to think of our guests. Drake — he seems to be rich and smart, and I don't care what kind of old stuff he's after. But this Crow? Hardly ever says a word and seems to be glued to his master."

"Bodyguard, I'd say."

He nodded. "Yes, but — I don't know what to make of them."

"Friends," Syreen added.

186

"Friends? Like in *old buddies since childhood?* They don't look like they were bred in the same environment."

"Friends like in *I have a new steady,*" she disagreed. "Sex partners."

Stephan shook his head. These two? "Shouldn't I have noticed? Oh."

"I know you lean that way, too. Of course, I have no proof. But when I met them, I was the only woman in a gay bar."

"In a *gay bar?* You?"

"I wasn't aware when I entered, and once I was inside, I didn't care. It was a nice place, and then Drake approached me. Next we were talking business."

Stephan chuckled. "May I ask another question?"

"Sure."

"In the guild hall, you called me your maintenance magician — do you really expect me to do real maintenance stuff?"

"Yes and no. I know you're not trained for it. You're a soldier, so you received basic training in maintenance, like me. You can read the manuals and make sense of them. However, I think you're also a smart guy who can fix a cooker with any tool just at hand. So if our little baby here should ever need repair while we're far from any dock, I'm sure you'll do your best. Am I right?"

Stephan watched her. Again, this was so different from what he knew of his former — dead — superiors. "You are right, Sir — Syreen. For you, I'll do magic, whatever it takes."

PART FIVE—LEAVING

CHAPTER FIFTY-EIGHT

Syreen flicked her finger. "Kyris Orbital Base for *Raydancer*. Bye, folks. I had a nice time with you."

She had to wait for the answer some centicycles and rechecked her controls and instruments. Everything looked as it was supposed to. Had she missed anything? No. The embassy knew she had a contract—to reconsider options, she had put it—their *field reconnaissance* hadn't produced new intel yet, and the buoy was safely stored away. Provisions were plenty, so she only had to keep her passengers and crew happy somehow. That would be the hard part.

"*Raydancer, you're welcome to Kyris anytime. Good journey.*"

"Thank you," she replied, and triggered the intercom. "Prepare for jump in two."

Their destination was an unnamed star some light years off the direct route to Brannock that probably hadn't seen visitors for megacycles—if ever after having been charted. There was no regular connection to the web of trade routes, so no merchant would go there, and pirates couldn't gain anything there either. However, it was a powerful star, good for recharging, and the star map had shown Syreen the favorable jumps. In fact, the two long jumps would be cheaper with regard to energy consumption and in turn cause less stress to the hyperjump projectors than the best possible of the four short jumps across Skye to Brannock.

She had seen it in the map, and the computer had proven her right. It was a seven-sigma jump, leaving a risk of nineteen failures per billion due to unknown, uncharted obstacles or random disturbances of the hypercontinuum. That wasn't bad compared to the usual six-sigma level for primary charted routes—with a three point four per million risk—or the still acceptable five-sigma level for secondary routes with over two-hundred failures per million. A failure there could mean a major damage to the hyperjump projectors, a significant course deviation, or—rarely—the total loss of the ship in question.

So she felt entirely confident when the computer triggered the jump.

Chapter Fifty-nine

Drake shook his head and watched the clock. A quartercycle had already passed since the announcement.

"Anything wrong?" he asked aloud, hoping the pilot could hear him. "Is there a delay?"

There was a brief delay. Then the lieutenant's voice came over the intercom. "Sorry, I had to check the neighborhood first. Seems we're alone here. I'll run another scan before unfolding the collectors, but you can unbuckle."

"We didn't jump yet," he objected and glanced around. "Or did we?"

"Sure we did," she answered. "The jump went as smoothly as planned."

"I didn't feel it. Every jump I've made so far caused at least some dizziness, depending on distance, and shouldn't this have been a longer one?"

"We made a seven-sigma jump. You shouldn't feel it."

He unbuckled, rose and walked through the corridor toward the bridge hatch. He knocked, and in opening it unveiled her happy smile.

"Seven, eh? On our way to Kyris we did a few sixes and many fives. I've expected a four-sigma jump and was willing to bear it to save time and money. I've never heard of a seven-sigma jump."

"The routes are out there. You only have to find them."

"And you did? An uncharted route, never done before, across twice the distance liners do in one jump, and you just spotted it in the map? You're lucky."

"Luck wasn't involved. I saw it. That's why I picked this route."

"Girl, either you're pulling my leg or you're a prodigy."

"Prodigy?" She frowned. "I'm just doing my job well. My instructors told me I'm good at navigation, sure. But nothing extraordinary."

"Well, this is extraordinary. Perhaps they never noticed because they never challenged you the right way, but I'd bet no explorer navigator could beat you."

There seemed to be a hint of sadness in her bright green eyes. Drake decided to change the subject. "What are our plans now?"

"As I said—I'll do another thorough scan of the system to rule out surprises, and then I'll start recharging. That shouldn't take long, as we didn't spend much, and meanwhile I'll calculate the next jump."

"A smooth one again, I guess?"

"Sure. Seven-sigma until Jakarta. From there, it may become a bumpy ride."

"Bumpy. Which is?"

"Uh, well, no more than six-sigma, perhaps five. I must check the local conditions once we're there."

"Well." His gaze briefly lingered on her chest, and then was attracted by her disarming smile again. "Should I fetch you a forwine while you're doing the scan?"

"Oh, that would be kind."

He turned away for the galley. He knew Syreen wouldn't admit it, but Lady Luck had led him to the best navigator in the entire quadrant. He deserved a little luck after having spent twenty years—the best part of his life—on his research and those frustrating last three kilocycles on Kyris.

CHAPTER SIXTY

The jump to Brannock went as smoothly as promised. Their approach left Herman with some time to daydream of himself and his commanding officer interacting in a very unprofessional manner. He felt some pressure on the seams of his uniform crotch, which he didn't want to show to their passengers.

He saw no way to find relief in the near future and silently cursed his fate. Oh, okay, he owed Stephan his life for finding the duct in time. No one else would have thought of that, but couldn't Andrea, for example, have escaped with them? The brawny private with the square face had never bothered to hide her small tits and her wild bush on the way to and from the showers. She had openly advertised the fact that she'd chosen temporary sterilization upon joining the army, and she had never hesitated to grab any swollen cock in reach, whatever the cause. During exercises, recruits going behind a bush for urgent needs at night had suddenly sensed a warm and gentle hand at their members, helping them aim, and more often than not had returned to their sleeping bags with a well-creamed shaft. He imagined Andrea as she was sitting at the campfire, always with invitingly spread legs, always with unbuttoned shirt like the guys, and always willing to pull down her pants.

Andrea's face changed to Syreen's, the unbuttoned shirt filled with firm, round domes, and his cock felt like exploding soon.

His self-control was somewhat impaired when he rose

193

from his chair — silently, so as not to disturb the sleepers — and went to the bathroom.

Chapter Sixty-One

Syreen felt slightly excited. The jump had been smooth again, and *Raydancer's* self-diagnosis had credited her with little to no wear of the hyperflight projectors. That would save her principal a lot of money for maintenance, and herself a lot of headaches for readjusting spare parts.

She was already scheduled for docking at Brannock Four's military orbital station, where she wasn't entirely sure whether she should consider that as an honor to a new commandant visiting the system or a precaution against a foreign battleship, as tiny as it was. In any case, the Brannock system with its three inhabited planets was currently well-defended by four heavy cruisers and three stingship bases, plus a few customs vessels. The port master's no-nonsense attitude had sufficed to make her pussyfoot into the system and voice her needs in the most polite way she could think of.

After switching off, she was mentally exhausted, but also still stirred up and a bit horny, so she went to the bathroom for a cold shower.

In the corridor, she met Herman, heading the same direction with a firm boner in his pants, radiating unsatisfied lust like an open converter hatch with heat, and unable to hide the desire for his commanding officer.

Combined with his tasty-looking carotid, he was a treat made to be consumed in any possible way. She couldn't help but push him through the bathroom hatch, unbutton his pants, and reach for his cock even before the hatch closed behind them.

With his pants dropping down to his ankles, he was defenseless when she pushed him down on the floor. *Stay.* He probably wouldn't have required her mental command, due to the way he stared at her bare tits as she pulled her uniform top over her head. She dropped it, kicked her boots away, tore her own pants down and off, and went on her knees to mount him. She was soaking wet, so she could instantly take him all the way in.

When she leaned forward, he reached for her boobs. She enjoyed his touch and paused, splitting her attention between his erection inside her, the demanding grab on her breasts, and the call of his carotid arteries. Her tongue felt her canines growing forward.

There was no way to stop. She started moving her pelvis, making him moan in joy, and bent all the way down to sink her fangs into his throat.

The subject of Herman's daydreams came across him and jumped right out of these dreams, with swollen nipples poking through her uniform front, with cheeks colored pink, pupils opened wide, breathing hard, and staring at him hungrily.

Hot.

When she pushed him into the bathroom and unpacked his cock, every cell in his body yelled, *Yes!*

She unwrapped her perfect tits while towering over him. *I must feel them.*

Next, she removed her pants, and when he saw the dripping wet, swollen pinkness wrapped in a cute black bush, he knew penetrating there was the only thing he'd ever do in his life from now on.

His wish was granted, and then she leaned down over him, and he thought it couldn't become any better, except if they could become one mind and share their lust.

There was a little sting at his throat, and a wave of excitement crushed into his mind, the stimulation of an unfamiliar weight pulling at his chest, the hard pushing of a large something between his wide-spread legs, the never-known sensation of movement inside him — and the sweet, sweet taste of human arterial blood in his mouth . . .

Yes! Syreen's body shouted out.

Yes! her mind agreed.

Yes! a presence, melted into her conscious, echoed.

There was a kind of flash when their joint minds and bodies reached the climax, when she felt her cock shooting her load inside her vagina, when she felt her hands tense around her tits, when she felt the doubled relief, when she felt the warm, powerful taste of life . . .

No! she cried out mentally. *No! I won't!*

She fought with herself to stop sucking, to remove her fangs from her victim's throat, to push herself up. She watched how the small holes in his skin slowly shrank with only one more little drip of blood escaping the bite mark.

Syreen felt his breath in her hair, felt his heartbeat under her chest, felt his pulsating cock inside her pussy, and thought with relief, *I didn't kill him. I didn't suck him empty.*

She looked down at her subordinate. This wasn't acceptable conduct from either side. This wasn't advisable to maintain discipline. This should never have happened.

Only, it had felt exceptionally good, too good to ignore.

She struggled with herself. Should she make him forget? She was sure she could order him so. But was that fair, considering what they just had experienced together? No. She couldn't keep that memory for herself alone. There were only two things — *Forget the bite, and don't talk about our sex to anyone. Oh my.*

CHAPTER SIXTY-TWO

Herman felt worn out and weak, like if he'd skipped breakfast after an endurance training run, but he didn't care. He'd grit his teeth and do his duties as always while secretly enjoying the memories of his surprise encounter.

Man, that girl's hot! Once she's loose, there's no limit. That's once-in-a-lifetime sex, and yet — he remembered her smile when she had raised her pelvis, letting go of his cock and then of his load, which had slowly run out of her and dropped down on his tool. He had remembered the promising flash in her green eyes when she had leaned down once again and licked his sperm together with her own goo away from his erection.

He remembered how she had then taken a quick shower and redressed before his eyes, pretending he hadn't presented her with his unfailing boner, and how she had winked at him through the closing bathroom hatch. A promise for the future, he was sure.

He also remembered the long, cold shower he needed to get his tool stowed away, not easy with the reverberations of these strange feelings of a hard something forcing its way inside him. Had he truly taken part of her feelings? Was such a thing possible?

If their minds were indeed so tightly linked together, that might be an excuse for forgetting all discipline — it simply had to happen eventually.

Now Syreen had left with Stephan to pay the local commander a polite visit, which was good, as Herman currently couldn't guarantee anything with her near him.

These crates had to go up on that rack, and the stuff currently stowed there had to be moved down and forward.

"Need help?"

That was a voice he had rarely heard so far. Crow. The man was waiting at the hatch to the cargo compartment and peeking inside.

"Yes," he said. "Come in."

CHAPTER SIXTY-THREE

Stephan quietly trotted along with his superior and the *honor guard* the local authorities had sent them. The local soldier wore a white jacket with golden seams and buttons, blue trousers with red stripes, black boots, white gloves, and a saber at his side which didn't look entirely ornamental to Stephan.

In any case, they couldn't complain about his professional hospitality. They had been welcomed and been kindly asked to follow to a more convenient place.

This place wasn't far from their dock, probably to ensure they wouldn't learn more about the base than absolutely necessary. Nevertheless, Stephan compared the corridors' size, paint, lighting and air conditioning with the little he had experienced before—Kyris and *Raydancer*—and decided the Brannock people were either working on a very tight budget or neglecting maintenance or both.

In comparison, their guard's gear was as tidy as could be, matching his manners. Perhaps the Brannock people were *people* people?

Thinking of such topics could—almost—make him forget contemplating the news about his crewmates. Both Herman and their commanding officer had been radiating such joy as he hadn't seen ever before, together with a telltale smile that didn't leave much to the imagination.

While as a soldier he had to consider the possible repercussions on discipline and everything, as their fellow in fate he welcomed the development—the tension between the only two straight people aboard who were attracted to each other and inhibited by regulations had been noticeable. It was better to vent it than to let it lead to trouble, wasn't it? As their commandant surely was no slave to regulations, she wouldn't have trouble living with her *weakness,* and Herman — well, he'd follow his cock's demands, as most males did.

Of course, the situation hadn't improved for himself. Stephan had certainly lost his prospect of turning Herman to the queer side — he no longer was the only relief in reach. If he needed relief for himself, he had to work even harder on Herman, check out their passengers, or try the straight side once again. He had to admit to himself that he was a little bit curious about Herman's experience. If there was any woman worth testing his own alignment with, it would be this one.

Syreen contemplated the conversation ahead of them. She sensed the curiosity masked by professionalism in their guard, as well as in Stephan's mix of approval, sexual attraction and worries, but decided to ignore both for now.

A Captain McArthur had been announced as her host. What could he want with her? And what would she be willing to tell him? All the considerations she had discussed with Lord Persson applied to Brannock, too, plus she wasn't commanding the only warship in this system. She'd better be very cautious.

Their honor guard stopped at an open door and waved them inside. "This way, please."

The large conference room was empty but for eight chairs and an oval table with a carafe and four glasses on it. She didn't smell anything and decided the colorless liquid had to be water.

The door closed behind them.

Syreen motioned Stephan to take a chair and did the same, facing the doorway. When he cleared his throat, she shook her head, supported by a very gentle mental push to please be quiet. They'd be patient.

A quartercycle later, the door opened again, and a mid-fiftyish man with gray hair briskly marched in, hardly gave her time to rise, and reached out a hand to shake hers.

"Captain Richard McArthur, Brannock Marine Infantry. Lieutenant Syreen—ah?"

"Just Syreen, no surname. Nice to meet you, Captain."

"Yes, yes. Have a seat, please." He didn't wait for her to follow his advice, took the opposite chair and folded his hands on the table. "Okay, let's keep it short. Your arrival raised a few questions, not to mention concerns. It doesn't happen often that a single warship visits another star nation unannounced. I must demand a few explanations. You will understand that."

"Of course I understand, Captain. Go on."

"Okay, thank you. So, what's your business in Brannock, Lieutenant?"

"Mainly resupply. Basic needs. Food, drink, utilities."

"Where did you come from?"

"Kyris."

"Directly? I know that system. Usually, traders stop at Skye. Why did you skip Skye?"

"For efficiency. I'd have needed two more jumps to go through Skye."

"And by what route did you come here?"

Syreen quoted the unnamed star's catalog number.

"That's not a common route."

"No, it isn't. I think it's rarely used."

"So. Who authorized you to deviate from known routes? Is such recklessness allowed in your *Fleet?*"

"Captain McArthur, the use of seven-sigma jumps isn't considered reckless in the Duchy's Fleet."

The seven-sigma made him pause, but only for a moment.

Syreen could sense his impatience and disapproval.

"Lieutenant, that may be, but surely you still need author-ization. No mere lieutenant can make such decisions, I'm sure."

"Any Duchy Fleet lieutenant would be entitled to do what-ever's necessary to fulfill her contracts and use her own good judgment in absence of superior officers."

"So you thought trying a different route showed good judgment, *Lieutenant?*"

"Preferring two seven-sigma jumps over four six-sigma jumps proves good judgment, *Captain.*"

"Which you can easily say in hindsight, Lieutenant."

"Captain, I assume that Brannock Marine Infantry officers are sufficiently qualified to judge considerations on interstel-lar navigation—in any case I can assure you that I had chosen that route because I knew in advance that I'd do two seven-sigma jumps."

Stupid, she chided herself. *Now you've attacked him directly.*

The captain frowned. "So. And you are qualified to know such in advance?"

"I am." She forced herself to calm down—and radiate some calmness, too. "I scored first in my tenure's exam. There is no award for cross-tenure scores, otherwise I'd have earned that, too."

"Oh, yes. Awards—you're wearing some decorations there, Lieutenant. May I ask what this long row of small stars should tell me? One for each system you visited?"

"No, Captain. One for each spaceship I killed."

That made him pause and swallow hard. "Pirates?"

Syreen decided to smile. "The last one. All the others were armed warships who shot back. That's why I'm wearing this star—" she pointed at the four-ray silver star at her chest— "for commanding a spaceship in battle."

"Mmm. Well, I think I'm supposed to ask for the other

insignia now, before we continue our interrogation."

Interrogation? So. Syreen moved her finger to the five-ray star with halo. "Awarded for a hyperflight command. Any Duchy skipper visiting you would have one."

McArthur nodded. "I see. And the galaxy? Navigation, I presume?"

"No, Captain. It's the sign of the Duchy's current Fleet Commander in Charge. Which means I'm the Duchy's high-est-ranking officer on active duty overall."

"Overall?"

"Across all services. In the Duchy, Army or Marine officers cannot command Fleet, regardless of rank."

Syreen could sense his embarrassment. Other than what he might have assumed, she outranked him by far. Should the Brannock military want to get even, they'd have to send her an admiral, not a *mere captain.* In terms of cock size compari-son, she had won.

"Captain, why don't we go on with your questions? After all, we're not here to discuss our organizations. I'm a skipper visiting your system. I command a warship suited for escort duty, and after my last escort mission to Kyris, I entered an exploration contract with two paying passengers."

"Exploration?"

"Exploration," she acknowledged. After all, that was part of her public registration. "And that's why picking an unu-sual route is no special deal for us."

"I didn't know the Duchy dealt with exploration."

"We don't advertise it."

"Okay. May I ask where you're going next?"

"You may ask, Captain, and I may not answer."

The officer frowned. "I'm supposed to find out."

"And I may change my mind the moment I undock. So I could tell you anything, and you'd have no way to verify it. Why not leave it at that? I don't want to tell you lies."

"Please," he said. "If you can't tell me a destination, I have to make one up for the report. Our computer won't let me get away without."

Syreen considered that. "Oh, well—have you ever heard of Silver Seven?"

The captain shook his head. "No."

"That's where we're going, our final destination. Only you won't find that name in your records."

Now he smiled. "Such happens. Too bad—our internal revision will burn some midnight oil before they give up."

She smiled back. Some things were universal—like foolish computer programming or the dislike of internal revision among officers on active duty.

He tapped his pad, shrugged, nodded, tapped again, and then pushed it aside. "Okay. So much for the records. Pardon me for being curious—how can a lieutenant become fleet commander?"

Syreen was well aware that her interrogation was far from over, but she was willing to play the game to stay on McArthur's good side. "Well, it's complicated. For one, promotions must follow regulations—must be approved by a senior officer, and of course, even a fleet commander cannot sign her own promotion. You see the problem?"

McArthur nodded and smiled.

"For two, while the process of dropping out of the line of command is simple—regardless whether you die, retire, or call in sick—it's not as easy to return to active duty. Imagine an unfavorable sequence of events . . . well, details about the Duchy's current military organization are of course classified."

"Of course. However, as you mentioned a battle command and multiple kills, some may have been killed in action?"

"I can't confirm or deny that."

"Your presence alone speaks volumes. From the

remarkable line of stars I can only conclude you were more successful than your superiors."

"I may admit that I was quite successful, yes." She sensed that Stephan was about to say something and would give away more than she was willing to tell. She glanced at him and sent a gentle mental disapproval.

The private only smiled, not even aware he'd received a specific message.

I'm getting better at that. Subtler.

McArthur waited, but she didn't elaborate on the subject. Finally, he harrumphed and spread his arms wide. "Well, I think that's it, then, Lieutenant. I wish you good luck on your further journey."

She gave him another friendly smile, rose and nodded. "We should return to our ship now. Thank you, Captain McArthur, and have a nice tencycle."

Their honor guard would surely already be waiting outside.

CHAPTER SIXTY-FOUR

R*aydancer* trembled when the docking clamps were retracted.

Syreen frowned. The mechanism might have suffered damage from earlier docking maneuvers and not been repaired yet. She knew it couldn't have been her own arrival — like at Kyris, her approach had been as smooth and gentle as the touch of a feather.

As smoothly, she now steered her corvette away from the dock, letting it swing around and slowly gain speed.

She eyed the communicator panel. Would the Brannock people feel the need for another chat? If not, she wouldn't impose her presence on them.

A few centicycles later she dared to send more power to the engine. Her controls were telling her it was all-clear, provisions were restocked, her passengers and crew were happy — happy to leave this less than hospitable system, she guessed — and her next jump was already calculated and prepared. Why did she feel unrest?

She checked the three-dimensional plot of the Brannock system. The four heavy cruisers were spread around the system to guard the main incoming vectors, which meant they also guarded the outgoing vectors. Of course, no sphere open in all directions could be effectively blocked by only four ships, but hyperjumps rarely started and ended close to a star's rotation axis, but rather on the rotation plane — that was how the mechanics of hyperflight worked. By convention, incoming jumps ended on the plane, while outgoing jumps would be performed slightly above or below.

In either case, four warships could shield one quarter of the plane each, and if those heavy cruisers harbored a few sting-ships, those could reach any incoming ship before it could effectively endanger the inhabited planets.

Or they could intercept a departing ship before it had reached the necessary fifty percent light speed for a jump.

The recommended fifty percent, she corrected herself. A lower entry speed multiplied the cost of a jump and put more strain on the projectors. However, how much was the multiplied cost of a seven-sigma jump compared to a regular six-sigma jump? For example, when jumping at forty percent? Or twenty?

She had to teach *Raydancer's* computer a few new formulas to find out. A forty percent jump was still cheap in comparison, a twenty percent jump prohibitively expensive.

Her current trajectory kept her clear of the two closest heavy cruisers, but she still had an odd feeling about them. When she checked their vectors, she found nothing conspicuous. Neither of them had reacted to her departure or her choice of vector.

Old gal, you're seeing phantoms.

Nevertheless, she checked the hyperdrive controller programming and changed the safety code regarding entry speed, so that it would allow slower entry depending on the overall power consumption — any solution no more expensive than a five-sigma jump should be accepted — and then prepared a few more solutions for her next jump. Not acting by the Books had saved her ass before. Who knew when she'd need additional options next time?

Herman knocked at the bridge hatch.

The hatch slid open, and a lovely female voice replied, "Yes?"

His hand entered first, carrying a mug of forwine. Syreen inhaled the smell and smiled. "Thank you, Herman."

"We didn't hear a word since we departed. I thought you might need one."

"Oh, sorry, yes." She took the mug out of his hand and placed it into a recess underneath the control panels. "Thank you. I've been calculating a few jump alternatives."

"There are alternatives?"

"Sure. Have you ever thrown anything on target?"

"Yes, why?"

"Think of it. You can throw up or straight. Depending on your impulse, the object can hit the same target."

"Ah. Yes. With darts, I do the latter—quick and almost straight. With trash, the former—a high arc to the basket."

"See? You got it. Several alternatives. Now consider you could do the same to the right or left, too—the options are endless, as long as you don't have to consider obstacles."

"Obstacles?"

"Like a sergeant blocking your way. You wouldn't want to hit him—neither with a pointy dart nor with trash."

Herman grinned. The idea of throwing trash at a sergeant had never occurred to him. Darts—well, that was the sort of accident you could get away with if the sergeant was foolish enough to step into the line of fire.

He'd have hoped for time for another passionate interlude, but his commanding officer only took a sip from the mug and gazed at her panels. Duty first, he understood that.

She suddenly frowned and replaced the mug, and at first, he could see no reason. A few taps on her panels produced a curve diagram with four significant peaks and several less intense echoes.

Her eyes and fingers rushed across the controls. A moment later, data sheets with prominent three-dimensional images appeared. Herman couldn't tell exactly, but they looked like warships.

She cursed. Next, the klaxons went off and the lights turned red. "All hands, general quarters," she commanded calmly. "Now."

CHAPTER SIXTY-FIVE

Syreen didn't know whether her crew had let their passengers exercise the proper reaction to an alarm, but she received four confirmations within half a centicycle. That was excellent.

She studied her plot before activating the intercom.

"Okay, folks. Here's what happened — a flotilla of warships just arrived in this system. The hypershock data tells of one battle cruiser and three light cruisers, and unless they're following a friendly invitation, this is not what you'd send for a polite visit. My preliminary assessment is — they might outgun the locals, especially as Brannock must protect three planets while the newcomers can move as they like. However, if Brannock's stingship pilots are good, the price might be high."

She called up another diagram.

"They arrived in our quadrant, but about twenty-nine degrees off our trajectory, increasing. The big ship wouldn't be able to intercept us, the light cruisers would have to make up their mind soon, and in any case, we could change course and outrun them — unless they brought stingships."

Or long-range missiles, but I'd better not mention that. It's bad enough.

"I don't plan to stay and watch the spectacle. This isn't my circus." Although the four *Associated Planets* warships were her monkeys — enemy and legit targets — she knew any battle would be short, heroic, and futile. "We will continue our flight, ignore requests to bring *Raydancer* about and jump out, if they give us the time." *What will they make of an AP corvette with Duchy transponder signal?*

"I so agree," Drake said from his seat. "I don't want to see my lifework spoiled on the brink of success by some local quarrel."

That brought murmurs of agreement.

"I ask you to remain seated, in case I need to do sharp maneuvers."

"What, now?" Drake asked. "Even if they tried to intercept us, that would take cycles, wouldn't it?"

"Please."

"Oh—it's okay for now. Just curious—perhaps you can explain once we're out. I'm quiet."

Syreen smiled. He wasn't bad. Open to reason, with a sense for good and bad timing, what else could she ask for?

Now was the time to recap everything her battle instructors had told her, plus the respective chapters from *Raydancer's* manual.

Would she need shields? No. If one of the battle cruiser's gunners were able to hit at that distance—and she knew what it took—they'd be toast with or without shields. The situation might change if stingships came after them.

She checked her aft laser controls, and then *Raydancer's* medium pulse cannon. It could be pivoted to a hundred and fifty degrees all around and thus shoot backward, but the remaining thirty degrees—where the muzzle eventually pointed inward for maintenance purposes—still left a large cone where only her lasers could fend off approaching stingships—or long-range missiles.

She knew all tricks in the Books and a few others. This situation might call for one of the others, she mused, and began preparations.

CHAPTER SIXTY-SIX

The expected call came late, but it came.

"*This is Brannock system control. All ships cease acceleration and await further instructions. Repeat—all ships cease acceleration.*"

Syreen did nothing. *Raydancer* followed its course and accelerated toward jump speed. There were no obstacles in her path, so it was quite plausible that a slightly less diligent skipper would leave the bridge alone and the ship on full automatic. A nap, a meal, a shower—each would require extra time to return to the pilot's seat. Each excuse could buy her precious time.

Would the flotilla commander know about her? There hadn't been any battle cruisers involved in the Duchy raid, and although messenger drones were fast and frequent, spreading the news should still take a few tencycles. He still might know about the raid in general and be curious why an AP corvette signaled a Duchy flag. She wasn't inclined to enlighten him.

After ten centicycles, she triggered her radio.

"Brannock system control, this is *Raydancer*. Did I read you right? All commercial vessels are to cease acceleration?"

With a little luck, this could delay their actions until it was too late. She was still in range for small and fast stingships, although that would become a tight race.

Not much later, her plot showed two dozen new symbols. Stingships, as expected, starting from their cruisers.

Syreen sighed. Why couldn't they let her depart in peace?

"Raydancer, *this is Brannock system control. Cease accelera-tion, bring your ship about and await our boarding party for inspec-tion.*"

Another flock of symbols appeared on her plot. Now the Association battle cruiser had deployed his own stingships, and those were in a much better position to intercept her.

They're in this together. In that case, they'll have to suffer the consequences together.

"Brannock system control, this is Duchy Fleet corvette *Ray-dancer,* Lieutenant Syreen speaking. I herewith confirm the re-ception of your request to bring about and await boarding, which constitutes the announcement of an act of war. I am willing to accept your revocation and admittance of error if you cease all other hostile activities, primarily the attempt to intercept my ship by vessels incapable of anything but attack. Moreover, I expect you to take measures against further hos-tile advances by third parties in this system, which I must re-gard as piracy unless accompanied by a clear declaration of war."

Drake looked at the little ship's crew's grim faces. "She's not serious, is she? There are — what — eight big warships in this system and she's taking them on?"

"She's serious," Herman said. "The way she talks, she knows what she's doing. I'm not at all inclined to rot in some cell until interstellar lawyers found out we're innocent — if they bother to accept our case and if they still find someone to defend. So I'm glad she doesn't give in easily."

"But — with this toy?"

"It's not a toy, it's a corvette, and they'll learn soon enough it's got sharp teeth. And it's much more than she had when she destroyed that dreadnaught."

"A *dreadnaught?*" Drake gasped. "She didn't mention that."

"One of the stars on her chest," Stephan chimed in. "She

boarded it and destroyed it from inside. Single-handedly. If she thinks she can handle this, she already has a plan."

Syreen had a plan. It was based on the assumption that the Association ships were the most dangerous opponents, so she turned *Raydancer* away from them. This increased the time they'd need to catch up with her, took one Brannock stingship wing out of the equation and decreased the time for the other to get her—while placing them into her pulse cannon's firing field.

While they had time to consider her offer, she had time to get a better aim—better than triangulation, with a continuous flow of data that she fed into her impromptu formulas.

Raydancer's computer provided her with the stingships' shape. It seemed to be a standard design, copied by many star nations—only not the Duchy—consisting of a slender body and two short tail wings that could be helpful for planetary maneuvers. As targets, these ships were much smaller than pirates, but she had plenty of time to refine and calibrate her formulas.

"Raydancer, *this is Brannock system control. You entered our territory uninvited and thus submitted to our rules. You will do as commanded or suffer the consequences.*"

Fuck yourself. "Brannock system control, this is *Raydancer.* I entered your system voluntarily and on the assumption that you follow the fundamental universal customs. My plot tells me that you're continuing your hostile pursuit while refusing to declare war. I will treat this act of attempted piracy as appropriate. Receive my last warning now."

One centicycle later, Syreen approved *Raydancer's* calculations and triggered her pulse cannon once. She counted to three before firing eleven more shots. If the Brannock pilots were smart, they had used the short pause to break formation. If not, if they were still where computed, twelve stingships would now be one winglet short — over a distance of two light minutes.

Five centicycles later, *Raydancer* provided her with pictures of twelve consecutive flashes, each illuminating a lengthy shape. With relief she registered that she had indeed hit the tail wings and not the bodies. They should be able to return to their carriers or at worst be collected by an evac shuttle.

Next, her plot showed the stingships decelerate. Obviously, their wing commander had got the message — those hadn't been lucky shots but well calculated hits. She could shoot them at will long before they'd come close enough to hurt her.

This left her with twelve Association stingships on her heels. Syreen ran another calculation. They'd be close enough for a long-range shoot before *Raydancer* reached forty-eight percent light speed. So she recalculated her jump for forty-five percent.

Before she transmitted her calculation to the hyperdrive controller, she received another call.

"Raydancer, *this is Brannock system control. Congratulations for your precise shooting.*"

Which was quite an understatement. She had scored twelve impossible hits on moving targets — again — and thus written a new page in the Books.

The speaker went on, "*We're grateful for your understanding. While we're not interested in open hostilities with the Duchy, we must ask for your pardon with regard to the current distribution of power within our system.*"

Put differently, he'd rather stay on her good side but couldn't afford to get on the Association's bad side, not twelve stingships short, even though their damage had given him the excuse to cease pursuit.

"*This message is on a tight beam and will not be logged in our systems. Good journey,* Raydancer."

CHAPTER SIXTY-SEVEN

The light of another lonesome sun shone on *Raydancer's* body and collectors, recharging her capacitors and batteries.

Inside, passengers and crew had gathered in the passenger room. It was Stephan's turn to serve drinks, and he cautiously set the tray down between their chairs.

Only when he had passed the mugs around and taken his own seat, and they all had taken a first sip did the lieutenant take a deep breath and nod.

"You might have questions."

Stephan could think of a lot of questions, but as far as he knew, their passengers were still unaware of the Association's raid on their home, and he suspected Syreen would prefer to keep it that way.

"What in all nine hells happened there?" Drake started. "That's — uh — unprecedented."

"I agree," the lieutenant said. "Let's start with the known facts. Associated Planets sent warships to Brannock, strong enough to discourage resistance, but not overwhelmingly so. We can't know what they came for and we can't be sure what they told the locals, but I assume the request for closing down the system and inspecting all vessels was their idea. You can legitimately conclude they were searching for someone or something small enough to be carried on a starship. Well, the local authorities decided to follow their friendly suggestion, and when I didn't immediately comply with their instructions, they sent two stingship wings after us and requested boarding. However, uninvited boarding is a hostile act any-where in the known universe—either an act of war or an act of piracy."

"What's the difference?"

"Well, once the boarding party declared war, you may expect to be treated according to the Geneva convention—don't ask me where that term comes from—while otherwise you can be kept hostage or just find yourself being spaced. As a Duchy officer, I must protect civilians from acts of piracy at any cost, and that's what I did. Before you ask—I don't know yet why they so stubbornly refused to declare war."

"At least until you shot them," Drake said. "I mean, that's what the plot showed, wasn't it?"

"Yes."

"Whereupon they decided to let you go. Does it mean you'll add more stars to your uniform?"

"Not one," Syreen disagreed. "I shot their tail wings off."

"Across that distance? That's—"

"Impossible," Stephan chimed in. "As it's impossible to score a hit across that distance at all, but our skipper did it, twelve times. That must have given them something to worry about. I mean, I'm not navy originally, but I found time to browse our library—with our pulse cannon, we might barely pierce a big tank's armor . . . unless that single shot hits a weak point. Now, she showed them she can shoot a moth's eye across half their system. They may safely assume she can hit a cruiser multiple times in the same place—once to erase its armor, the second time to shoot through the hole and kill their reactor. At least that's what I'd expect."

There was silence. After a while, Syreen gave her maintenance magician a mischievous smile. "Stephan, that's a great idea. I must consider that next time."

"Wait," Drake intervened. "What next time? Do you expect another such encounter?"

Syreen took another deep breath. "I wouldn't say I expect it, but I can't rule it out, either. I mean, why should a large star nation like the Association decide to alienate its neighbors in such a violent way in the first place? And if they do, for whatever reasons, where will they stop?"

She had a clear idea about the reason—their search for that *relic*—but wouldn't talk about it. Instead, she focused on her principal. "Do you perchance have an idea what they might be after?"

"What do you mean?"

"Well—the navigation data you gave me. It must be rare and valuable. It must originate from somewhere. Could it be someone wants it back?" She sensed his growing anger and sent out a gentle soothing touch. "Please—I don't want to accuse you, but we must consider all possibilities. Could we otherwise have stirred up an hornets' nest?"

He relaxed a little. "I wouldn't know how. Nobody ever took interest in my research. And about the data—I agree, it's rare, and it's valuable once you know how to read it. You know, it was just a useless old relic in some old museum in the Sirius sector, in open sight to the public. I knew of a research paper that described a damaged navigation library that looked quite the same. The Sirius relic didn't look damaged, though."

The term *relic* triggered her excitement—briefly. "How did you learn about it in the first place?"

"It's cataloged, and the museum catalog is available in many libraries across the sector. No big deal to find it."

So the same information had been available to the Association before they started their raid. Unless they had been very careless, they had known about and discarded it. And careless wasn't quite the right attribute she'd credit them with.

"Go on. So you recognized it as an old navigation library."

Drake nodded. "Undamaged, yes. From the research paper I had some clues about accessing such a library — those researchers had made several attempts and found the basic protocol, only it wasn't detailed in their paper. I had to dig up a few other sources to put it together. Then I needed the right tool to access it with, and with that tool I paid the museum a visit. In short — it worked, and a few centicycles later I had a copy on my pad. The museum exhibit remained untouched and undamaged. Nobody seemed to have noticed — and why? I had asked permission to examine it, I had applied my pad, done some electromagnetic measurements they might have detected, and the rest was garble."

"Garble?"

"Garble. That's what I downloaded. Garble — encrypted data. I had to decrypt and interpret it, which I eventually did. My only clue was — it should be about stars and planets, as that's what the research paper had said."

"Why?"

Drake leaned forward. "Because they found it inside the wreck of an alien starship."

"That raises another question," Herman said into the silence. "If the damaged relic was found in a shipwreck, where did the whole part come from?"

"Another alien ship?" Stephan suggested.

Drake shrugged. "Of course I tried to find out about its origin, but the original source wasn't recorded. As it seemed, some merchant took it as compensation from a passenger who couldn't otherwise afford the trip, and sold it to a collector who donated it to the museum. There were no records on that unknown passenger, and you can't start searching for witnesses to events that happened a megacycle before."

"What does it look like?" Herman asked. "Do you have a picture?"

"I do." Drake passed his pad around.

They all admired the artifact.

"Looks like a cross between a heart and kidney," Stephan observed.

"Like a living thing," Herman agreed and shuddered. "But it doesn't move, does it?"

"No," Drake confirmed. "I didn't touch it myself, but it's said to be warm — more like a piece of cloth than metal."

"Strange," Herman said.

"Did you tell anyone about it?" Syreen asked.

"Not until now," Drake said. "So I think we can rule out for now that they're following me. They'd had plenty of time to contact me on Kyris, but they didn't, and then you came along."

"Coincidence?" Herman asked.

"If my research and the events around taught me one thing," Drake said, "it's this — there's no such thing as coincidence in the universe. No. Someone triggers an avalanche of events that eventually hit us way down the stream, and although we don't know how they relate, they can all be tracked back to this single cause. Perhaps you should now tell me about you. Could they've come after you?"

"I don't think so," Syreen said.

"Why?"

"I'd prefer not to elaborate on that. It touches classified information."

"Fuck!" Drake's sudden outburst startled them all. "I don't care about your military secrets. While I'm aboard this ship, I'm sharing your risks. Am I not entitled to know what those risks are?"

The lieutenant sighed. "Yes, I think you are. Even more, after you've talked about your secrets so openly." Then she summarized the sequence of events that had made her leave the Duchy in a foreign ship, however without mentioning her detailed intel on the Association's primary goal.

After she had finished, Drake remained silent for a while. Finally, he shook his head, and then gazed around. "So we're flying in a stolen ship? Or would you prefer the term *borrowed?*"

"I'd prefer the term *captured,*" Syreen disagreed. "I've boarded a pirate vessel and claimed this corvette as my prize. However, for the records I must state that I'm on a secret mission by command of the dreadnaught's skipper."

She waved and tapped her own pad, and *Raydancer's* computer produced a text.

Drake began to read. "Top secret . . . next available hyper-flight-capable vessel . . . issued to Lieutenant Syreen . . . signed — that's an admiral's signature!"

"Of course it is."

How sweet this pout looks on her, Herman mused.

Their passenger threw up his hands in mock despair. "I give up. This doesn't make any sense. Why should they attack your home system, and then send you away on a top-secret mission with one of their ships?"

Syreen shrugged. "I have no clue why they attacked us in the first place. They could have come and asked us anything, instead they came to kill. To me, it's a madman's deed."

CHAPTER SIXTY-EIGHT

A knock at the bridge hatch tore Syreen from her musing. "Come in."

She looked up when Drake made one step through the door.

"Thanks for granting access to your sanctum." He winked. "I hope it's not bad timing."

"Oh no, it's okay. I've just calculated our next jump. No big deal."

"If it weren't, every merchant would do seven-sigma jumps and save the maintenance cost. I'd guess you found some intuitive access to navigating that no other can copy."

She considered that. "You may have a point there, and you must be right about the first one. Indeed, I can't see why someone would want to do expensive jumps if there were better options."

"You could probably earn a fortune by charting and selling such routes."

She smiled at the idea. "I might earn another fortune by not selling such routes—if I asked the right people."

"Who would that be?"

"The military. Knowing how to travel long distances and arrive with almost full capacitors gives a huge strategic advantage."

"Oh. That alone might be reason enough to come for you, then?"

She glanced down his slender body, across the bulge in his black leather pants, and up again. "I always thought men would come for my tits, not for my brains."

He returned her examination without real interest, although she didn't wear her jacket in the pilot chair, only her skin-tight top. "Yes, I can understand how you got that impression. While you can't hide your tits, it's easy to miss your brains when you don't advertise them."

"Thank you."

"You're welcome — I came for another reason, though."

"A pity."

"Thank you. Not this time."

Syreen appreciated the smile he showed.

He gazed outside. "Do you think they were coming for you this time?"

"Nah." She repeated her reasoning. "Their commandant must be curious about an AP corvette under Duchy flag, but he can't know the reasons. He'll surely report back, and then the hunt is on, but they don't have a clue where we're going."

"Can't they guess?"

"Not really. Even if they extrapolate our route from Kyris to Brannock, there's still a score of options, with Jakarta being one of a dozen. And with the recent encounter, we shouldn't return via Brannock anyway. I fear I've burned that bridge."

"I can't argue with that." He shrugged. "These are troubled times. I should be concerned, but there's nothing I can do."

"You can. Continue your mission, and perhaps whatever we find might make a difference." She gave him an encouraging smile, complemented by a gentle nudge.

His face lit up in return. "Okay. One more thing."

"Yes?"

"The stations — my postponed question."

"Oh, that. Well, I can't tell in advance when I might have to dodge."

"Dodge what?"

"Oh, a pulse or a laser beam, for example."

"I thought those come at light speed."

"Yes, why?"

"How can you know you must dodge, then?"

Syreen paused. *He's right. How can I know?*

"I've got no clue," she had to admit. "But I did it before. Otherwise I'd be long dead."

She remembered her first battle. How had she known when to leave formation? Cap might have wondered, too — but he hadn't been given the chance to ask. Other potential witnesses were now symbolized by the stars on her uniform.

"That's extraordinary."

"Yes." *And you don't worry about it now.*

CHAPTER SIXTY-NINE

Arriving at a new star system became routine. Announcing her arrival with a brief explanation why an escort arrived without a merchant, negotiating docking fees, stating resupply and maintenance demands — where the spare parts for a heated pulse cannon muzzle could have raised a few eyebrows, but didn't — and programming the approach didn't cause her a headache.

The Jakarta port authorities appeared very relaxed to her, although, like at Kyris, she seemed to command the only warship in the system. When *Raydancer* approached the large orbital wheel, she could see a possible reason — a few stingships docked to the spokes. So they weren't entirely defenseless. Not that it would help them should the Association show up here.

She opened the intercom. "Okay, folks, in a few cycles we'll dock at Jakarta Orbital. Provisions and parts are coming to the dock, the usual drill."

"We won't let them inside," Stephan acknowledged. "What about the maintenance guys?"

She smirked, although her crew couldn't see it. "Would you feel better knowing some stranger tampered with our cannon?"

"Definitely not, Sir. Okay, I'll try my best."

"Relax, Stephan. These parts are designed for easy maintenance. I could do it myself — in fact, I'll check your result, so that we both can be sure we didn't miss anything. Okay?" She made a mental note to remind him of her preferred form of address.

"Yessir."

"Thanks. Listen on. I've been invited for dinner by the Jakarta Admiralty. I deemed it wise to accept and stay on their good side. I've been asked whether I'd bring company. Drake, do you want to join me?"

"You need a second pair of ears and eyes? Sure, I'll be glad. Lieutenant, may I offer Crow's service to assist your crew in securing our ship? He's well versed with such tasks."

"I accept. Oh—and I'll leave you my gun behind. Just in case."

"Glad to learn you have one, Lieutenant. Again, may I propose to leave it with Crow, while your crew takes care of their duties?"

"I support that, Sir," Stephan added.

"Settled, then." Was she too trusting? No. Drake and Crow needed her pilot services, and she could make sure Crow returned the gun if she *asked* kindly enough.

"Herman, would you please take the bridge? I need five to refresh for my visit."

"Sure, Sir."

She could almost hear his disappointment, even without her enhanced senses. He surely had different ideas. But she'd have to focus on the upcoming docking maneuver—she had to meet the dock in place, time, and speed, before it rotated away from her tangential approach path. The Jakarta port authorities had strongly proposed to take her ship in remote control, but she wouldn't grant any outsider access to her computer—who knew what they'd leave behind? *Just a basic nav program, sure, which needs to access the drive parameters, of course, and then must overrule pilot controls, naturally, so please allow full skipper privileges, gladly, and the program will deinstall after docking, yeah, and honesty is your second name, bastard? Over my dead body.*

CHAPTER SEVENTY

Jakarta sent them a six-head *honor guard,* armed with short swords and tasers—weapons of choice for space stations and starships, as the wielder didn't have to worry about accidentally piercing parts of the hull.

Was it wise to take Drake along? Syreen mused. *In case of trouble, I must protect him, too.*

Or, if Jakarta held any grudges against the Duchy, his presence might prevent them from premature actions.

She wasn't surprised that they had docked at the military part of the wheel, that they had to pass several checkpoints, and were scanned for arms—the poor guard patting her down made a point of examining her chest and then her thighs, and she touched and amplified his excitement mentally, whereupon he grew a boner he couldn't hide, which in turn Drake ogled with obvious interest so that the guard blushed and lost his voice.

After that checkpoint, she and Drake exchanged knowing glances. Their honor guard didn't miss that, and all six blushed, too.

Their guard was still inappropriately embarrassed upon arrival at the admiralty's dining hall, where the visitors were passed to another group of guards who politely asked them inside, into a room decorated with wood-print wallpapers and imitation candle lighters.

Two older men in dress whites with gray at their temples, prominent bellies, and enough salad on their chests to dress a company—well, at least a company of exotic dancers—

interrupted their chat and turned to the new arrivals.

Both had four wide golden stripes around their sleeves, one topped off with a five-ray star, and the other with a crown. The latter turned to her and held out his right hand.

"Lieutenant Syreen? Welcome to Jakarta, and nice to meet you. I'm Fleet Admiral Jorgens, head of the Royal Jakartan Fleet, and this is Admiral Povannian, my second and head of the Royal Jakartan space forces."

She smiled and shook the offered hand. "Nice to meet you, Sir. I'm Lieutenant Syreen, Fleet Commander in Charge of the Duchy Fleet and all supporting services. This is Mr. Dragutin Petran, my business partner and principal for my current exploration mission."

They had to change positions to execute all combinations of handshaking, exchanged further hollow politeness, and then they were asked to take a seat at the small round table. Syreen was asked to sit at the Fleet Admiral's right, and Drake came to sit across from her.

The table was already richly set in white and green, with silver cutlery and crystal glasses, and Syreen had to suppress a brief flash of panic when she saw the arrangement. Then she remembered her lessons in *social activities*. The Duke took pride in his military people's good manners, and they had to show it during the annual Defense Appreciation Days, where each member of Fleet or Army was invited to a festive dinner at one of the ruling families' houses—or their orbital suites, respectively, which she always volunteered going to. No, she wouldn't put her home to shame.

Well, at least as long as the food doesn't move on its own.

CHAPTER SEVENTY-ONE

To Syreen's relief, none of the seven courses moved on its own. She couldn't recognize it all, but most seemed to be some kind of vegetable, fruit or crop, as the locals preferred intensely spiced meals. There were no raw grubs on the table.

Their hosts were as generous with regard to their local produce of wine. Syreen treated it with care and noticed Drake doing the same. No Duchy officer should appear drunk at any time, and under the current circumstances, it was even less advisable.

She couldn't read their hosts' minds, but their distaste and greed told her volumes. They didn't voice it, but at home, Lieutenants weren't invited to Admirals' dinners. Was it the same here? *Bet you're after my ship. No escorted merchant, no registered route, so no witnesses and no one knowing when I might go missing. An opportunity not to pass up.*

All through the meal, they had only exchanged trivia. After the table was cleared, Fleet Admiral Jorgens smiled, nodded, and began, "Well, Lieutenant Syreen. I'm eager to hear your exciting story. I learned you had to strain your cannon recently."

"Just a few practice shots," she said. "With the recent increase in piracy, any diligent skipper should be prepared, and as I knew I'd find spare parts at Jakarta, I didn't have to hold back on the last leg."

"Ah yes, you didn't mention your route yet."

"No, I didn't."

They smiled at each other.

"Were you happy with your practice results, then?"

"Oh, yes. I scored twelve of twelve, as envisaged."

"Difficult shots?"

"Moving targets, no bigger than a stingship, long distance."

"What's *long distance* for you?"

"Two light minutes is."

The admiral frowned. "You're kidding. Such a shot isn't possible."

"I'd show you my log if it weren't classified, but I assure you I hit my target. Each time."

His gaze wandered across her chest. He seemed to recognize the symbols. "You're living a dangerous life."

"I'm a soldier. Danger's part of it."

"You don't fear for your life?"

"Fear kills. I trust my skills and judgment and act as necessary."

"Even in a standoff?"

"If the situation requires, I change the rules. Maybe I should tell you about a recent pirate encounter?"

"Please. I always like to hear first-hand news."

So she told him about the *Light of Mandalay* and *Hardigan's Hauler.*

There was a hint of fear in him after she had finished.

"You'd have shot the merchant?"

"No." She returned his gaze. "But I'd have shot a second pirate without hesitation, and then looked for survivors. You know the true meaning of the word *ultimatum?* It's the last you see or hear of me before I act as announced. I don't play games."

"What if you couldn't?"

"That would mean I severely misjudged my options, which is very unlikely—but of course, I'm not immune from mistakes."

Fleet Admiral Jorgens smiled, but it was a fake smile.

"Indeed. What if someone politely asked you to surrender, and you were unarmed and far away from your ship?"

Drake stirred. Like herself, he had noticed that the question wasn't entirely hypothetical. Syreen was glad he kept quiet, as the situation was tense enough. Admiral Povannian seemed to be prepared to intervene, although she couldn't spot any weapons on him.

"Well, I'd politely ask the respective person to fuck his own ass and then watch him tear his own cock off to follow my instructions. Should that require more time than available for a tactical retreat, I could still tear his throat out with my very sharp teeth. Hypothetically." She copied the fake smile. "Note that *unarmed* is a relative term."

"With a score of armed guards outside, that would be an unwise move."

"I agree," Syreen returned. "Like it would be very unwise to anger a warship skipper with a well-adjusted pulse cannon."

"Which is currently under maintenance, I heard."

"Is it?" *You doubt it.*

That was the moment Povannian reached under the table and produced a small but nasty-looking needle gun. "I think it's time to quit playing."

CHAPTER SEVENTY-TWO

Syreen squinted at the armed admiral. *Time to quit playing? Okay. Shoot Jorgens.*

Aghast, three men watched Povannian changing his aim. Then he pulled the trigger. Jorgens' chest became lined with tiny red specks.

When the Fleet Admiral dropped to the floor together with his chair, Povannian tossed the gun away with an expression of disgust on his face.

Leave the gun, secure the door, Syreen sent at Drake.

She turned to the shooter and showed him her fangs. He didn't look tasty, and she didn't even enjoy the sudden fear and realization in his eyes, but he'd been warned. She *acted as announced* while Drake was occupied, and bit the Admiral to suck a large portion of blood before she literally tore her victim's throat out with her fangs.

Refreshed and strengthened, she licked a few drops of excess blood from her lips before she rose. She couldn't help the blood stains on her uniform, but she could wipe her face with a napkin.

"That was a scam," she told Drake. She had to order him to ignore the gory scene so that he wouldn't throw up. "He needed a scapegoat for his own leadership ambitions. Good that you didn't touch the gun. We'd better leave now."

"You think they will let us go after this mess?"

"Keep silent and stay close to me. They have more important things to tend to."

She opened the door. *Ignore us.*

The guards closest to the door peeked inside and uttered a surprised cry, answered by multiple excited questions. Discipline dissolved.

Next, she focused on one of the guards in the rear ranks.

Shoot your superior.

The surprised soldier raised his taser and stunned a non-commissioned officer closer to the door. In the following turmoil, Syreen and Drake left unmolested.

She kept her order up until they had passed the last checkpoint. With quick strides, they reached their dock, where a small detachment of soldiers guarded *Raydancer's* airlock.

"Hurry," she suggested. "There's a riot at the admiralty. Rumor has it one of the admirals attempted a coup d'état."

Their leader only needed a little mental nudge to follow her suggestion.

As soon as the small company had disappeared, she tapped the outer hatch.

"That was easy," Drake commented. "I wouldn't have thought we'd get out of that mess alive."

"Hey, you're with me," she said cheerfully. "Come, we're not through yet."

As soon as the outer hatch opened, she pulled him inside. The following brief pause was welcome to take a deep breath, get her pulse down and take her stained jacket off. When the inner hatch moved aside, she saw Crow lowering his gun and smiling. She smiled back and reached out her hand to collect the gun, and he delivered it.

"General quarters, all hands," she commanded and activated alarm locks, lights, and controls. "We're leaving in two."

Two centicycles was all the time Syreen needed to drop into her seat, buckle up, activate her panels, scan the local stingships' positions—still docked—and compute an initial departure course.

She got four clear signals from her crew — she tended to include her passengers in that term now — and triggered undocking.

Her radio quickly came alive. "Raydancer, *this is Jakarta Orbital. You weren't cleared for departure.*"

She triggered her mike. "Jakarta Orbital, this is *Raydancer.* The guards at our dock were called away because of some riot. I won't stay docked while you're sorting out your internal problems."

"Raydancer, *you're not allowed to depart. Return to your dock or we must take measures.*"

"It's not like I could just pull back a few meters, Jakarta Orbital," she argued, buying a little more time. "Moreover, what measures are you considering? This is a Duchy Fleet starship in free flight in a friendly star system. I'm entitled to leave whenever I like."

"Raydancer, *I read you accelerating. Cease that or suffer the consequences.*"

She rolled her eyeballs. *Same ol' same ol'.*

"Jakarta Orbital, I may advise you of universal law. You may declare war on the Duchy and enter battle. Or you may take hostile action against a Duchy vessel without declaration of war and be treated like a pirate's nest."

"*A pirate's nest? You wouldn't —* "

"I wouldn't hesitate to shoot. Consider well. I will regard any stingship launch as a hostile act."

That left her counterpart speechless. Meanwhile, she gained speed and distance. *Don't force me to do something we'd both regret,* she prayed, and began the calculation for a twenty percent light speed jump.

CHAPTER SEVENTY-THREE

Drake could feel the tension inside and around their little ship grow like Cyraceean water grass, and quietly snuggled into his seat. He still hadn't entirely grasped the past events. How could a polite dinner invitation turn into chaos so suddenly? And once it had happened, how had they been able to get back to their ship alive?

He couldn't say how much he appreciated what the young lieutenant was doing for him and his mission. As an officer, she probably could have stepped out any time and asked for repatriation, and very likely would have been granted it. She might have lost her prize—such small ships seemed to be in high demand currently—but not risked her life. Instead, she treated his mission as if it were her own and invested much more into it than he could've asked for.

He couldn't say how much he appreciated *how* she performed in her role, how she led much more experienced and more senior officers around by their noses and outmaneuvered other navy units superior in numbers and firepower.

Still, it was scary. Until he had hired her—and it had seemed like a good idea back then—he had peacefully traveled from star to star on dull passenger liners, been treated with respect at any port, been welcomed in any orbital station, and as soon as he had found a ship and a skipper willing to accept his mission, every star nation they visited seemed to can universal laws and customs only to get her ass.

If only they were just after her ass, and tits, and pussy. No, they wanted to steal a warship, and he didn't want to imagine a universe where such behavior became customary.

There were so many questions to be asked, so much to talk about the events on Jakarta Orbital, but he didn't dare to disturb her while she surely was doing her best to bring them out of this system. What if the Jakartans had a similarly good pilot, or one who could score a lucky hit on *Raydancer?*

Only this jump, and we're on our way. Only one more jump, and we're on our own. Until then, he'd be quiet.

Syreen didn't dare to take her eyes off her plot for long while calculating fire solutions and better hyperjump alternatives in parallel. How effectively had she intimidated Jakarta's port authorities? Would they dare to act without backup by their admiralty? How long would it take their military to sort out what had happened?

Bullying my way out of a foreign system seems like it will become a bad habit. When I'm done with this mission, the Duchy won't get any foot on the ground here in terms of diplomacy. On the other hand, what they were trying to do wasn't the best of diplomatic arts either.

She wouldn't even relax when *Raydancer* had gained too much distance and speed for any daring stingship pilot to catch them before reaching the full fifty percent. With her current bad luck, an Association warship would enter the system the very moment she reduced her attention.

Nothing happened, though. Then the computer triggered the prepared seven-sigma jump, and they were gone.

Their next destination system was empty. Firstly she deactivated *Raydancer's* transponder. Next she did a thorough scan, then a second, and then she recalled the alarm and triggered the collectors to unfold.

With a deep sigh, she leaned back in her seat and closed her eyes.

Herman had expected the worst when their skipper returned with their principal, her uniform jacket already removed before the inner hatch even opened, and issuing general quarters before telling anything about her invitation. The following cycles were at best difficult — Drake not saying a word but sulking in his seat, and Syreen too occupied to announce anything from the bridge.

He exchanged glances with Stephan and Crow — in unvoiced agreement, they remained silent and waited for things to come.

If he hadn't known what a seven-sigma jump felt like, he wouldn't have noticed it, but he felt relieved, as it marked the end of their escape.

Their passengers had noticed, too, and looked up. He only shook his head, copied by Stephan, and they leaned back and waited. Another while later, the lights went back to normal.

When Herman went to see their skipper, knocked, waited in vain, and finally dared to open the bridge hatch, he found her deeply asleep. He quietly called Stephan to take the bridge and Crow to lend a hand, and together they carried her to her cabin and bunk.

He removed her boots and glanced at Crow. His crewmate shrugged, so he continued with her stained uniform top. The presence of another man made it easier for him to ignore her well-formed naked chest this time, and so he managed to remove her uniform pants, too.

She'd never looked so delicate to him. He had to absorb the sight of her once again before gently placing the sheet over her shoulders. Stephan and he were already taking care of everything they could to unburden her, but there was still so much only she alone could do — no wonder her body had finally claimed the long-needed rest.

He held her clothes up and pointed at the stains. He'd take

her uniform to the refresher and return it later.

Not for the first time on their journey, Stephan examined the control panels on the bridge from the pilot's seat. He felt lost among all the symbols. Okay, this was radio — not needed — and that was the hyperdrive — don't touch. He could recognize the plot of *Raydancer* and a solitary star. As long as nothing else showed up there, they should be fine.

There was a status bar with digits, slowly growing. *Capacitors, aha.* He found a highlighted symbol right next to it. Collectors — okay, that made sense.

The rest could be anything. Guns, drive, whatever. He didn't care. As long as he could tell when to wake their skipper, they should be fine.

Her sudden breakdown told him that this wouldn't suffice in the long run. She needed a second, be it Herman or he himself, and the sooner the better. Never in her class, but they had to be more than a fool with a tool when taking the bridge.

Was there an online manual? Indeed, on an otherwise empty panel. He started to read.

CHAPTER SEVENTY-FOUR

Syreen felt lonely. There was so much emptiness around her, with slowly rolling waves tugging her back and forth. A distant presence reassured her, wordlessly telling of peace and continuity. All was fine, except for a brief itching that called for her attention. She tried to stretch toward it and felt her feet tangled. She struggled, and when she stretched again, she pulled the blanket off her shoulders.

Only now she realized she was stark naked and lying on a flat, soft surface.

I've been asleep. Where am I, and how did I get here? She felt around. *Question one — on my bunk aboard* Raydancer. *Question two — well. My pants and top are gone. Can't remember taking off my shoes either. Does it matter? No.*

It took her some effort to get up. A glance on her tac — in its place on the table — told her of two cycles sleep. She must have needed it, and the way she felt, she could have slept more.

So why did I wake up?

Stephan scratched his head again. The AP manual was a mess. It was okay to only look up a symbol or a specific panel layout, as long as that panel hadn't been customized. It didn't help at all to get a comprehensive overview — comprehensiveness obviously hadn't been the manual authors' goal. The glossary only mentioned the basic terms he already knew and ignored the jargon used all over the manual. So this was officers' literature.

Army recruits got plain and simple instructions, with clearly defined terms. Every army manual listed all the terms used, even though every recruit had to learn them by heart.

Hmm — do navy officers learn their stuff by heart, too?

Or perhaps the Duchy had a different approach to manuals in general? Without another sample, he couldn't tell.

Despite all the confusion — when a tiny symbol flashed in the plot, he remembered what he had read about it. *Raydancer's* sensors had received the blip of an arriving ship, the echo of its hyperjump.

This can't be good.

They were far off any commonly known route, so the newcomer could hardly be an honest merchant. This left the options of a ship gone astray, another explorer, a pirate on the run, or a military ship on a special mission, in the order of ascending probability, where the latter most likely meant trouble.

Raydancer's capacitors were almost fully charged. So it could do no harm to fold its collectors. He tapped the respective symbol.

With a little luck, they'd remain undetected. Everything else would be the lieutenant's call, he reckoned, and reached for the intercom to wake her.

Syreen had only just put her cleaned top and pants back on and was reaching for her left boot when the speaker chimed.

"Yes?"

"Skipper? We have a new arrival in the system."

A new arrival? That can't mean anything good. "I'm coming!"

She ignored her boots and hurried toward the bridge. Stephan had already freed the chair for her. "I've folded the collectors."

"What? Oh — good choice, Stephan. Well done."

Would it help? It had taken away the risk of telltale

reflections from the large collectors, but of course all the reflections having happened during the last two cycles of recharging were still traveling all over the system at light speed. Depending on its position, the bogey could well come across one . . . Where was it, actually?

The blip had originated farther away from the central star, and about forty degrees forward with regard to *Raydancer's* current trajectory. So the collectors hadn't obstructed its view on the central star, and hadn't reflected the starlight toward the bogey. Most likely, the stranger's first scan hadn't unveiled their presence yet.

A thorough search — like the one she always did upon arrival — would inevitably give *Raydancer* away, though. She couldn't sit the situation out. It was better to act soon, before she closed up further on the stranger.

Situation — the bogey was much faster than her, decelerating, and approaching the central star. With *Raydancer's* current trajectory and speed, the bogey would reach their mutual course's intersection before her.

Options — she could change her course outward and away from the bogey. He'd have to invest even more power to slow down and turn, but if it was a larger ship, he might deploy interceptors or missiles, which would both get her before she could jump. Poor choice.

Or she could accelerate forward and try to get ahead. The bogey only had to keep its speed to follow and intercept her. Bad choice.

Or she could . . . would that work? She began typing the formula for a new solution.

Stephan watched her enter cryptic formulas, wipe diagrams around and adjust parameters, first with amazement upon her obvious mastery of these arts, and then with growing concern, once the plot started to show their own trajectory as a green line and the new arrival's potential courses as a yellowish cone opening toward them. There was also a red line curving toward the green — probably the other ship's quickest way to catch them.

What really worried him were the following changes Syreen made to her own plot. The green line moved closer and closer to the star symbol — she didn't really plan to fly through a sun, or did she?

Then she added a new, blue symbol. It terminated the green line before it could reach the star.

"It could work," she mumbled. "Let's see." And, louder, together with activating the intercom, "General quarters. High gee in two. Prepare for dodges and a hard jump later."

CHAPTER SEVENTY-FIVE

Syreen's plans encompassed three major factors—firstly, high acceleration to gain as much speed as possible across as little distance as possible while closing up on the central star. Secondly, getting as close to that star as possible to make pursuit and targeting harder for their unknown potential opponent. Thirdly, jumping out of the system with the gained speed before getting too close.

You don't jump in the close vicinity of a star, their instructors had told her. *You'll inevitably end up inside that star, as the hypercontinuum is warped around stars.* After all, that was the reason why merchant routes needed extra jumps—navigators always had to plan their routes far enough away from every star they might pass.

Back then, she'd been about to ask why you couldn't incorporate the star's effects into the equations. She had bitten her tongue and patiently waited until her instructor had shown her the lengthy list equations for the standard approach. To modify this system was unthinkable—it was way too dangerous to fiddle with a half-understood, established, workable system, when any glitch might cost a ship and the lives of its entire crew.

These arguments no longer applied. She understood the system and its limitations, knew where to iron out the edges, replace suboptimal simplifications, correct mistakes. She had already changed some calculations, added or replaced parameters, and made the system both more flexible and precise, and thus allowed their small corvette to truly dance through hyperspace, and now, in open space and not in a stuffy class-room, with that big star in reach, it felt only natural to incor-porate its presence.

However, she could also recognize where her instructors' caution had come from. If someone tried a five-sigma jump that close to a star, he'd end in hell. If someone tried a poor six-sigma jump, he would be toast, too — even with her modi-fied equations. It had to be perfect.

So she refined and reworked her calculations until she was confident to have several solutions — one optimal late jump and several emergency backups.

Meanwhile, the bogey had noticed them, and changed its course for pursuit before calling.

"Unknown vessel, cease acceleration immediately, activate your transponder and identify yourself. This is APS Gorgon, *Captain Jerome Mouton speaking."*

No threat? By the Books, Mouton couldn't have a safe aim yet, as his *APS Gorgon,* according to *Raydancer's* library a light cruiser, didn't own missile launchers. He could suspect the unidentified corvette on his plot of being another Associated Planets starship, in which case he knew she had data on his armament.

As far as Syreen knew, there was no way to trace a hyper-jump. Once a ship was gone, it could have gone anywhere. *APS Gorgon* hadn't belonged to the small flotilla they had met in the Brannock system, and any ship arriving there after *Ray-dancer's* departure couldn't have reached this system yet. Ba-sically, Captain Mouton couldn't know about the recent events in the Jakarta system either. The only fact he might know, depending on his orders, was the raid on the Duchy, but that didn't count here, as she was operating an Associated Planets starship, from all he could tell.

So why had he come here, to this remote star?

Compared to what she had learned so far, the Association's navy was by orders of magnitude larger than any other navy in this galactic sector, but could they really afford to send out a five-dreadnaught fleet to the Duchy, battle cruiser flotillas to inhabited systems and light cruisers to uninhabited, nameless stars by the score?

Their leaders had to be desperate or insane, and if they were, what did that mean for their followers? Specific, merciless orders without reservations regarding interstellar laws and customs . . . like attacking another nation without a declaration of war.

They probably wouldn't care about losing a corvette *just to be sure.*

Syreen decided she had nothing to say to them. She wouldn't even grant them knowing her name. Later, when they put all the pieces together, they might conclude it had to be her, had to be *Raydancer,* but they could never be sure. Leaving them with doubt was the best she could do.

APS Gorgon continued to close up, *Raydancer* continued to accelerate toward the star, and she continued to guard her cockpit and ignore Captain Mouton's calls.

A tingling, the hairs on her neck standing up, made her hand at the flight stick twitch. *Raydancer* frantically jumped a few legs to the side, just before its sensors registered the stray emissions of a passing pulse shot.

CHAPTER SEVENTY-SIX

That bastard was shooting at her—and darn close, too. If Syreen hadn't dodged the shot, they'd be toast now.

She had to ignore the excited shouts from the passenger compartment acknowledging her sudden dodge. Firstly, she had to change their trajectory significantly to get *Raydancer* out of the danger zone, as she had to expect another sequence of shots. Secondly, she had to adjust her flight plan to that change. Thirdly, she had to recheck and potentially recalculate her jump solutions. Fourthly, she had to make up her mind what she'd show him.

She could have returned fire—and scored—but in order to get her single pulse cannon aimed, *Raydancer* had to change course by about thirty degrees—which would spoil all her other plans, would bare her flank to the enemy's teeth, and would allow him to cut some more distance off.

She could stick to her course, taking chances to dodge the next shot, too—and now wasn't the time to puzzle how she could foresee and dodge an energy pulse coming for her at light speed—and thus showing him her impossible luck.

Or she could trigger a jump at only thirty-two percent light speed right now, unbelievably close to a star, and make him rack his brain over what might have happened to her.

The last option had one big advantage—it reduced his further influence over her actions to zero. She liked that thought.

"Crew, prepare for hyperjump in one."

One centicycle later, they were gone.

PART SIX—ARRIVING

CHAPTER SEVENTY-SEVEN

After that last unwelcome and unfriendly encounter, Syreen decided to keep their stay in the next system short. She did her thorough check, as always, but wouldn't decelerate during that time, and wouldn't unfold the collectors for recharging. Instead, she let *Raydancer* further accelerate to gain the advisable jump velocity, and started to calculate the jump to RAK-11.

A knocking at her door interrupted her.

"Yes?" she asked.

The hatch opened and Drake peeked in. "Sorry to disturb you. I know we're still on general quarters, but I thought you might have forgotten—and other than your crew, I can still claim I'm a civilian."

His smile was disarming.

"You're right, I forgot." She cancelled the alarm. "Sorry—that last encounter put me on edge."

"Thanks. Now that I already interrupted you—may I ask what happened there? From the plot display it almost looked as if we dodged a shot?"

"We did."

"So you did it again."

"Yes."

He stared at her as if she had grown horns—at least that's what she read from his face.

After a pause he asked, "How?"

She shrugged. "I can tell you the facts. I pulled the flight stick, *Raydancer* moved, the shot passed where we'd been just before. That's all on the ship's log. It's deducted, but also a fact—had I not pulled, we would be dead now. The unsolved puzzle is, why did I pull? I can't tell."

Drake shook his head. "How can you not know? That's miraculous."

"You're the researcher, you tell me. What explanations can you offer?"

"Ugh. You were lucky?"

Syreen considered that. "Yes, I was, in a way. However, my instructors always told me there's no such thing as luck, only hard work and diligence. The little experience I've collected in my youth tells me skill may be helpful, too."

"Okay." Now Drake smiled. "So if you didn't work your ass off to dodge that shot, it must have been your skill. Precognition?"

"What do you mean?"

"That you can see things before they happen."

"That . . ." Syreen knew he was wrong there. "That doesn't feel right. I can't see the future. I mean—that's not how it was."

"How was it, then?"

"Uh, well . . ." She tried to remember. "I don't know. I had a feeling, like someone standing behind me and breathing down my neck, and I . . . I felt I had to evade that, and I did."

The researcher shook his head again. "Doesn't make sense. Hmm—have you had that feeling before?"

Had she? With a shrug, she repeated, "I don't know."

Drake looked at his toes, musing, then at her face again. "You already told us. Remember? When you said why we should remain buckled up. You said you can't tell in advance when to dodge—but you also admitted you'd done it before."

She recalled that discussion. "Oh. Yes, I think I said something like that."

"So—somehow you know when you're being shot at, but

only very briefly before, right?"

"Right."

"So you can only see — no, feel — the very near future. Wait, no. Can you tell how long that pulse had to travel from the moment it was shot?"

"Sure."

"Can you tell how much time you needed to react to that — uh, breathing down your neck?"

"Only guess."

"Do it. Tell me."

She frowned, shrugged, and turned to her controls. She understood where he was heading. Could it be?

The ship's log told her when she had pulled the flight stick. She subtracted her own usual reaction time, as stated in her training results — where her instructors had already commented that her live performance clearly excelled her simulator results. Next, she took the distance from her pursuer, divided it by the speed of light, again subtracted it from the moment the shot had passed, and stared at the results.

"Well, space me!"

Drake dared to step closer and lean over her to see what she had commented upon. He noticed her slightly humid smell, not unpleasant, but indicating her need for a break. Their pilot had to be fresh and alert.

Without context, the two groups of numbers wouldn't have meant anything to him, but he could easily spot two pairs of date-time values. One clearly reflected the shot, and the other had to be her own. The two couldn't be mistaken, as the pilot's dodge command had to be before the shot's arrival.

The respective first date-time values came in reverse order — she had felt that *breathing* after the shot had left the pursuer's cannon, within less than a millicycle.

"The hypothesis is," he concluded while stepping back, "that you can sense shots directed at you the very moment they're fired. Faster than light."

"Impossible."

"Have you ever heard of Ockham's razor?"

"No."

"If you have multiple explanations for a given phenomenon to choose from, the simplest one is also the most probable one. Do you have any simpler explanation? Oh, and you already threw out luck—or chance, or fate, which are basically the same."

"No." She took a deep breath. "I don't have any explanation, and despite the evidence, I'm not yet ready to accept that one."

Drake slowly nodded. "Sure. We can claim too few samples."

That made her smile again, and he had to admit to himself that he appreciated this smile.

"What are our next steps?"

"I'm just calculating the next jump, and then we're gone. Should be done within the next quartercycle or so."

"Shouldn't we—you—have some rest?"

"Right after that jump. Once we're in an uncharted system, I doubt the Association will come for us again. That will be a big relief and make my rest easier."

"Oh. If you put it that way, I think we can do without rest here, too. Would you like a mug of forwine with your calculations anyway?"

"No. After the jump, yes."

"Well." He nodded and left. When the hatch closed behind him, he sighed. She was hard on herself, and he actually liked her. A good teammate, that was what she was, accepting a heavy responsibility for all their well-being.

Then realization struck him. Whatever her supernatural

skill was, precognition or premonition or who could tell—
without it, they were already dead.

Chapter Seventy-Eight

Syreen's panel clearly showed their destination, but the respective star couldn't be found in *Raydancer's* library. The ancient data collection added quite reliable position data, and also told of its planet, but had nothing on the hyperspace between. From her computer's point of view, it was a jump into nowhere, and from her own point of view, it was a flight *on sight*.

What could she expect? Vision and data agreed — there was no other star interfering with her preliminary hypercorridor. There was no evidence of dark stars, dark matter or other major obstacles. And yet . . .

The hypercontinuum harbored other dangers. Ruptures of the universal structure, energy potentials unable to discharge other than to a passing ship, gravitational sinks of yet unestablished wormholes, or the — so far only theoretically postulated — improbability bubbles.

Lucky explorers could report on such dangers in hindsight, although — according to the Books — it took very smart scientists and complex computer calculations to deduce their presence from the data of a completed but deviated jump.

She had a gut feeling on the space between, and she was willing to trust it. So she reduced her hypercorridor to a much narrower channel with far fewer legitimate solutions. After readjusting some parameters, she had a complete hypervelocity-hypervector pairing and ran it through simulation.

The computer signaled a warning — no reliable data — but no objections. Only now she felt insecure. Should she really dare such a jump, or was it reckless?

No, that's just cold feet. She wiggled her bare toes. *Literally. I haven't found time to get my boots yet. There's nothing reckless in this calculation, only thorough preparation.*

So she announced, "Prepare for jump in five," and released her solution to the hypercontroller.

There wasn't much left to do—rearrange her controls, log her approval of a non-standard jump, and prepare *Raydancer's* sensors for additional recording.

Herman felt the now familiar tickle of another smooth jump and took a deep breath. *We made it!*

He looked around into smiling faces—Stephan's, Drake's, yes, even Crow was smiling and gave him a thumbs-up.

"Your lady is a maven," Drake said. "She's taking to hyper-jumps like a fish to water."

Stephan grinned. "Yeah. Talking of water—should we make a draw for the bathroom?"

"The skipper's first," Drake suggested.

Stephan said, "I'd agree—only she won't make use of her privilege until her system scan is complete. So perhaps we should make sure she can feel comfortable in our presence."

Drake nodded. "That's a nice way to put it. Yes, I think we should make ourselves more presentable. You two go first."

Surprised, Herman asked, "Why?"

"You're crew, you must go. We're just passengers—we should go, we want to, but we're not facing disciplinary measures if we don't."

"You would," Stephan disagreed with a smirk, "but I get your point. Herman, I think it's your turn."

"Mine?" Herman frowned at his friend.

"Your turn. Firstly, you're the one she'll want to look at most, and secondly, it's your turn to prepare breakfast, so better get your ass moving."

The idea of breakfast appealed to Herman, while the reminder about his affection for their commanding officer triggered a tingle in his loins. *A cold shower will help.*

Syreen sighed. Yes, they were indeed alone in this system, at least as far as *Raydancer's* sensors could tell — and with regard to other starships only.

RAK-11 had one planet, apparently with a solid surface, and at a distance that principally allowed habitable conditions. Until they came closer, she couldn't tell whether there'd be life forms to encounter or even talk with, and before she approached that planet more closely, she had a few other things to tend to, among which some more rest wasn't the least important.

So she sketched a course toward the planet that would give her some time to complete the tasks on her list, submitted it to the computer and triggered *Raydancer's* collectors to unfold.

Syreen rose from her seat. *Now I'll get my boots, take a comfort stop, pick a quick brekkie, and then take a nap.*

When she opened the bridge hatch and caught the first smell of breakfast, she rearranged her plans. *Boots can wait.*

From what she could see through the open passenger compartment hatch, her fellow travelers seemed to be waiting for her. "I'll be with you in two."

CHAPTER SEVENTY-NINE

Stephan tried to hide his amusement when his commanding officer joined them barefoot, and really struggled not to laugh out loud when he saw Herman's reaction to her appearance. He had to admit that she looked cute — tasty, others would say — without her boots, but Herman's puppy eyes were too much.

She graciously thanked Herman for preparing such a good breakfast — a deserved praise, Stephan agreed — and then tackled it like she'd been starving.

Stephan didn't let his own serving cool down either. So they all enjoyed their meal rather silently.

Once they had all finished, Drake raised his forwine mug. "A toast to our skipper for having navigated us through troubled waters unharmed. Cheers!"

"Cheers!"

The lieutenant didn't deny the praise. After the second sip, she added, "Well, I have to admit that the jumps went rather smoothly. I'm rather concerned about the hostile activities, though. The Association bullies its way across the small star nations, and nobody dares to stand up against them."

"How should they?" Drake asked. "This galactic sector was a peaceful — not to say dull — place. With its share of piracy, of course, but I've never heard about war or such. So, while I'm far from knowing much about the overall situation, the few examples I learned of — Kyris, Brannock, Jakarta — seem to be typical for navies in this area. You only need enough firepower to protect your home system against marauders while the one or two larger vessels you have are on escort duty. Why spend a fortune on warships?"

"You're right," Syreen agreed. "That's what our superiors told us, too. Our skirmisher wings could protect the Duchy against any reasonable number of attacking pirates, while our destroyers could do escort missions or hunt a pirate down. Large enough to operate independently, harbor rescued survivors or arrested pirates, provide medical emergency treatment and even take a beating by pirates — swift, fast, and with heavy pulse cannons to deal out. It worked for megacycles. However, the Association is different."

"They operate larger ships," Drake noted.

She took another sip. "Much larger. Cruisers, whether light or heavy, okay, that's a question of range, too. If you have to cover a larger chunk of space, you need units that can operate independently for a longer time — without maintenance dock or resupply."

Stephan's gaze came to rest on her toes, while she went on.

"More stuff to carry around, more departments, a few shuttles aboard, and the hull grows. Let me put it like this — corvettes are built for compactness and single-hand operation, destroyers for firepower, frigates for speed and escort missions, cruisers for independent operation. All okay. However, battle cruisers and dreadnaughts are built for just that — battle. So, the Association is prepared for war, and I don't know why."

Drake leaned forward and examined her toes, too, before he said, "Well, although it happened before my birth, there have been interstellar battles. It's in the history books, and I've read a lot of them during my research."

"I fear we've somewhat neglected that topic in the Duchy," Syreen admitted.

Stephan couldn't remember anything about battles in the sky — his superiors probably hadn't seen the need to burden infantry with such useless stuff.

Drake placed his own mug down. Herman cocked his head, and Drake nodded. Herman rose to fetch another.

Drake scratched his head. "Let me sum it up, as some of the details are sickening. During the era of expansion, there were many territorial conflicts, over who found which planet first, over valuable resources, or just with regard to location, when a single system was separated from others. That's a bit like our current place—we're far away from the Duchy, with several other star nations between. In the past, sometimes the more powerful players decided to expand their boundaries and swallow the smaller nations in between. Sometimes, such conflicts were solved by short battles, sometimes the display of sufficient strength would tone their aspirations down. Toward the end of the same era there were a few, well, disagreements between single-planet nations and large merchant corporations. Some of the big players decided to take the law in their own hands, equipped their cargo ships with guns—officially, as defense against pirates—and used their wealth to occupy those nations who couldn't afford their own navy yet. Some of the larger nations agreed to put an end to this behavior—as their governments clearly saw the danger of being consumed, too, once the corporations grew large enough—and sent out their fleets."

"The guild wars," Syreen remembered. "There was a reference in the pirate regulations."

"Correct. If I remember rightly, the name came later—the merchant guild was founded by honest merchants to distinguish themselves from the corporations, and they suggested extending guild laws to any interstellar trade, banning any serious armament from merchant ships. The guild was seen as the winner, and that's what the war was named for." He paused. "The worst I read about—and I really had to force myself to only skim the records—were the missionary wars."

"I never heard of that." She looked at Stephan.

Stephan shook his head. "Me neither."

Drake lowered his voice. "It was a war — or better, a bundle of wars — about religious beliefs, and about imposing them on others. Back then, drones were deployed to hit a planetary capital at about half light speed, or large amounts of plutonium dispersed in the atmosphere — in any case, the goal was to render a planet uninhabitable and eliminate the entire population."

Herman almost dropped the mug he had just brought, and quickly set it down before Drake. "But that's barbaric."

"It was, yes. These conflicts only lasted a few months. After that, the other star nations had agreed on a charter against such actions — and on a firm statement. Three different religious nations were identified as the main arsonists and were each asked for unconditional surrender. One complied — they had to accept being isolated and disconnected from space travel. The other two trusted in their faith and took up the fight. Their navies were wiped from space — and their planets were annihilated."

Syreen frowned. "How do you annihilate a planet?"

"There were no details in the records I read, but basically, it was about throwing large rocks at them." He reached for his mug. "Well — that's why there are warships."

"They must be megacycles old," Syreen mused.

"Sure, but still operational. Don't ask me why."

"The question remains," Stephan chimed in, "what the Association is doing here — what they're searching for, why they're swarming out in numbers, and why they think they have to send out battle cruisers. After what you said, normal cruisers would be perfect for the job. Don't they have enough cruisers?"

CHAPTER EIGHTY

Syreen smiled at Herman when he brought her another mug of forwine. "Thanks."

He beamed at her. "You're welcome, Sir."

Aware of his affection toward her and her own more physical needs, she knew she was supposed to discourage him, but she couldn't and wouldn't want to spoil her cheerful mood.

"Let's drop that subject of warships for now," she proposed. "I don't think they'll follow us here. They don't have the data, and—"

"And they don't have the pilot who could do it," Drake interrupted her.

"Maybe not, or maybe they do. But first, they need to know where to go. Only then comes the question how to follow us here."

Drake frowned, "Could they tell? From our jump, I mean."

"No. Up to today, it's impossible to determine the destination of another ship's jump." Or was it? Syreen considered the idea. "Maybe the aftershock's strength could give you a rough idea of the impulse applied—but then, a powerful five-sigma jump could cover the same magnitude of distance as a weak six-sigma jump, while a weak five-sigma jump renders the same shock as a strong six-sigma jump."

So close to a star—where a jump should be impossible at all—even picking up the aftershock should be hard.

She focused on Drake. "We agreed that you'd tell me the whole story before the last jump. Due to that bothersome encounter we were forced to jump first, but I think now it's time for your story. After that, I'll check our pulse cannon—Stephan, I didn't forget that—and then we'll talk about how we should approach the planet ahead." Once they'd settled that, there'd still be time for a shower and a nap.

Her principal nodded. "I know, I promised you. I had reservations first, but after what you've done, I think you truly deserve to know. Well, where do I start?"

Drake paused, but nobody seemed to feel inclined to give him a cue. "Okay. You might already have guessed that I'm researching ancient alien races and their legacy. It's not exactly a profession, and it's not entirely scientific interest. You could call me a treasure hunter in the broader sense. I have the time and the funds to afford such an expensive—well, my friends call it a hobby. My grandfather collected records and a few artifacts, and the stories he told triggered my curiosity on those who populated this galaxy before us. I read everything I could get my hands on until I eventually found this alien navigation library that brought us here. Frankly, I have no idea what we might find here, but my sources give me hope that those star systems which no longer exist in our data might harbor something valuable to find—I mean, how do you hide stars when they're out in plain sight for everyone? Someone made an effort to erase them from our memory."

Their skipper nodded, but it was the maintenance guy—Stephan—who asked the crucial question. "What's worth such an effort? Rare elements, or something dangerous?"

"I asked myself the same question, naturally. Why would someone try to hide this planet and not another? I didn't suspect raw material, though. Something valuable, maybe, but something that can't be found anywhere else—and I daresay, there's no chemical element we haven't found somewhere else already. Something dangerous—yes, but if it were just a threat, why couldn't it be eliminated? The few hints we have about ancient times tell of planetary surfaces bared of any life form — erased to the molten core, just to make sure. We found such evidence. If they were so powerful, they wouldn't just hide a danger, but fight it — or place a warning."

"Sounds reasonable," Stephan agreed.

"So, if it was no danger to them, it might be a danger to others? I mean — what kind of weapons could erase an entire planet? We don't have such means of power. What if those items were safely hidden away — in case they might be needed again?" He spread his arms. "Only, when this ancient race disappeared, or left, or whatever happened to them, they weren't able to collect all their stuff."

"Weapons?" Stephan asked.

Drake nodded. "There are insinuations toward that in the records. Note that we don't have anything in writing from them, only fragments like the navigation library. But there's old lore — rock paintings, cuneiforms, and other things, by contemporary races. Mostly extinct, too, but their records were the subject of human research for megacycles. So researchers found images of interstellar visitors and their actions. In very few cases, open combat."

Before the maintenance guy could ask, he added, "Yes, there may be weapons. I doubt we'd be able to understand or even apply them, but there must be a lot of stuff around — primarily, knowledge. That's what I'm after."

Syreen made a straight face. *I don't believe a word. No wonder — I can sense you're not entirely honest. The idea of those weapons gives you a thrill. Who wouldn't want to be the first to get his hands on one?* She kept her mouth shut and listened on. *Access to an ancient race's ultimate weapons? Won't happen on my watch.*

"There are a few clues," Drake went on. "The images all show bipedal creatures — uh, two legs, two arms, two eyes, proportions roughly the same as ours. However, that's not entirely reliable, as it also applied to the respective race creating the image. We have the records of the damaged alien starship — where the library came from."

Syreen sensed a rise in his excitement. Was that what he was after? Another alien starship, this time undamaged?

She waved her hand toward Drake, to encourage him to continue.

He said, "I brought the protocol I used to access that navigation library. Maybe if there's another such artifact on this planet, it will answer."

That made her sit up straight. "You mean, we should broadcast our arrival to anyone down there and hope for a friendly invitation?"

"Sure — oh, I don't think the planet will be inhabited. It wouldn't make sense to pick a hiding place where the local populace will discover the hidden treasure themselves, would it?"

"Maybe not. Okay, we haven't registered any electromagnetic emissions from the planet yet, so that might indicate it's deserted — or it might indicate the populace isn't interested in radio. However, you say there might be a super weapon, and you say its original owners were hiding it from unauthorized access. Wouldn't it make sense to protect it somehow? And if so, what automatic defenses would we trigger?"

"Valid point." Drake nodded. "However, with the correct protocol we may as well be regarded as authorized."

"Would you bet your ass on that?"

He gave Crow a side glance, and shrugged. She could sense a mix of emotions — reserve and curiosity, doubts and disappointment. He wasn't ready to give up.

"Tell you what," she said. "We're not exactly in a hurry. Let's have a look at the planet first, do a thorough scan of its surface, and postpone that general call."

He calmed down and relaxed. "Yes, you're right. It took me years to find this place—no need to spoil it all by some premature action. We'll do it your way."

For now—he didn't voice it, but she saw it in him.

Herman used the pause to chime in. "Does this *ancient race* have a name?"

Drake shook his head. "None we'd know of. That's why they're commonly referred to as the *Forgotten People*."

CHAPTER EIGHTY-ONE

Scored! Syreen couldn't hide her excitement. This sounded indeed like the same race connected to the *relic* for which the Association was searching. Only the Association was searching known planets, while she now had found an un-known — deliberately *forgotten* — planet.

Drake hadn't missed her reaction. "You've heard about them before?"

"Yes." She briefly considered what she could give away. "I told you of my brief visit to the Association dreadnaught. The *Forgotten People* were mentioned in their mission order."

He took his time to digest her statement and nodded. "You had also mentioned your own intel that would give my search credibility — that's what you meant?"

"In general, yes. I thought if they were searching for stuff from the past, anyone could be searching for stuff from the past. I didn't know you were after the same."

"We still don't know whether they're searching for the same stuff," he objected. "It's not unlikely that they're trying to find that weapon, though. That would explain their deter-mination."

He spread his arms. "I can't even rule out that I'm the trig-ger."

"How's that?"

"Well — while I didn't actually advertise my research, I couldn't entirely keep it under cover, either. I mean, I'm no navigator. I needed a few hints to even find the right sector to start my search, so I had to ask people who knew about astronomy. Maybe the word spread, someone added up the details, and then someone decided, *hey, we should be the ones to find that place first.* Worse if they knew what I'm searching for."

"Worse indeed," she said sourly. "Many brave soldiers died."

She sensed his indignation before she saw it rising in his face, and hastily added, "Not that I'd blame you. That's the Association's responsibility alone. As I said before, they could have just asked."

"And told everyone what they're looking for?" Stephan objected. "No—I can see why they didn't advertise it."

"It's cynical," Herman added. "The postulated existence of an ancient weapon, where nobody knows whether it truly exists, triggers war for it."

"Which reminds me," Syreen added with no little sarcasm, "that I promised to check our pulse cannon."

CHAPTER EIGHTY-TWO

After an extended, refreshing nap, Syreen decided, *I need another shower.*

She had needed one after the maintenance check to feel clean again. Now she needed another to feel fresh. She picked up her uniform leggings for the short walk to the bathroom, arranged them to slip inside, and then changed her mind.

Her clothes needed refreshing, too, and with three gay males aboard and one already seduced straight one, the effort of dressing decently was pointless. After what they'd been through together, she didn't rely on her uniform for their respect. So she grabbed her shirt, coat and boots and ambled forward.

She shouldn't have worried—Stephan held watch on the bridge, with his back toward the open hatch, and the others were in the passenger compartment, probably still sleeping. Nobody noticed her nude walk.

Six centicycles later, she was clean, awake, and decently dressed, and stepped into the galley for a hot forwine.

Herman was already there and handed her a filled mug. "I reckon you want one of these."

"Thank you, Herman."

He smiled. "I woke up and found the bathroom occupied. Well, I quickly counted heads—it had to be you. So I decided to have a mug ready for you."

Syreen took the mug. He wasn't finished yet. She could sense his worries.

He fetched another and filled it. "I had an idea."

"Yes?"

"The Association. They're determined, almost desperate, if not to say mad. They'll do anything to get that artifact first, and if it's a weapon, they'll do the impossible—like you did, where you are neither desperate nor mad. Would you agree?"

She nodded. "Go on."

"Well—they came to the Duchy for something. But not the weapon? There's something missing in the story. Anyway—by now they should have sorted most things out. They're two prisoners and a corvette short. The corvette left the Duchy shortly after the dreadnaught accident. That's the first piece. The second piece is Brannock—another corvette like the missing one. We didn't meet them at Kyris or Jakarta—maybe they saved those systems for later?"

Syreen contemplated that. "I'd have to check the jump routes. The quickest are not always the shortest."

"In any case, sooner or later they'll learn about our visit there, too. The guild logs our arrival toward our contract, and every ship passing through propagates the guild database changes. No big deal to find out. No doubt they'll also learn about our latest escape from that *Gorgon*—as soon as that skipper reaches a system with message drone traffic." He waved his mug. "Five pieces to put together, but that's not everything yet. Our mission's in the guild database, too, right? A Duchy officer, an AP corvette, a researcher possibly connected to the Forgotten People. What does that add up to?"

She felt a cold shiver running down her spine. "I see."

"Yep. This corvette's searching for that super weapon. There's a sequence of stops—with the *Gorgon* reporting the last sighting. After that, we disappear. No further visit to any inhabited system. We must know something they don't. We must have found a way. If I were in their shoes, I'd send ships to every star around. How long until they recognize they must have a blind spot?"

"Not long."

"And once they do—what does it take to solve the puzzle? I'm just a dirtbug—no argument please—but I ask myself, how often do skippers look out of their windows to see what their computer won't see?"

"Most try to avoid that. The emptiness around can be hard to bear."

"Okay. And even if they do, it's not obvious. You don't say, hey, *I don't know that star over there, it's not on my map,* right? But eventually they'll get there, and once they do, they'll find this place. I'd be curious. No—in fact, I wouldn't be, I'd try to get away as far as I could, but I'd expect them to be curious. And if they are, they'll try a jump. Right?"

"I can't find a flaw in that theory." She sighed. "You're right. They'll come here."

"Yes. It's just a question of time, isn't it?"

CHAPTER EIGHTY-THREE

I've botched it, Syreen mused. *I left a clear trail but for the last jump.*

However, even in hindsight she couldn't find any way to avoid it, except for not accepting Drake's mission, and that would only have deprived her of the little lead she had against the Association.

"Thank you for pointing it out." She drank her forwine and placed the mug on the counter. "Can you take care of this? I'll go and try to guess how much time we might have left, with the number of jumps, drone schedules, and all."

"Sure."

Herman mirrored her confidence now — or had she projected it? She shrugged inwardly and went to the bridge.

Stephan turned around when she entered. He quickly cleared the seat for her. "No incidents, Sir. I took the liberty of folding the collectors once we were fully charged."

"Thanks, Stephan. That's fine. You should take a rest now — I'll need your help with the buoy once we reach orbit around Silver Seven."

"Silver Seven?"

"That's the code name for our destination — it was my last official call sign."

"Oh. Lucky number?"

"Something like that."

"Good idea. Okay, I'll snuggle in my seat now."

"Sleep well."

"I'll try."

He disappeared, and she sat down and started checking her data. But her thoughts returned to the buoy. Should she deploy it? Or was it better to pretend they weren't there?

No. There's no point in hiding. They'll do a thorough search for Raydancer *anyway, and unless I find the perfect hideaway, this will just buy us a tencycle or so – during which the Association can claim the system, then call our presence illegal and shoot us at will. With a Duchy buoy, however, they're the intruder and I can shoot. I might even have a chance to score – unless they come in numbers.*

So far, she had played it more or less legally – from wearing a Duchy badge aboard a hostile dreadnaught to the open appearance at Kyris, Brannock and Jakarta. The only infringement she could be accused of was not showing a transponder signal, and that could be called self-defense after the Association's Duchy raid.

Moreover, the latter was a minor personal offense that wouldn't jeopardize the Duchy's integrity. While she was always ready to ignore the Book on technical issues and internal regulations, she'd play by the rules with regard to interstellar customs. That determined the buoy's fate.

Okay, back on topic. How much time do we have left?

Syreen arranged the incidents Herman had diligently mentioned as small blots on a timeline and in her plot. Next, she added the potential flow of messages as fingers reaching out from the blots. Some of the flows were given by drone schedules, others were just guesses – where their probability increased over time. Result was a complicated web of probabilities like, *the message on this incident will reach this node with this probability curve. The probability of all messages combined in this node increases like this.*

The probability curves didn't run entirely asymptotically – except for the last encounter, all messages were eventually transported by drones, kicking probability up to one. Syreen hadn't included the unlikely loss of a drone into her model. There she had to play safe.

Once a node had reached sufficient overall probability — which included the Association being aware of the facts — how long would it take them to decide on their actions, gather enough units and start searching?

This would add more complexity. No. Of course, any single skipper could act on his own, but that wasn't the question. When would a well-organized search start?

Which nodes were prone to decision-making? Primarily the Duchy, where a mission command was allocated, and then, of course, the central planets. They'd have ships ready there or could collect them on the fly in the systems they'd pass. How many jumps would it take them to get close?

A military operation meant fewer recharge stops, but that didn't matter in total — the final recharge would only take as much longer.

She contemplated her model for a while. *No, stupid. Once a node reaches the threshold, the information will be actively passed on. That accelerates propagation.*

So she added the respective rules and examined the results again. She didn't like what she saw.

Drake sighed and eyed the list again. Whoever had procured their provisions had been diligent and pragmatic, but totally lacked a sense for the finer sides of life. Of course, this journey was no luxury cruise, but a little more attention here and there . . .

His gaze fell on the last entry, *miscellaneous.*

Why, if every other item was well categorized?

He tapped it, and a second list unfolded before him. He only needed one glance at the first two or three items to let out a gleeful shout. Only the finest of Kyris specialties! Carefully selected for the fastidious palate, and in surprisingly ample quantities for such a small vessel.

He resisted the urge to choose all across the list. Whoever had compiled that list — and failed to categorize it — deserved proper praise and attention.

When he heard the bridge hatch open, he wiped the list away and ordered another mug of forwine.

Their pilot appeared with the proverbial clouded gaze, but her face lit up when he handed her the fresh mug.

"What is it? Trouble ahead?"

She took the mug and then a sip and said, "You could say so."

He waited patiently.

"We have sixty tencycles at max, then they're at our door, just one jump away."

Drake didn't have to ask who. "Sixty tencycles? What will happen then?"

"They will jump in, and once they locate us, they'll shoot first and ask later. So either we'll fight or sneak away."

"Do you think we can?"

"Depends. The later they spot us, the slower they are, the better for us, as we then can rely on our better acceleration. Where I assume that we're still dirtside." She took another sip. "Of course, should we leave before they arrive, our odds are much better."

"But that's not what we came for."

"No? I thought so — we come here, find and collect some ancient treasures, and then run as fast as we can. That would be the wisest we could do."

"Unless we find something we shouldn't leave to them."

"Yes."

He felt pierced by her gaze. "I mean, uh . . ." How should he put it so that she wouldn't misinterpret his intentions?

"They're definitely the last ones I'd grant free access to an ancient super weapon, that's for sure," she said. "So if there were any chance they could deploy it, we'd have to sabotage it."

Sabotage it? No, she's right. However, they'd still need time to do that.

"You said, sixty tencycles at max."

"Plus one jump they yet have to find."

"And how long are we safe from them?"

"Safe? You mean, worst case? Ten tencycles, perhaps twenty. From then on, their odds grow."

"That's not much. How much time do we need to scan the planet before we land?"

She laughed. "Where we don't even know what to look for? Any number of kilocycles."

"No, I mean, until it's safe to land."

"Oh, that." She crossed her legs and leaned to the wall. "I'd like to do one full scan. That will give us a first insight into the planetary structure, seismic activities, the weather patterns, plus we'll have a full map to pick our landing point from. And in case there's something striking, we won't miss it."

"How long?"

"Oh, I must calculate that—three tencycles, perhaps?"

"That would leave us seven tencycles for search and investigation. A bit tight, wouldn't you agree?"

"What are you up to?"

He grinned. "Well, yeah, if we agree that blocking the Association's access to a super weapon is the primary goal, I basically see two options."

"Which are?"

"One—we broadcast my protocol, receive an invitation and have a look."

"Not likely. What's the other?"

"We broadcast my protocol and trigger the weapon's internal alarm. We're wiped from the sky, and anyone arriving after us, too."

She stared at him. He enjoyed her consternation for a moment, then he raised his own mug. "However, as I certainly prefer to live a few more kilocycles, I'd propose to send that protocol through a relay. If the relay is shot, we can still sneak away — or use that information to determine the weapon's location."

There was an understanding smile growing on her face. Not for the first time he wished she had a cock.

CHAPTER EIGHTY-FOUR

Turn after turn, *Raydancer* orbited Silver Seven, its cameras recording stripes of the planetary surface, its computer trying to recognize artificial structures or at least uncommon formations.

Daylight images changed with infrared patterns. The small crew watched the collected images in shifts, now and then picking a strange-looking spot, magnifying it, and then discarding it.

Syreen tried to remember what her instructor had said about unknown planets, aside from *Check your library.*

Unknown planets had meant *unknown to a Duchy skipper on an escort mission,* not *uncatalogued.* It had meant approaching a potential pirate's nest on an otherwise charted planet, where the great explorers of the past had already recorded dangerous creatures and features.

This planet was a blank sheet of paper. They could only assume that an ancient race would pick a tectonically stable planet to hide and store its treasures. That didn't mean anything with regard to its wildlife, though.

Did this planet have any wildlife? Most of its surface seemed to be covered by wide sand plains and scattered rocks. The deep scan data showed some large subsurface caverns and narrow tunnels connecting them, where caverns and tunnels extended deeper than the scan could tell. The tunnels didn't seem to follow any regular pattern, and some might be filled with water. The scan hadn't found any hints of processed metal, but of course, there was ore, and the red-yellowish sand contained its share of silicates and iron oxide. Oxide—yes, the atmosphere was basically breathable, only with lower pressure than humans felt comfortable with. Water and oxide should imply animal life, but what kind?

One planetary rotation took eleven cycles. Days were hot and sunny, nights were cold and pitch-black. The rhythmic change caused a matching regular rise and fall of heating and cooling air following the terminator, accompanied by strong storms.

The buoy was deployed in a high orbit, ready to announce the Duchy's claim on the RAK-11 system to any chance visitors.

Syreen saw no reason not to land. Whatever the planet might offer, *Raydancer* could bear it. Whether her passengers would want to take a walk was a different question.

But where should we land?

CHAPTER EIGHTY-FIVE

Drake fought with his frustration. *Nothing! Not even a single ruin!*

Of course, hiding a secret super weapon and whatever came with it on an uninhabited desert planet made some sense. It also made sense that a simple, even if thorough, scan from orbit wouldn't give it away.

He didn't know exactly what he had expected to find. Some kind of city, some kind of temple? Something like the pyramids that had been found on other human colonies? Or a nice row of shelves for self-service?

No, surely not. But in his dreams, there had been sequences of cues, cryptic for the ordinary man, but easy to follow for the well-educated researcher, with each puzzle leading him closer to the reward.

Near the end of the third tencycle, their skipper had disappeared behind the bridge hatch. He tried not to regard it as a way to avoid discussion, as that didn't match his image of her, but he'd really preferred her saying something about their results — or the lack of results.

Now their planned initial scan was completed. Their corvette continued to orbit the planet — he still couldn't entirely come to terms with that strange name Silver Seven — and record images, but he didn't expect any news from that second run.

They should discuss their approach.

Syreen could sense Drake's frustration and impatience through the hatch. She could understand him. Their mission would be so much easier if there was a big sign *Enter here* in a prominent place on the surface.

If we don't find a place to start our search, perhaps we could at least find a place to hide Raydancer? *Some of the caverns are large enough, so what about their entrance?*

The idea of inserting a long, tube-like object into a deep cavern triggered other associations in her, but she shook them off. *Not now.*

She rose with a sigh and ambled over to her shipmates in the passenger compartment. They immediately turned their attention to her.

"Any news?" Drake asked.

She shook her head. "No. I checked the scan data. As far as we can tell from orbit, Silver Seven harbors no danger for *Raydancer*. Its air is breathable, although I'd recommend masks 'cause it's rather thin. The temperatures are unpleasant—too cold or too hot—but wouldn't kill us instantly either."

"So we could land and walk around," Drake concluded.

"In essence, yes. However, saying that there's no danger for our ship doesn't mean there couldn't be dangerous creatures. We just haven't spotted any yet. So if you decide to walk around on your own risk, get killed by some monster, and thus fail with your mission, don't come back to me with your complaints."

He smiled on the obvious contradiction. "You say we shouldn't go outside?"

"I say we should proceed with caution, stay close to the ship, be prepared for hostile activity, have always one person on guard duty with our gun. You know our little corvette has no sick bay. There's a medbox for immediate treatment of injuries, and that's it. Any serious case, and we must jump out—not to Jakarta, not to Brannock, and I wouldn't bet on Kyris. Got the picture?"

He stared at her. "I hadn't thought of that."

"Me neither. Sorry. Perhaps you should have chartered a larger ship."

"Like an Association cruiser? No, thanks." Drake spread his arms. "I'm happy with our small team, really. I get your point, and we'll be very, very careful once we go out—if we go out. I have no clue where."

Syreen placed her hands on the backrest of Herman's chair, forcing him to look up to see her. "There is no clue. This is an innocent, uninhabited planet, nothing to be found. No ores worth carrying around, no scenery worth a tourist stay, no rare or odd items. Traveler, recharge your capacitors and move on. It's the perfect place to hide something—and that's why I'm positive we will find something. I don't know yet what that something is, but it wants to be found."

Drake answered her cheerful attitude with a smile. "It wants to be found?"

"Yes—and that's why we'll call it. Your proposal. We send the protocol and see what happens."

"Via the buoy."

"No. I changed my mind. The buoy would broadcast our message all over the system, and we don't want to publicize that code. It's better to do it on a tight downward beam."

"And if we trigger an answer?"

"I'm willing to take that risk. As I said—if it's so well hidden for such a long time, it wants to be found, or put differently, the people who left it here had to make sure it could be found by their successors. So the answer to a polite call should be nonlethal."

"Oh, okay. Makes sense that way."

Sadly, she had to dim his enthusiasm now. "However, that means we'll have to do another tour around. We might be lucky and get our response early, or we might have to do the full drill, another three tencycles."

CHAPTER EIGHTY-SIX

It was no more than a blip, returned on a beam so tight that *Raydancer's* sensors could almost have missed it. It wasn't repeated, and it didn't tell much.

The brief message was easily decoded to a pair of coordinates, in a latitude-longitude fashion. The latitude wasn't hard to interpret with regard to the planetary rotation, but the longitude needed a zero to relate to.

The number was small. Syreen decided to take *Raydancer's* own position at the time of receipt as zero and analyzed the result. She arrived at one of the large cavern entrances she had considered as hiding places. *There's where you're hiding, friend?*

She triggered the intercom. "Guys, we have a destination. Prepare for landing in fifteen — the storm down there might cause a bumpy ride."

That would give her time for a comfort stop before beginning the descent, and it would give *Raydancer* time to complete most of its next orbit, which was the economic way to approach their target, especially if they arrived at the right angle. With a few parameter entries, she adjusted their course before she rose.

Drake felt excited. *Finally!* His idea had proven right — their call had been answered. Now they would set down, walk over, and marvel at the alien legacy. Finally, his investment would pay off — money, of course, but most of all, the time he'd spent to get to this point.

He hadn't made his mind up about the super weapon yet. Was it advisable to leave its control to a young lieutenant of some backwater star nation? Okay, she was smart, able, and so far very reliable, but also quick at the trigger. Did that qualify her as a super weapon's commandant?

Legally, she had the right to claim it. He didn't have to dig into the regulations. She had claimed the system for her Duchy, so any military installations they found were hers. She had only promised him to honor his *legitimate commercial claims,* as far as those didn't interfere with territorial claims.

So far, they hadn't found anything of commercial value. The commercially most valuable items were among the provisions in *Raydancer's* storage. If that didn't change, he might claim the recognition for discovering a new planet — and perhaps the blame for unleashing doom over the known galaxy — but otherwise remain empty-handed.

There was that little imp in the back of his head telling him, *only one gun!* Yes, he might trick their skipper into handing that gun to Crow, for standing guard outside, but what next? There was just one pilot on this planet, and he guessed she wouldn't be blackmailed. She'd rather let him shoot her crew than surrender the super weapon — and in cold blood, as she had treated that pirate from her stories.

His excitement gave way to resignation. He'd have to take the crumbs she'd leave him.

CHAPTER EIGHTY-SEVEN

Good timing, Syreen congratulated herself. The storms following the temperature differences around the terminator had moved on, the turbulences faded, and now she was approaching the cavern entrance with the sun in her back.

She preferred flying such approaches with open blinds and direct visual feedback rather than plot diagrams and numbers. There were too many things her computer might consider irrelevant when they weren't, and too many warnings about things that didn't bother her at all.

The entrance was more than wide enough to fly *Raydancer* in sideways and high enough to do the same upright, should she have desired it, so navigating was no big deal at all.

Further in, the light quickly faded. She decelerated and allowed her eyes to accommodate to the dimness outside the ship. When a large shape blocked most of the cavern's width ahead, she set *Raydancer* down on its landing gear.

She opened the bridge door.

"Come forward. You must see this."

One after the other, her shipmates poked their heads in and stared forward.

"Can you make light?" Drake asked.

"Give your eyes time to adapt."

They waited. Syreen could sense their tension — anticipation, curiosity, with a dash of primeval fear.

"It's huge," Drake said.

"What is that?" Stephan inquired.

"You tell me," she returned.

"Looks like an — uh — V-shaped dildo to me," Herman observed, earning grins and chuckles. "With a lot of bumps."

"Warts," Stephan objected. "Lots of warts. Warts on leg stumps — that's a spread-eagle if I ever saw one."

"And the joint?" Herman asked back.

"Shaved pussy. Sorry, Sir, but that's what it looks like."

Indeed, the oval shape with the vertical groove between the two — uh, legs — looks like a pussy. Why didn't I notice before? Because it's ugly with all the warts?

"I can't see anything like a hatch or airlock — unless it's that shape," Stephan said. "And otherwise — can you see that pointy cone above? The only part that's not round and wrinkled and bumpy."

"I see it," Herman agreed, "but it's not the only one. There's one at the end of each leg, pointing inward."

"Oh — yes, there. Antennae?"

"Don't jump to conclusions," Syreen interrupted the two.

Stephan nodded. "Sure. Just collecting ideas."

"No windows?" Herman asked. "Well, there isn't much to see around anyway."

"Except for us," Stephan reminded him.

"Okay, now that we've found it — what is it?" Syreen asked. "Drake?"

Their researcher had remained silent since he asked for light. Now he cleared his throat and said in a low voice, "I've seen a sketch of that. You remember? The alien shipwreck? Someone had tried to reconstruct its original shape. That *someone* got most of it wrong, but the similarities strike me as important. This is an alien starship, undamaged, a Forgotten People starship. The little we know about the wreck is that some of its parts were organic. That's why the researchers called it a *living ship*."

CHAPTER EIGHTY-EIGHT

Drake paused before the airlock. "Are you sure you don't want to come?"

The pilot shook her head. "No. I would really like to, but one of us must keep watch on the bridge, and you all deserve to go, after being so patient." She smiled and added, "I'll have a look around later."

"Later, then."

He entered the airlock, where the other men were already waiting, and adjusted his mask. Crow checked the gun again and nodded. Good Crow, always willing to stand aside in Drake's favor, always willing to cover his back—this way or that.

The two soldiers were professionally calm. Armed with cameras, scanners, backpacks and long knives, their task was to explore the numerous access tunnels to their cavern for potential threats—after their first look at the living ship, of course.

Drake would first examine the ship from all sides to find out where the entry hatch might be. He planned to diligently document every detail on the ship's outside and surroundings before even attempting to enter it. There had been too many reports on poor preparations and damaged scenes—if such a report really was all he could keep, at least it should be a good one that would collect praise from the scientific community.

Such would provide him with a foundation to collect funds for another expedition—after all, RAK-11 wasn't the only forgotten system. Now that he knew how to match his old library with current data, anyone could take him to another doorstep, and with this treasure trove, he'd also find another navigator willing to try a jump to the unknown.

"You coming, boss?"

He looked up. Crow was waiting in the dim light outside. His voice sounded muffled under the mask.

"Sure." He stepped out of the airlock, down the short ladder, and onto the cavern floor. A cloud of dust sprung up around his feet.

The air was cold, and he was glad of the robust evac suit that *Raydancer's* inventory had provided. It was supposed to shield the bearer against the cold of space as well as the heat of a star, against radiation, poison, acid, or sharp edges, and with the soft hood-helmet, it would be entirely airtight.

They had decided against the helmet, but accepted the mask that made breathing easier in the thin air. Wearing the mask was uncomfortable, and the oxygen-enriched flow tasted stuffy, but it allowed them more time outside.

The other men were waiting for him. He nodded and waved them forward.

The two soldiers glanced at each other, and then spread toward the caverns' sides, leaving him the center. Crow followed. In that formation they negotiated the uneven cavern floor with its ledges and dips.

He tried not to focus on the alien ship alone—and he was well advised there, as he learned when Stephan raised his arm and called, "Freeze."

Drake stopped at the edge of the rocky ledge, fought for balance, and then slowly set his free leg down next to the other.

The soldier pointed at the dusty area at the foot of the ledge where he'd been about to place his next step. "The scanner says it's going down three legs. Better check that."

He went on his knees and reached down with one hand. There was almost no resistance, the fine dust gave way like a pool of water. "Wow. Nasty surprise. Thanks, Stephan."

Stephan shrugged. "You're welcome. We should stick to the rocky surfaces as far as possible."

"I agree." Drake looked around. "We should have brought more light."

"In my backpack," Stephan returned. "I don't use it because its range is limited, and I prefer a dim overview over a sharp cone of light."

"Makes sense." He shrugged. "Okay, let's go on."

CHAPTER EIGHTY-NINE

They were standing between the two would-be legs and gazing at the ship's body. Compared to *Raydancer*, it was huge indeed — each leg twice as long and three times as thick as the corvette, and spread at about sixty degrees.

From this close, the surface appeared even more wrinkled, and that included the warts. A fine layer of dust covered every part facing up, turning it gray. In fact, the hull was more greenish than gray, but it was a sick, dull green.

Herman licked his upper lip under the mask. It tasted as stuffy as the air he was breathing. "To me, it looks more like a dead ship."

"Only no worms, no cobwebs, and no foul smell," Stephan added. "Kind of mummified, if you ask me."

Drake stepped closer to the body. "Well, if you store something away for gigacycles, you better prepare it against decay. I'm rather puzzled that there's so little dust."

"You've got a point there." Stephan raised his scanner and checked the display. "We get no readings beyond the surface. Impenetrable for this toy. It doesn't radiate anything but a little warmth, and there's no magnetic field. Might as well be a rock."

Herman shook his head and pointed forward with one hand. "This *rock* sent a tight-beam signal through all that stone over our heads. *Something's* still alert inside. So, I wouldn't try to rock this rock."

"You were the one who said it's dead."

"Nah. I said it looks like it's dead. Waiting to spring the

trap."

Stephan shrugged, glanced at Drake, and winked. "Not my trap."

Drake returned the wink. "Nor mine. We'll disarm it."

"Okay." His crewmate turned back to Herman. "Let's go?"

"Let's go." Herman pointed around the leg to their left. "That way. Once around the back, and then we'll work our way back to *Raydancer*."

"Sounds like a plan."

Stephan went ahead, as he had done in the past.

We're still at war, Herman suddenly realized. *We tried to run away from it, but here we stand, and the enemy's coming for us again. And again, we're exploring unknown caverns unarmed.*

Stephan tried to evenly divide his attention between his scanner display and the unfamiliar surroundings. He didn't like the shadows caused by the little light that reached that far inside, and he had even less taste for the darkness behind the alien ship.

After only two steps he had to admit, "We need the lamps."

"Either that, or our visors," Herman agreed.

"Visors? What visors?"

"Our own—the ones we used in the duct. I found them when I checked our provisions, and put them away. I thought they might prove useful here."

"And you didn't bother to tell me."

"No—I wanted to, but then we were so quickly preparing everything, and I had to fetch this and check that, and somehow I missed the opportunity. But I brought them."

"But you brought them." Stephan smiled, although he wasn't sure whether his crewmate could see it. "So, what are you waiting for? Out with them."

Herman quickly produced two visors and handed one to Stephan, who took it and put it on.

He activated it. "Whoa!"

"What?" Herman asked.

"Look for yourself."

He waited until his crewmate had activated his own visor. Together they admired the web of hair-fine lines covering the ship's entire body, indicating warmth. Not surprisingly, the lines joined in the warts.

They had marveled for a while when a flicker ran across the lines, forked into one of the warts and disappeared around the ship to the other side.

"Did you see that?" he asked.

"Yes," Herman said.

Herman watched two more flickers running across the fine web, each time different, and two or three centicycles apart.

"Fascinating," he decided, "but we have a task."

"You're right, we should check the cavern first. Let's find the monsters."

Stephan had only voiced what he'd thought, too, but Herman would have felt better without. He felt for the hilt of his knife — not the melee sword Duchy infantry trained with, but reassuring anyway. With the evac suit armor, he didn't have to fear claws or teeth, and he could deal out in kind.

Slowly, they worked their way around the rear of the ship, where the torso extended again as long as the *legs* were. He couldn't spot any remarkable features, and Stephan didn't point out any, either. Only more warts and wrinkles, and the occasional flicker.

When they came around the other leg, Stephan pointed forward. "See that?"

Herman tried to find out what he meant. There were three dust basins, and one looked brighter.

"The dust?" he asked.

"The scanner says that's a deep pit. It's warmer, and I wonder why."

"Physics isn't my strongest subject," Herman admitted, "but what if the fine dust can somehow keep the warm air? I heard something like that about feathers—uh, down feathers."

"Let me check that." Stephan approached the first basin— a dark one—and probed the dust with his knife. He touched rock after a few fingers. Next, he felt it with his palm. "Very smooth. Not deep, but more like soap. Slippery."

The next probe at the brighter pit went in all the way. Herman could see a little cloud of warm dust rise around Stephan's arm, and at the same time, the brightness around faded.

"I can't reach the ground," Stephan commented. "Well— the scanner says it's at least two legs deep. Enough to disappear in it."

"Or hide in it."

Herman smiled under his mask when his crewmate quickly pulled hand and knife out.

His scanner called for attention. He looked up, past the display, and believed he saw movement near the cavern's closer wall. Adjusting his visor didn't help.

"Over there," he said aloud and raised his scanner. Before he made the first step forward, he checked the cavern floor for dust basins and chose a safe path.

Stephan looked around. Whatever Herman had spotted, if there could be anything, there could be more. *Trouble comes in waves*, their instructors had taught them. *Expect the enemy to show you what they want you to see — and then try to see what the enemy tries to hide.*

Their instructors had been good, had taught them many useful things—and some less useful—and that had saved their asses until they had reached that duct. Sadly, it hadn't saved most of their mates, and their instructors had probably shared their fate, considering the Association's merciless approach.

This was probably the worst time to contemplate the others' fate. He'd better watch out — that was what their memory should remind him of.

Herman was cautiously approaching one of the larger, almost man-size tunnel entrances in the cavern wall. Stephan systematically checked the smaller neighboring mounds, eyed the deeper dust basins his crewmate carefully avoided, and also tossed the occasional glance over his shoulder.

When his gaze passed Crow, who was covering the angle between the ship's legs, the bodyguard signaled him to keep an eye on his back. Stephan returned the wave thankfully and focused forward again, where Herman had covered half of the way to the wall.

There was *something* stirring at another large tunnel mound.

"Stop."

Herman heard Stephan's advice and froze. *Discretion's the better part of valor,* he remembered. One of their staff sergeants had once dropped that line.

His scanner still showed nothing remarkable. Shouldn't their gear find any threat long before they could spot it?

Then another motion caught the corner of his eye — a little cloud of dust slowly sailing down to the ground before another tunnel entrance. What had caused the dust to stir?

So you're playing games with us?

He waved Stephan closer.

His crewmate frowned, but came. Herman reached into Stephan's backpack and produced two head lamps.

Stephan shook his head. Herman winked, focused one

lamp to tight beam and placed it on the floor to his side. He switched it on and adjusted it so that it illuminated just one tunnel mound. Then he stepped away from it.

Now Stephan nodded.

Probably with a grin under his mask. Let them come.

From the would-be safety of her cockpit, Syreen watched the little expedition spread around the cavern. Drake was focusing on the ship with Crow guarding his back. Herman and Stephan were searching for possible monsters in the tunnels around, while the one truly monstrous creature was waiting in her lair—she herself.

She sensed a growing hunger inside her, felt weak and tired.

I will have to feed again soon, and there are only four sources. How long will I be able to keep myself under control?

They had agreed to return to *Raydancer* before the sunset storms rose, not knowing how strong the gust would be outside.

Better play it safe, Drake had agreed.

He had no idea. It was probably much safer for them outside, but what did she really know about herself?

Now, in the relative safety of a remote, forgotten planet, hidden in a subterranean cavern, alone aboard their small corvette, she found peace and quiet to contemplate her strange abilities in depth for the first time. It was as if she had arrived somewhere, was no longer on the run.

I sense emotions.

That was something she could easily live with—most of all, because she could tune in and out of them. So far, she didn't drown in other people's feelings, rather noticing them like she noticed their facial expressions, in passing.

I control other people's minds.

This was a bit more unsettling, but also convenient. She

didn't have to, and when she did, it was for a good cause. Her cause. It came naturally to her, like breathing. She could subtly change people's minds — make them ignore her — or forcefully make a man kill another. She had no qualms about the latter, not when her own death would have been the alternative.

I suck blood.

That was the unnerving part. It came as easily to her as the other skills, but she couldn't accept it as natural. Biting other people? Feeding on their strength? And then watching the tooth marks disappear? Too much like magic for her taste. What kind of creature did such things? Surely not a human.

What can I do about it? Nothing. No facts to build upon, no answers. I can only live with it.

CHAPTER NINETY

Herman tried hard to keep his gaze fixed on the illuminated tunnel mound. Nothing happened.

This is not my business. I'm no scientist. I don't know what to make of this. And yet . . . He glanced at Stephan. *We're here to help Syreen any way we can. If staring at tunnel mounds helps her, that's what we do.*

Where the mound looked somewhat like a butt hole, and he'd certainly prefer to stare at a pussy. The latter was what Drake did now — staring at the alien ship's pussy — and that was odd.

The only straight guy around stares at assholes, and the gay bloke gets to stare at a pussy. That can't be right.

It couldn't be right, and it couldn't be what their skipper wanted — what their skipper needed. She was no scientist either, and she couldn't know any more about this planet and these tunnels than he and Stephan.

What she needed was someone with balls and brains to find out what was going on in these tunnels, and if their scanners wouldn't do the job, he had to.

So he made a firm step forward and paused. Nothing happened.

Two more steps. He watched — and a moment later, there was a little stir at one of the mounds ahead, however, not the illuminated one.

Herman squinted and prepared himself for whatever would come for them.

A few breaths later he realized again that nothing would

come for them.

"I'm sick of that," he said aloud. "Let's enter one of these darn tunnels and have a closer look."

"Is that wise?" Stephan asked.

"Nah, it isn't, but we won't get any wiser staring at those holes for the next cycles either. I'd say we need some tangible evidence before we have to return to the ship for the night, and if that evidence isn't willing to come to us, we have to go and get it."

"You're crazy."

"Not really. If there were anything we couldn't handle, it would have come for us. We're such a rare treat—the chance might not return for ages. Come on. We're just penetrating this planet's unknown ass, and that's standard procedure."

Stephan laughed out loud—but only for a moment, and then he quickly rearranged his mask, as it began to leak from his outburst. *Standard procedure, indeed!*

While his crewmate began to advance toward the tunnel, he shared a brief eye-contact with Crow, waved at the tunnel and received a nod. That was standard procedure, too—*if you're about to get lost in a dark hole, tell someone where you're going.*

He followed Herman, but remained a few steps behind.

His curiosity had to stand back.

The scanner in one hand, the other hand on the knife hilt, they entered the tunnel. Every two or three steps, Herman paused and checked his immediate surroundings. Every two or three steps, he shook his head before proceeding forward.

They were about twenty legs in when Herman raised one finger. He pointed at his scanner, then at the tunnel ahead, and continued forward very slowly.

Next, he crouched and held his scanner toward a niche in the tunnel wall. Stephan couldn't see the reason until Herman waved him to come forward. When he peeked over his crew-mate's shoulder, he spotted the culprits, too.

Five truly *monstrous* creatures were cowering in the niche and trembling—each about the size of his thumb, with four tiny legs, gray fur, pointy noses, large beady eyes and even larger ears, and a tail again as long as his index finger.

"Oooh, horrific," he commented. "Fierce, dangerous inter-stellar sabertooth mice?"

Herman nodded. "Don't know about their teeth, but other-wise—yes."

Chapter Ninety-one

R *aydancer* was trembling on its landing gear. The storm was howling through the cavern, playing on the large tunnels like on organ pipes, trying to grind the small corvette down with streams of fine dust.

Syreen smiled at the thought. Spaceship bodies were built to resist collisions with interstellar dust at relativistic speed. No mere storm could cause true damage — the worst they had to fear was reduced direct vision.

Of course, the internal systems had to fight their own battle against dust — inevitably, the expedition members had brought it with them, in their hair, their ears, in every crease and wrinkle. Luckily they had returned before the storm. Again, spaceship equipment was built for such challenges, where shuttles and corvettes were built to go dirtside and thus specifically good at it.

She sipped at her forwine mug and examined the panels — all green, no trouble. She had already reassured her ship-mates, should she do it again? *No, better not, it might have the opposite effect.*

Instead, she should distract them. She activated the intercom. "Herman, Stephan, do you have a moment?"

They were with her at the bridge hatch within the blink of an eye, with cleaned hair and faces and refreshed uniforms.

"Yes, Sir?" Stephan asked formally.

She smiled mischievously. "You're over that terrible encounter, are you?"

"Yes. After we terrified those poor mice almost to death,

we showed them an escape route and let them go. I wonder what they're feeding on, though."

"Oh, that." Syreen gestured toward her panels. "Look outside what's flying past our window — there are shreds of vegetation in the dust around us. During the calm periods, they might try to collect whatever's blown into the cavern by the storm."

"Ah — thank you. I was puzzled."

"You're welcome. I think you're entitled to be curious. After all, you're member of a research expedition." Syreen winked at him. "However, that's not why I called. What are your plans for tomorrow?"

"Plans, Sir? Uh — shall we do another mission outside?"

"What are your preferences?"

Stephan shrugged. "It surely beats sitting aboard and counting provisions for the umpteenth time."

"Agreed. What if I had another option?"

"Which one, Sir?"

"I'd say, Drake needs some tencycles to figure out how he can get inside. Meanwhile, I could teach you how to fly this baby."

"Fly?" Stephan glanced at Herman, who made the same clueless face. "Isn't that complicated?"

"The way I do it, it is. Finding optimized new jump routes is difficult. So is shooting at long range. So is winning a battle. Telling the computer to do basic stuff, however, isn't. I'm considering lessons in emergency piloting. Which means that you'd be able to reach an inhabited system if something happened to me."

Like if you must lock me away to save your lives.

CHAPTER NINETY-TWO

The morning storm had passed, the dust had settled again—or the old dust had been blown away, and new dust had taken its place—and Drake was examining the grooves with their flash patterns, using Stephan's visor.

He couldn't take his gaze off the ship's structure, followed the flickering traces across the body, but didn't dare to touch anything. What did these signals mean? Why didn't they follow a regular pattern—or was the pattern too complicated to recognize?

Now and then, he interrupted his observation to examine a wart more closely, or to search for breaks in the wrinkled hull. Nothing—his researcher's diligence wasn't rewarded at all. However, he wouldn't give up easily. If this approach didn't render any results, he'd try something else. There were still many options left.

Syreen occasionally looked out of the window or at her plot. The latter offered her a better overview of Drake's and Crow's position, but she still preferred the direct view. Perhaps she owed that to her skirmisher practice.

However, she dedicated the greater share of her time to supervising Stephan's and Herman's exercises. They were doing well for beginners. Both took a practical approach—they stuck to the basics, practiced their lessons, and mostly ignored the traps she set up for them. Whereas she herself would have tried to make the most of a training mission—even in the simulator — and thus most certainly would have sprung all those traps, the two soldiers refused to show any initiative. Their results were accordingly ordinary.

"Isn't it boring?" she asked Stephan after he had finished his latest task.

"What is boring?"

"Just going down the list, pushing buttons, straightforwardly?"

He shrugged. "I think we're supposed to do it straightforwardly. It may not appear very exciting to you, but even the most basic emergency pilot qualification is a huge step forward for a dirtbug private, and for me, that makes it exciting."

"If you're happy with that."

He turned to her and focused on her face, and she felt trapped by his gaze.

"I don't expect fascination from keeping my stuff tidy or cleaning my gun. Routine is good, diligent routine is better, paying attention to what you do is best. My life may depend on it. So I won't be easily distracted. Only when the straight route won't work will I try to improvise. And once I do, I'll try to avoid the pitfalls."

"What pitfalls?"

He didn't turn his gaze away. "The pitfalls that would teach us what surprises the universe may have in for us. The pitfalls every instructor includes into the setup. I surely haven't spotted them all, but I had an idea here and there that something smelled fishy, if you get my meaning, Sir — Syreen."

Syreen smiled. "Do the last one again, and try to find the pitfall. Follow the smell. Trust me — nothing will ever run as planned. You're too smart, and our time's too tight, to waste it with routine only."

"Shouldn't I learn it anyway?"

"Yes. You need to know the Book. But I trust you to learn

fast, so you can skip a step here and there." She sensed his reservation and placed a hand on his shoulder. "I know. Routine comes from practicing the same stuff again and again. You will have plenty of time for that later. Right now, I want you both to get up to speed. You must know how to fire and recharge before you learn how to clean your gun after battle — because the latter won't help you if you don't survive the first attack. War-time drill. Got me?"

He swallowed what he might have wanted to say. "Yes, Sir."

CHAPTER NINETY-THREE

Herman looked up from his panel and pointed outside. "Drake returns. The way he's trudging along, there's nothing new."

"Must be frustrating," Syreen said. "Seven daylight periods in a row, and absolutely nothing."

Herman suppressed a curse. He'd almost missed the now flashing collision warning symbol. He quickly retrieved the computer proposals, moved his finger toward the first—and then picked the second.

"Good choice," Syreen praised him. "You know why?"

"The first would have worked, too," Herman said. "But only for the moment. There was something wrong with the further trajectory. I couldn't tell instantly, but I'll check now."

"Do that."

A moment later, he looked up with a frown. "Screw me! Right into the central star."

"Exactly."

"But why?" He called up the log. "I mean, the computer should only offer me valid solutions."

"It is a valid solution, given you'll change the course again later. For collision prevention, the computer look-ahead is limited."

"Ah, I understand. So I should recheck after every such maneuver, right?"

"Every time anything changes, including your gut feeling."

"Like I check my gun every now and then."

"Like when you're on watch."

"On watch." Herman nodded. "That's exactly what a pilot's doing most of the time, right? The watch."

Drake scratched his head, shrugged, and smiled at Syreen.

"Nothing?" she asked kindly.

He spread his hands. "I'm through with my list. I measured, scanned, recorded every square finger, but there's no obvious entrance, no hatch, no airlock, no cargo bay, not even between those *thighs*. Those warts are everywhere, but for what? I could stare at this . . . *artifact* that's sprung from someone's nightmare for a kilocycle and never learn more. I tried everything. Well, everything but the library. That's my last idea—take the library, walk up to the door and ring, uh, send the protocol again. See what happens."

"Open sesame."

He laughed. "Like that—where the Thieves from the Association don't have the key either. They don't even know of the treasure den yet."

"Just tell me one thing. You found no entrance, but you'll walk up to the door. Where?"

Drake smiled again. "I'm no expert, but if you want to penetrate anyone, there's one prominent spot—between the legs. I'd bet on that."

"You'd dare?"

He waved his hand. "Hey, it's a starship, not a trap. It's meant to carry people, so yes, I dare. What's the point in inviting us down here and then not granting access?"

"If you put it that way . . ."

"Yes." He cocked his head. "You want to come along tomorrow?"

The lieutenant needed a moment of contemplation before she answered. "Yes. Yes, I suppose I deserve a walk outside."

"That's settled, then." He turned to Crow, who was

patiently waiting behind him. "We'll take a shower to remove the dust, and then we'll meet for dinner, okay?"

CHAPTER NINETY-FOUR

Syreen followed Drake and Crow through the airlock. When she set her foot down into the dust on the cavern floor, she realized that this wasn't just the first time she had set her foot on a new planet — this was her first time ever conscious visit to any planetary surface.

From the moment she'd been found on Base Four to her assignment to Silver Wing, she'd been everywhere around Fleet, including the huge survival training complex on Base Two, but never dirtside.

So how does it feel?

She glanced toward the cavern entrance, toward a surface without a ceiling, bathed in RAK-11's bright light.

What would it feel like walking under the open sky? No walls, no ceiling, no shield, nothing to protect against the open space?

With a shudder, she turned away and focused on the cavern.

Walls around, roof and floor. Otherwise, no big difference. Same gravity as aboard, which is no wonder, as I deactivated the artigrav when we set down. I'm still breathing canned air through this mask.

Her gaze went down. *Dusty. Yes, I'm outside for a few millicycles and already feel dusty.*

After a while, she added, *and I'm still hungry, tired and weak.*

The hunger had caused unrest in her sleep, and the lack of sleep made her feel weak now, but she couldn't do anything against her hunger. No meal could satisfy her longing — it didn't help at all that Crow's evac suit ended below his tasty throat.

"Come on. I'll show you where you can walk safely."

She approached him. "I'm okay. I've read the reports. It's just the first time on a natural surface."

"The first? What do you mean?"

"That I spent my entire life in space — until today."

"You've never been on a planet?"

"Never. As far as I know, I was born in space. I was raised in space, trained in space, and I lived and worked in space, until today."

"That's remarkable indeed. Well — maybe that's where your intuitive grasp for space comes from."

She considered that idea, and then shrugged. "Maybe."

"How does it feel for you?"

"Dusty."

Drake laughed, and Crow chuckled.

"Come," Drake said.

After another glance at the brightly lit cavern entrance, she followed him.

CHAPTER NINETY-FIVE

Syreen marveled at the living ship with its warts and wrinkles while walking along one of its legs behind Drake. Every two or three centicycles, she felt a little shiver inside. The regularity made her pause.

"What's up?" Drake asked.

She only raised one hand and removed the evac suit glove.

"Hey—you think that's safe?" Drake tried to stop her.

"Yes." She placed her palm firmly on the rough surface of the next wart. It felt warm and flexible.

The next shiver came, and it ran through the wart under her hand. It was the ship. How could she feel it without being in touch? Was that another effect of her sensitivity?

She waited another moment, but nothing happened. Disappointed, she took her hand away. "Okay, move on."

"Nothing?"

"Not really."

Her principal headed on toward the *crotch*, if it could be called that. From this close, the vertical groove inside the oval shape could still be taken for a pussy. But there was no knob, handle or latch to open it with—would it need sexual stimulation?

She smirked at her own naughty idea. Drake didn't notice, as he was holding up his ancient library toward the groove and trying to trigger any reaction.

A flicker caught her eye. It had run across a wart near the oval, and had been accompanied by the already familiar shiver. She walked over and reached forward with her hand.

"Almost," Drake said. "Let me adjust this—here. And—go."

Syreen turned around. Expecting something special to happen, she automatically chose the next support in reach—the wart.

The oval contour became a blinding circle of light, tearing the cavern from its dimness. Flickers and sparks ran all over the hull.

"I made it!" Drake yelled and retreated a few steps.

Now the central groove also showed a line of light. It grew more intense, and then opened like a cat's pupil. Not like a door, rather like a soft curtain, it widened to the size of the oval.

Syreen tried to see past the bright light. There was a large hall behind the opening, like a cargo compartment or a hangar, surely large enough even for a corvette. Rows of containers were lined up along the side wall as far as she could see inside, most likely continuing far into the dim background.

No, not containers. They look like eggs. Not inappropriate for a living ship.

CHAPTER NINETY-SIX

Drake smiled at his pilot. Then he remembered his mask and waved toward the opening.

"Want to come in?"

The lieutenant returned the wave. "After you. Congratulations. Your idea worked in the end."

He nodded. "Crow, you want to come, too?"

Crow acknowledged by approaching them, but he diligently waited until they had entered, then followed last.

The hangar-like room was well lit by several hundred lights all around the floor and ceiling. The lighting evened out the warts and wrinkles of floor, walls and ceiling.

"Not much difference to outside," Syreen observed. "The same surfaces, same dull-green colors, same lack of sharp angles."

"The same lack of obvious hatches," Drake agreed. "But well illuminated, and less dust."

"No dust. And large enough to easily harbor two corvettes." His pilot headed to the left side, seen from where they had come.

The only obvious difference was a gap in the row of containers, but he followed. What had she spotted there?

She was pointing up. There was a recess in the non-corner where wall and ceiling met.

"Yes, and?"

"It could be a kind of opening."

"Your guess is as good as mine." However, he stepped under the recess and gazed up. "Okay. And now? I just say *up, please?"*

The recess seemed to grow, and then it opened like—uh, yes, like an anus. When he glanced down, he found Crow and Syreen staring up at him. There was no floor under his feet, and yet his feet seemed to rest on solid ground.

The technology behind wasn't difficult to understand— *tightly applied artificial gravity together with a solid force field* would do the trick. However, only the most pretentious venues—and a few luxury cruisers—afforded gravity elevators with their complicated adjustments and expensive maintenance, and even they used opaque platforms.

Aboard this ship, it didn't strike him as showy. He could accept it, just as he could accept a kind of pussy-shaped curtain where a solid airtight door should be.

The elevator pushed him through the hole to a brightly lit, narrow corridor running along the hangar's side. The ceiling was high enough to let him stand upright, but not much more. He stepped away from the hole, and it closed. Drake made one full turn.

Toward the *legs,* the corridor turned outward. It seemed safe to assume it would continue into the leg. The other direction passed numerous recesses—probably doors—toward the rear end before it turned and widened. Despite the lighting, the wrinkled, dark-greenish walls made him feel uncomfortable.

The hole in the floor opened and Syreen rose through it. She waited until he had made room for her to step forward.

"Crow will stay down in the hangar," she announced. "Anything striking here?"

He pointed rearward. "I'd say, that way."

"Yes—looks like an invitation."

Syreen was torn between her curiosity about the strange ship and a growing disquietude stemming from her subliminal desire for blood. In these unfamiliar — not to say spooky — surroundings, it was even harder to control.

Every now and then, a dim flicker ran along the walls, accompanied by the now unsurprising although still not familiar shiver, and reminded her how odd this place was.

She felt tension rising. *Any sudden noise now, and I must scream.*

It didn't help her at all that she could sense the same tension in Drake, too, so she focused on blocking that sense out.

This way, she almost missed the moment when Drake turned around the bend and entered the room at the end of the corridor.

She heard the gasp, looked up and past him.

The room was distinctively different from the rest of the ship. First of all, the greenish floor, walls and ceiling were not wrinkled, but instead showed a much denser pattern of warts. The ceiling in the room's center was twice as high as in the corridor, coming down all around like a dome.

As before, the room was well lit from indirect sources.

Most striking were the two installations in the center of the room — a large, reclining chair-like structure and a basin at its feet. Those were the only two visible features, aside from the entrance they had used and a similar exit at the opposite side.

It couldn't be anything but a chair, despite its decorations. It was of the same greenish material, and it rested on a central trunk, supporting a kind of trough that rose toward the ship's rear. The forward bottom of the trough forked into two bent grooves. The upper end offered two more grooves along the trough and a separate hollow shape at the top. Every part of this entire shape suggested it was made to support a humanoid body.

There were a few arms — tentacles? — with pad-like forms around the head rest, and there were more pads in easy reach for hands, plus a few to the sides of the legs.

The whole structure seemed to be made from one part.

There were no seams, assembly grooves, or fixings. There was no separate padding, either.

There were more warts around the chair's back, but the most prominent feature was a kind of flight stick right where the pilot's crotch belonged, and a shorter stub below. The flight stick pointed toward the head, though.

"You'd have to impale yourself on that stick to sit down here," Drake commented silently, and then looked around.

Nothing stirred in reply to his remark.

Syreen nodded. It reminded her of her skirmisher's stimulator — or of Stephan's erect cock. "This might be the recreation room."

Drake stared at her. "Seriously?"

"No."

He took a deep breath. "You almost got me there. What's that in the headrest?"

She followed his cue and spotted two pimples with rather sharp points. Anyone leaning back in this chair would have his neck poked.

Now that she had recognized them, she found similar pimples in the leg grooves, one to prick each thigh.

"I've seen such before," she said.

"Really?"

"It should be classified information, but right now, I don't care. The Duchy skirmishers are equipped with stimulators and syringes. When the pilot assumes her seat, the syringe injects psyjuice into her thigh, making her senses sharper and her reflexes quicker. The stimulator serves as reward — the more you score, the more sexual stimulation you get."

Drake cocked his head. "You mean, they fly with a dildo in their pussy and get an orgasm for kills?"

"That's what I did, yes."

"You did." His gaze seemed to scrutinize her. "You are drugged and abused to kill more efficiently?"

She shrugged. "That's what Fleet crew are for. Efficiency."

"I can't believe that."

He meant something different, but she didn't correct him. "Our instructors told us it's an ancient technology that most other star nations don't use anymore—the psyjuice recipe is top secret. However, the Duchy is one of the oldest and most traditional star nations in this sector. They've preserved the old methods."

"And forced them on you."

"Oh, no, it's entirely voluntary. You're told in advance, and it's perfectly okay to pick a different career path. However, it's also a reward to be selected as a skirmisher candidate—only the best pilots are invited."

"So you're proud to spread for your nation."

She hesitated. There was disdain in his statement, and she couldn't ignore that.

"Yes, I am. I step into the front line to be shot at, injured, mutilated, fried, to suffocate or freeze in space, whatever, and to be masturbated by my skirmisher on my way to death. I'm proud to be more efficient that way and able to kill more enemies before they can kill me and my wing mates. Once you accept the brain fuck it takes to become a soldier, that little privacy between your legs no longer counts."

He frowned, but didn't avoid her stare. After a while, he said, "Well, put that way, it makes sense . . . somehow."

CHAPTER NINETY-SEVEN

Syreen watched Drake trying to elicit another reaction with his library device protocol. They had searched the room for a similar object but to no avail—and they had no clue where else to search for it.

Drake failed. He turned to her. "I'll have to find the right message. Give me some time."

"Sure. I'll have a look around."

In fact, she feared losing control and biting him. Her unrest continued to grow—surely also fed by the threat from the Association. Time was working against their little expedition.

She took the other exit and checked the corridor there. It looked the same, but close to the room's exit, there was a recess in the floor. She stepped on it, and the floor opened.

Syreen had to resist the urge to jump back. Instead, she impatiently waited for the elevator to take her down. She passed several levels where she could have jumped off, where a corridor ran toward the other side, but remained still until she had reached the lowest level. There, she walked down the corridor until a recess in the forward wall caught her attention. She approached it.

As she had almost expected, a curtain-like oval opening parted before her. It led into another short corridor with two curtains to the sides and one straight ahead. She chose the latter, and when it opened, she saw the hangar before her and Crow quickly spinning around to her.

She spread her arms, and he relaxed. He turned to guard the larger opening again, and on her way out, she passed him wordlessly.

The walk through the cavern helped her calm down and relax—even with the need to watch for dust ditches. With no innocent victims in immediate reach, she could forget her worries about her hunger.

The worries about the Association remained, as well as those on this mission. She had agreed to come—and, in essence, lead her enemy here—hoping she could find and take the *relic* first.

But was this living ship the *relic* the Association was searching for? She recalled the secret orders the admiral had read for her. It hadn't exactly described what to search for, only that the item had to be ancient—and the orders had insinuated an item small enough to be carried by a corvette, to be transported back to the Association as quickly as possible. This living ship surely was too big, and any similar item would long have been found in the Duchy anyway.

However, the ship could be such an ancient super weapon. How did that match?

Logic, Syreen.

The orders hadn't claimed the *relic* to be an ancient super weapon. It would give its owner superior power—perhaps grant control over such a living ship? After all, they couldn't have found the only one. Where had the damaged library come from? Where had the intact library come from? What if the Association had already found such a ship?

Well—if they had found one, they'd find another soon, and it would be as useless as the first without that darn *relic*.

She felt an unusual warmth on her skin. Without her noticing, her musings had guided her outside of the cavern. When she looked up, she saw a bright light shining down on her—RAK-11.

CHAPTER NINETY-EIGHT

Syreen quickly retreated a few steps back into the shadow of the cavern entrance. The bright light made her feel uncomfortable, and the heat on her skin reminded her of her instructors, who had explicitly warned them against exposure to solar radiation. The sunlight could burn their skin—it wouldn't instantly kill but would make their lives very, very unpleasant.

However, she had checked RAK-11's spectrum, and the ultraviolet part was very weak. So she should be safe for a few centicycles—if the radiation was the only danger she'd face outside.

I'll take that chance. Who knows when I'll find another opportunity to walk under an open sky?

She made one bold step forward, then another, and another, and then across the line that divided shadow and light.

Syreen kept her face down.

See, I can do it. I can walk under an open sky.

Next, she forced herself to look up and around. She saw dust, and rocks, and more dust. Only the colors were so different. She saw yellow dust, orange dust, red dust, occasional blue or green specks on the gray and red rocks. She saw a horizon. She saw sky above the horizon, with different hues of blue and red again.

The sight is limited dirtside. You never see the entire sphere—but a lot more detail. Dusty detail.

She forced herself to look further up, look up to Silver Seven's central star again. *No cockpit pane. No sealed suit.*

There's just air between me and you.

The bright light hurt her eyes. When she looked away, it took a few millicycles to regain her sight. That was no surprise—every starship pilot was taught to avoid looking straight into a star.

The most unusual experience was the sweat forming on her forehead, although she wasn't exercising. *That's the heat,* she concluded. *I'm not used to that, either.*

CHAPTER NINETY-NINE

A little draft tugged at her hair. Syreen turned around and saw the dust rising on the horizon. *Is it that late already?*

The evening storm was approaching, so she turned around and entered the cavern again, to find reassuring safety aboard *Raydancer*. She could use a shower now, and then a hot for-wine.

Herman was waiting for her right behind the inner hatch.

"Good that you're back. Stephan's on the bridge. Three centicycles ago, *Raydancer* registered four jump echoes."

"What?" She pushed him aside and entered the bridge.

Stephan made an attempt to free the pilot seat.

"No, stay there." She placed one hand on his shoulder and held him down. "They can't come for us within the next cycle. Let me see the interpretation."

Stephan retrieved the analysis panel.

"See those peaks?" he said. "Four significant echoes, like in the lessons you gave us. One larger ship, three of the same size, and — uh — five sigma?"

"Very good job, Stephan." She patted his shoulder. "What does our library say?"

"That would have been next," he replied and tapped a symbol. The result came quickly.

"Old friends," Syreen commented. "The battle cruiser with its light cruisers from Brannock. More than sufficient to keep a single corvette at bay, even if her pilot can do precise shots, eh?"

"What will happen now?" Stephan asked.

"Well, they will soon pick up the buoy beacon telling them they came to the right place. They'll scan the system for us and find nothing, as our own transponder is silent and we're well concealed. They'll approach the planet, position around it, and make sure nobody can get away past them. Then we're stuck until they find us."

"Which won't end well for us."

"No." Syreen sighed. "So we better leave before then. I'll go and get Drake. He's not back yet, is he?"

Stephan shook his head. "No."

"He should be. Storm's coming. Well—I'll hurry."

"Should I go?" Herman offered.

"No. I'm still wearing the suit and the dust."

Drake didn't look up when he heard another person entering the living ship's command bridge. He was sitting on the basin's edge, the library in one hand and his pad in the other, and waiting for the latest sequence to complete.

"Drake, we must leave now," the familiar female voice said.

"Give me two."

"The storm's coming up."

"This is my last attempt."

He could feel her impatience, but he was also aware of his own frustration. He had spent the entire tencycle experimenting and not gained anything. No, that wasn't right—he had gained access to the ship. However, after this initial quick success, the total absence of any reaction until now was unsettling.

His throat was dry and he felt a headache beginning. *Dehydration,* he decided.

"The Association has arrived," she said.

That made him look up. "Where?"

"At the system's border. They came with four warships, the ones from Brannock."

"So we're busted."

"Unless we manage a quick retreat, yes. However, I fear they might be able to intercept us anyway. We need time to accelerate, while they can keep their speed advantage — or we wait until they've decelerated, at which time they're close enough to shoot us anyway."

"Please." He raised his pad. "The last one's running. Let me finish it."

She shrugged. "Won't make much difference. However, I fear it won't help."

"No?"

"I guess you need some key to start this baby. Or, more precisely, I guess you need some physical device to legitimate yourself. I fear that's precisely what the Association's searching for at my home."

"So?"

"I mean, you don't think this is the only one, do you?" She walked over to the chair.

"Uh — well, no." He gazed at her, then at his library. "No. You think they already have one?"

"If there can be one, there can be many. If there can be three — this one and the ones the libraries came from — there have to be many."

He frowned. "Can't deny that logic."

"So . . ." She spread her arms and dropped them again. Her left hand dropped on the would-be flight stick, and she froze, her eyes and mouth wide open.

CHAPTER ONE HUNDRED

Solitude.
Patience.
Hunger.
Weakness.
Tiredness.

All these emotions passed through Syreen in a single moment, giving way to another.

Excitement.

The stick under her fingers stirred. It rose and became hard, like a boner. At the same time, she could sense desire, passion, and excitement growing in her mind—but those were not her own feelings. Those were the feelings of a stranger, like she had sensed the feelings of other people before, only this time, these weren't people's feelings. These were the *ship's* feelings.

It was calling for her.

There was another voice calling for her, too.

"Syreen, are you okay?"

"Syreen, shouldn't we leave now? The storm . . ."

Drake watched the young lieutenant slowly taking her hand off the cock-like shape and reaching for the neck of her evac suit. She pushed the opener and let the suit slide from her shoulders, revealing her skin-tight uniform shirt and pants.

A well-toned body, he had to admit, not for the first time.

Her face above the mask seemed to have turned a bit red.

This impression was confirmed when she undid the mask. There was a clear red-white boundary. *She must have been outside.*

She still looked like she was in a trance when she took off her shirt, and then her pants.

Female strippers usually didn't turn him on, but she wasn't stripping for an audience. The matter-of-fact way she removed her clothes was unnerving.

He wanted to rise, to stop her, to take her away — but no, he didn't. He was supposed to wait, not interfere.

Syreen only half-consciously noticed Drake's intention of interrupting her actions. She instructed him not to.

Next, she climbed into the chair, which seemed to give way or support where she needed it. She cautiously balanced over the stimulator, probed her own excitement and wetness, and then lowered down on it, accepting it inside her. When she sat down in the trough, the other plug nicely found its place inside her butt.

She hadn't tried a double penetration before, not even anal intercourse, nothing but a finger inside her ass, but here, it felt natural, and it increased her excitement.

After placing her legs and arms into the respective grooves and reclining into the trough, the chair shrunk to her size.

Perfect fit, as it should be.

Oh! There was a brief pain when the pimples pricked her sensitive thighs, but an arousing kind of pain. With that large device in her vagina, she could momentarily only think of sex.

This didn't change after the two pricks in her neck. Instead, she felt another rush of excitement — somewhat like psyjuice, only far more thrilling. Her perception jumped to a new level. She felt a warm, wet sensation around her cock, a breathing body in her lap, the presence of two other life forms inside her. She sensed the gravity holding her resting body down to the planet, keeping the planet in orbit around its star, pulling the star along with all the others around the galactic center. She heard stars singing their solitary melodies. She saw the light fade at the cavern entrance and noticed the increasing rush of air around her open mound—hadn't it better close?

All the time, she also felt the tingle in her crotch, the presence of a big, warm boner, gently vibrating . . .

Syreen took a few heavy breaths.

This weakness disturbed her. She needed more sunlight on her skin, had to drink gravity and cosmic radiation—perhaps should even feed on something substantial soon. The long time spent waiting had drained her powers—it had taken more time than foreseeable.

The waiting was over now. With a young, strong and healthy pilot, there was no more need for hiding away—except for that inconvenient presence of four potentially hostile warships, the arrival of which hadn't remained unnoticed.

No, avoiding conflict was no option. Without a significant period of feeding, entering hyperspace wasn't possible. Trying to remain hidden would leave the initiative with the enemy and wasn't advisable. Moreover, the current location wasn't favorable for fighting at all. Last but not least, the enemy provided a significant power reservoir that should not be wasted.

Surrender? Yes, the enemy's surrender was an option, too. In that case, most resources could be spared for later consumption or given quarter in exchange for useful services.

So fighting it was. The available power had to be applied wisely, though. A surprise attack would be best. The situation demanded a clever stratagem.

Syreen's head felt like it was wrapped in thick layers of insulation padding. There was too much information to process, too many sensations to follow—not to mention the stimulation inside her anus and her vagina.

I'm ready to come.

– Not yet. –

What was that?

– I am the ship. –

The ship . . .

– My symbol in your language would be Assiduous. *–*

It should feel odd to talk with a ship. It should feel more odd to have a mental chat with a ship. But most of all, it should feel odd to have a mental chat with a ship while having its boner in your own pussy.

– This was your first deep integration. –

I'm not used to processing this amount of information.

– You will adapt soon. –

I don't know if I want to . . . at least not yet. I need a clear mind to devise a strategy. This . . . oddity doesn't help.

– It is my purpose to guide you. It is your purpose to direct me. We were created to join. –

This was too much for a mere human.

– You are no human. –

Syreen's thoughts circled around that statement, *you are no human.* What should that mean? She'd been born human, raised, human, looked like a human . . .

– You are not like the others. –

No, she wasn't. Not lately. She had to accept that she was different. But this . . .

– You are of the People. –

The People?

– Your ancestors, my creators. But you are one of the few female People who can sense hyperspace, who can thus control a living ship. You are a Navigator. –

CHAPTER ONE-HUNDRED-ONE

Drake watched with horror how the lieutenant stripped as if no one was present, how she mounted that weird seat stark naked, how she allowed this—this *tool* to enter her private parts, saw her body flinch when the chair stabbed her—in her soft thighs, then in her neck—and had to watch helplessly as the living furniture closed around her legs and upper arms, leaving her tits and pubes bare to any bystander.

She took a few heavy breaths, and then froze. Her gaze turned into a dead stare. No more blinks, no more breathing, no motion at all. Had that goddamn chair killed her?

It's all my fault. I hired her, lured her on this mission. For me, she fought at Brannock. For me, she broke up with Jakarta. For me and my cursed mission, she jumped where nobody had jumped before. And I opened the gate into this ship, took her to this place. Now I can't even move my hand to cover my eyes, can't turn away, forced to watch her last breath.

Her eyelids fluttered.

Next, her chest rose, her nipples hardened. He recognized the signs of arousal and wasn't surprised when her pelvis slightly moved, as far as the chair's firm hold allowed.

But then she relaxed, and he gained hope—before she tensed again, stared at him, clenched her hands to fists. Suddenly, he was free to move, but no longer wanted to turn away.

What by all demons is going on here?

Still, the shock sat deep in Syreen. Not human. Her existence, the image she had created of herself, was shattered . . . but in a way, that was helpful, too, as that image had no longer matched her recent experience. Wasn't it better to be a different race—People—than having to accept the role of a flawed human?

Her gaze fell on Drake, who looked like he was pinned down by her sight alone.

He swallowed hard. "Syreen?"

"Yes."

Good to hear my own voice – something familiar, at last.

Drake's face wore a worried expression. "Are you okay?"

Good question. Define okay. "I am unhurt."

"Despite those—uh . . ." He pointed at her thighs.

"Oh, that. That's just a feed."

He shrugged and tried a smile. "You seem to have triggered something."

"What? Oh—yes, of course. I'm connected with the ship now."

"What do you mean, connected? I mean, I see the, uh, feed, but otherwise?"

"I mean, I'm in charge of this living ship now. I'm accepted as its pilot and skipper—well, *Navigator* is the correct term."

"Oh." Drake seemed to fumble for words.

She suddenly became aware that she was openly presenting her wet vagina to him, that he could clearly see the ship's penetration into her.

This isn't exactly the best way to earn respect. Well, I can't help it now. There are important things to tend to.

"Drake, we're going into battle."

PART SEVEN—FIGHTING

Chapter One-Hundred-Two

Stephan felt useless. He could loll in *Raydancer's* pilot chair and juggle all the screens around, but he couldn't do anything about the enemy's approach except watch it evolve in the plot display. As long as the small corvette remained hidden in this cavern and inactive, the enemy's beacons were the only clue they got.

His skipper's thorough scans had usually taken at least a full cycle. The Association seemed to be more hasty—Syreen was only gone for a quartercycle, and they were already spreading out. The big boy was advancing toward the planet, while the three light cruisers were moving in different directions. Stephan couldn't do the math, but they had surely calculated some method to cut off any escape route.

He assumed that even one medium pulse cannon could do some damage to a light cruiser, but how many hits were needed to eliminate it as a threat? He couldn't know, but he knew about infantry tactics against heavily armored vehicles—either you had a truly big gun, or you had to hit and run, preferably covered by your mates.

They didn't have a truly big gun, they didn't have mates to give them cover, and Stephan wasn't optimistic about the *run* part either, even though he'd credit Syreen for multiple hits first.

Their odds in battle weren't promising—and yet, in this situation, he'd prefer to fight. Hiding in the tunnels for the rest of his life, trying to live off those mice? No, that was not an attractive choice.

The intercom symbol flashed. He waved toward it. "Stephan?"

He sat straight up. "Sir? I didn't notice you returning."

"I'm still aboard the living ship. I will take *Raydancer* in."

"Sir?"

"It fits inside our hangar. I will call again when it's done, so that Herman and you can come over."

"Sir — does that mean you found the key to the living ship?"

"I'm the key, Stephan."

The moment Syreen voiced it, she realized the deeper truth in her statement. She hadn't needed any legitimation but herself, no antique device to start this ship — no *relic*.

I'm such an item from the distant past myself. I am the relic.

— Pardon? —

Those warships — they're searching for an ancient device, which they believe they need to control the power of the Forgotten People — to control you.

— That is a misconception. No device can replace a Navigator. —

Their intel is fragmentary. They're dangerous anyway, and I will do something about that.

— We will, skipper. —

We. But first, we'll take care of Raydancer.

— Raydancer is a nice symbol for such a dead tool. It is easy to control. I will harbor it, if that pleases you. —

So *Assiduous* had already hacked the corvette? Syreen suppressed a shrug, as her shoulders were tightly held in place. She had to think up a plan.

Once the Association had completed the system scan — and taken notice of the Duchy buoy — they'd take action. They had to expect one corvette in the RAK-11 system — a swift and fast little ship. The light cruisers were best suited to hunt it down, so two of them would spread out above and below Silver

Seven's orbital plane, one would cover the star-ward escape routes, and the battle cruiser would approach the planet itself, blocking any outward route in its reach—and as it could deploy missiles, according to *Raydancer's* library data, it could reach far.

— This library is useful. May I incorporate it? —

Of course, get your copy.

Under different circumstances, she'd have tried to run—tried to shoot her way past one of the light cruisers and jump, or even jump before shooting. But until *Assiduous* could travel the hypercontinuum again, this strategy couldn't work—as leaving the ship behind was out of the question.

— They wouldn't be able to operate me. —

They would make sure nobody can operate you. If necessary, by destroying the planet.

She closed her eyes and imagined a plot. *The timing is crucial. The big tank can't be close yet, but the cruisers must already have split up. Only in that way can I get them one by one. Given we have the firepower to shoot a light cruiser.*

— Given. —

That was something. *Can we take a beating?*

The ship remained mute, which Syreen didn't take as a good sign. We'd better not, that was.

I must know.

She sank back into deep integration.

The power level was low, *low* as in, *you might wring a few more drops out of it if you try hard,* nothing compared to a ship at the peak of performance. The ship was literally thin-skinned—armor, shielding and self-repair supplies were close to none. However, the ship wasn't stranded and was no lifeless wreck. Even an almost-dead living ship could move faster and more swiftly than a corvette, could suffer an occasional hit in a less critical area, and could deal out hard a few times, *hard* as in *one strike and you won't want to stand up, two strikes and there's nothing left to stand up.*

Which meant *Assiduous* could win any one-on-one duel if it could shoot first . . . so what was the effective range? The current three to five light seconds was manageable against lasers and pulse cannons but not against missiles. Missiles required different considerations.

It's somehow like fighting naked, Syreen mused while pulling her mind out of deep integration again. *Which is exactly what I'm used to, what I've been trained for.*

She felt like she had returned to her skirmisher. The stimulator in her vagina, the sting in her thigh, the psyjuice — only better — and a swift and delicate ship that shouldn't be hit.

I can do it.

Meanwhile, the evening storm had reached full power. It wasn't advisable to move around outside, as it wasn't advisable to open outer hatches.

For *Assiduous,* the storm didn't count. The ship directed *Raydancer* toward the central hangar gate, with the curtains — or lips — parting just enough to allow the ship inside, but not the dust. To Syreen, it felt like a penis penetrating wet labia, and triggered her arousal again.

Using an entire corvette as dildo — extravagant, isn't it?

The tool in question had meanwhile settled down inside the living ship, firmly held in place by custom-shaped clamps. She watched and sensed Stephan and Herman leave *Raydancer* with their belongings and step onto the hangar floor.

They exchanged a few words with Crow, who then entered the corvette and reappeared a moment later with Drake's and his own luggage.

She only had to open the right hatches to guide them to the rooms prepared for servants aboard, where they could drop their stuff and refresh.

CHAPTER ONE-HUNDRED-THREE

Herman was quite curious to see his commanding officer's new workplace. He imagined a much larger bridge with plenty of screens and plot tanks and dashboards and panels with blinking and moving symbols—and then he turned around the last corner.

"What?" was all he could say when he spotted the chair with Syreen in it. His gaze ran across her red-and-white face with bright eyes and a distant smile, down her *oooh so sweet* boobs with hard, erect nipples, her bare belly, down to her hipbones, where he spotted her creamy wetness all over that big, slowly pulsating rod.

I'm the one who should be inside there now. I'm the only one who should be inside her, when all the others are gay. This — this is perverse. So wrong.

Stephan and Crow pushed their way past him. Drake was sitting on the edge of a kind of basin and unabashedly staring into her crotch.

So wrong.

She turned her head, and her gaze fixed on him. Suddenly, he couldn't turn away, couldn't even look down anymore as she spoke.

"I will do what needs to be done to protect my shipmates, complete my mission, fulfill my duties as the Duchy's Fleet Commander in Charge, and navigate this ship in battle. This is what I've been trained for all my life, and it's no difference to riding a Duchy skirmisher — well, aside from the gawkers."

He felt mentally stripped down by her scrutiny.

She continued, "I do my duty whatever it takes, and there's worse than a flight stick in my pussy. You'd better learn to accept that."

"Yes," he murmured, suddenly feeling ashamed for his prejudice. Considering their situation, they had other issues to worry about than a weird-looking pilot seat or their skipper's dress code.

"Pardon?"

"Yes, *Sir.*"

Syreen sighed inwardly. The last thing she needed to worry about was a lovesick, jealous crewmate. This time, she had brought him back to brutal reality without applying mind control.

"Find yourself a seat—you too, Drake, you're blocking the plot. That's all hands, general quarters, please."

Assiduous provided the necessary seats by reshaping some parts of the wall behind her chair. Somehow she had known that such a feature was prepared—some information seemed to trickle into her mind subliminally. She also incidentally noticed that this way the sight of her crotch could no longer distract her shipmates, unless she swiveled her chair around—which she did now anyway.

"Okay, folks. Welcome aboard the new Duchy flagship, the living ship *Assiduous*. Together, the two of us feel confident that we can handle the Association flotilla should they opt for fighting. This is Duchy territory, even if newly claimed, and this time, I feel prepared enough to protect it. Most importantly though, I'm not willing to leave my new mate to them."

She saw approving nods and grim faces, and also a little curiosity.

"Let me explain a few things. Firstly, *Assiduous* is a living ship with his own conscience—and I can't tell whether he's an artificial intelligence or a natural being. In any case, we're supposed to treat him with respect, like every other shipmate. Secondly, once the fighting starts, I will deep-integrate with him, that is, we will join our minds. I may appear absent to you."

"You did that before, right?" Drake chimed in.

"Yes, I did. This integration makes us both much more efficient, as there's no delay between thought and action."

"How's that possible?" Herman asked. "Is it—is *he* made flexible enough to link with humans, or was it your pilot training?"

"No, Herman." She shook her head—as far as her headrest allowed. "No, *Assiduous* isn't flexible, but very picky with regard to his pilot. This ship was created by the People, nowadays called *Forgotten People*, to be commanded by *Navigators* of the People only. My Duchy pilot training and experience may have helped, but the decisive factor is that I'm a *Navigator* of the People myself."

Syreen watched their reactions while checking the enemy's progress in the back of her linked mind. They still had a few centicycles left while the warships approached or further split up.

Drake just sat there, frozen, open-mouthed, staring. Crow had raised both eyebrows. Herman looked like he was about to cry.

Stephan smiled. After a brief pause, he said, "For a member of some millennia-old, supposedly extinct race, you've aged exceptionally well, Sir."

There he touched a sore spot. She didn't return his smile.

"I'm a foundling, Stephan, dropped in a corner of Base Four, and subsequently found, raised and trained by Fleet. I don't know my parents or origin. Or, I should say, I don't know the link to my origin? For all I know, I'm twenty-three."

"Twenty-three?"

That sudden outburst came from Drake. "Uh, sorry—I wasn't aware that you're still so young. I mean, uh . . . I don't know what I mean."

Again it was Stephan who unabashedly broke the silence. "Why are you telling us, Syreen?"

"Because we're in this together. We're shipmates on this mission. We share the risk, and while I can't share all the gain—this ship—with you, I can at least share the facts with you. You're entitled to know what we're fighting for and who you're traveling with."

"What are we fighting for, then?"

"I will do whatever I can to deny the Association access to the Forgotten People legacy. No, let me put that differently—I will deny their military access to instruments of power. Everything else can be negotiated."

Stephan was still cheerful. She focused on him.

"You must understand one thing. While I'm not at all eager to end my young life so early, I would rather destroy this ship and myself than let them get us. Now that you know the truth—or as much as I know about it—this is your last chance to opt out. You can still board *Raydancer* and stay here until it's all over."

The private's face became very stern. "Sir, I told you once before—I support your cause any way I can. You're my commanding officer, the best superior I've ever had and may ever have. I believe in your skills and your odds. We will prevail."

His optimism lacked foundation, but served her well anyway. Most importantly, his acknowledgment of her role as his superior—his acceptance of her humanity after her confession—helped her.

She saw the same approval in the other men's faces, saw them nod, and even the taciturn Crow said aloud, "I agree."

Meanwhile, the approaching flotilla had slowed down and spread out enough to give her a chance for picking the first target. She let her chair swivel around.

"Prepare for takeoff."

CHAPTER ONE-HUNDRED-FOUR

Syreen raised *Assiduous* very cautiously from the cavern floor.

— Don't be timid. —

I never flew any ship into an unmoving obstacle, and I won't start that here.

Instead, she turned a bit to the left, a bit to the right, legs up, legs down, leaned right and left, moved a few legs forward and back, until she gained a feeling for the ship's reaction.

Next, she memorized the cavern's open space until she felt confident to find her way out blind.

Okay.

Upon her mental command, *Assiduous* leaped forward, reached sonic speed just after exiting the cavern, and swung skyward.

— That was not *timid. —*

Any complaints, mate?

— It is not advisable to exceed established safety limits. —

I never fly by the Books.

Her trajectory would keep the planet between *Assiduous* and the battle cruiser. Flying without an active beacon, the enemy had to rely on its detectors or visuals to spot her.

— We're not easy to detect, skipper. Raydancer's *sensors wouldn't be able to spot me yet. —*

Visuals, then. If we obstruct sight of other stars. I might be able to avoid that.

The battle cruiser was still decelerating toward a high orbit around Silver Seven. Two light cruisers were on their way out, and one was coming after her without being aware of that fact.

The longer she could remain undetected, the better were her odds to take them on, one by one. She couldn't afford to wait to be spotted and give them time to reassemble.

Would they bother to blast her buoy away? The small but expensive device was still announcing the Duchy's claim on this system. The Association couldn't have failed to notice, and thus had received their first warning. She would issue another final warning — once.

While *Assiduous* accelerated away from planet and enemy, she considered possible variants of early detection and prepared the appropriate actions in addition to her favored course of events.

How good were they?

CHAPTER ONE-HUNDRED-FIVE

They were good, Syreen observed, and their sensor equipment was obviously better than *Raydancer's*, which didn't surprise her. With such limited space inside a corvette, there had to be a tradeoff.

Detectors for minor moving gravitational anomalies like the pattern that *Assiduous'* drive produced needed a certain antenna distance to determine not just the anomaly's existence and strength but also its location. The distance between a light cruiser's bow and stern seemed to suffice.

They seemed to need quite some time to make sense of their data anyway. Once the first light cruiser came nearer, its crew spotted *Assiduous*. The cruiser skipper didn't hesitate to adapt his course to an interception vector. As Syreen had decided not to show off but fly more slowly than they potentially could, he had to take his prey as granted.

So his call and its content were almost predictable.

"Unknown vessel, this is *APS Lamia*, Captain Koyago speaking. You're requested to cease acceleration immediately and keep your current vector, otherwise we'll have to take action against you."

This was the right moment to trigger her own beacon. It identified her as *Assiduous* from the Duchy, with a new, temporary registration number.

Like her caller, she started with what he already knew. "*APS Lamia*, this is Duchy starship *Assiduous*, Lieutenant Syreen speaking. This system belongs to Duchy jurisdiction. You and your flotilla showed clear hostile activities upon

341

entering this system. You just announced further hostile action. Without an advance declaration of war, you have thus committed an act of piracy. The Duchy has a strict zero-tolerance rule with regard to piracy. I'm nevertheless inclined to consider your behavior as precautionary, if and only if you start deceleration on your current vector within five centicycles upon receipt of this message, and you refrain from any further action that could be regarded as hostile. There will be no further warnings."

Her main plot — the one she had conjured up for the benefit of her shipmates — showed a green sphere around the living ship and *APS Lamia's* vector toward this sphere. The moment *Lamia* entered this sphere — which would happen in three centicycles — the light cruiser could no longer escape her unless the skipper dared a thirty-percent jump.

APS Lamia didn't start deceleration. Instead, the other Association warships, which had surely received Captain Koyago's first message, changed their course to intercept *Assiduous*.

Syreen sighed. Some people didn't know when to stop.

Time for dancing.

She closed her eyes and entered deep integration.

CHAPTER ONE-HUNDRED-SIX

The central star's light and radiation warmed her skin and fueled her powers while its song told of life and change. Syreen enjoyed every note, every facet.

She had a different song to sing now, though.

Koyago sent another message. She gladly accepted the time he bought her.

"*Assiduous,* your Duchy won't help you here. Give up your futile attempt to confuse us and surrender unconditionally, and I promise you respectful safe custody."

This offer deserved no reply.

Another six centicycles passed by, and they called again.

"*Assiduous,* you have been warned."

You, too.

She stepped out of her trajectory, just in time to evade a first, probing pulse shot. Her excitement rose. She followed her initial maneuver with a turn and firm deceleration.

The distance to her pursuer shrank quickly. She dodged another shot.

Not yet.

The tension in her legs, between her knees and clit, quickly grew, from tingle to itch to heat, and her arousal grew with it. She wanted to spread and found out she already had. She hadn't felt so alive for much too long, and now — oops, dodge — she'd enjoy every aspect of it.

Close enough.

A spark jumped off her — *Assiduous'* — clit, guided by the field her knees projected, and hit *APS Lamia,* sliced through its shields like they were paper. *Ah!* The enemy ship's emissions were cut off. Only its inertia kept the light cruiser going.

Without power, light, oxygen provision, the other ship would be a flying coffin. Every active appliance, including the ship's reactors, had been toasted, and she didn't want to imagine the secondary damage caused by excess reactor heat. A few people aboard might still be alive, though, and their emergency power packs and evac suit oxyboxes might still work.

With an inward sigh, she surfaced from deep integration.

"*APS Lamia* survivors, you are allowed to deploy shuttles for later collection and abandon ship. Any hostility from your side will void your distress status and subject you to collective extermination."

Syreen wondered whether anybody would be able to answer her.

"*Assiduous,* this is Lieutenant Munro, officer in charge of *APS Lamia.* We have wounded crew. Will you pick us up?"

"Negative, Lieutenant Munro. I will not slow down as long as other hostile warships are active in this system. Moreover, I cannot offer you medical attention as I don't have any. You're on your own."

She felt some relief when she registered a shuttle beacon signaling distress. So they weren't entirely helpless.

Her next decision would probably seal the fate of another cruiser. She picked the one that was only slightly closer and changed her course accordingly.

It took the other skippers a few centicycles to project her new destination. They basically had two options — one, the light cruiser would try to run away from her, or two, it would steer system-inward and try to join with the other two warships.

They chose a variant of the second option, with the third

light cruiser heading for *APS Lamia* and the battle cruiser on an interception course.

"What was that?" Drake asked into the silence. "What kind of weapon did you apply?"

"It could be called an EMP cannon. It sends an electric charge through the enemy ship and grills any active appliance, shields, guns, drive, reactors, and life support systems."

"Deadly."

"Not immediately. Of course, people can suffer electric shocks if their systems are poorly shielded — but that would be a flaw in everyday operations, too. People can be hurt by side effects, like excess reactor heat. But most only have to start their emergency packs."

Drake tried a smile.

"Seems you've already won. You only have to apply it three more times."

Syreen didn't reply immediately. Instead, she focused on her scan results, which now told of her about some additional opponents — not entirely unexpected.

"Three more times?" Drake repeated.

"Negative. The primary problem is — I need to be close enough. Closing up to a light cruiser is risky — it could have hit us three times — but closing up to a battle cruiser is a nightmare. Closing up to a battle cruiser that's accompanied by another light cruiser plus a wake of stingships would be suicide."

He shrank back. "What will you do then?"

"Attack — and try a new trick."

Chapter One-Hundred-Seven

Syreen ran one simulation after another. Each ended reliably with *Assiduous'* destruction, some earlier, some later.

– This is not advisable. –

No, of course it isn't. However, the simulation doesn't cover all parameters.

– Which ones are missing? –

I can sense shots before they reach us, so I can dodge some.

– This is impossible for lightspeed shots. –

No, it's not. I did it before. Three times in our first duel.

– These incidents were registered. So that wasn't luck alone? –

It had nothing to do with luck. I knew of the shots before they reached us, so I dodged them.

– This is unheard of. –

So this was not a common trait among the People?

Syreen wasn't eager to rely on her premonition alone. She'd chance a great deal, but she preferred better odds if she could find any.

Now that two warships and twelve stingships were coming for her, and she was turning to take them head on, she would work on her odds. Again, she merged with the ship's mind.

Ick.

Wading through tough molasses wasn't her favorite pastime. Every mental step took what felt like cycles, only to apply a few changes at her destination, and then do another strenuous walk to the next place.

The effort paid off. Once she'd completed that task,

Raydancer's controls were hers.

She examined the plot again. The battle cruiser, identifying itself as *APS Griffin,* had slightly reduced its acceleration to let the light cruiser *APS Harpy* close up before engaging *Assiduous.*

The stingships assumed a shield formation around *APS Griffin.* Of course, they couldn't know yet whether *Assiduous* could deploy missiles, so they played safe. *APS Lamia* had already paid the price for underestimating its opponent.

You are not safe.

The formation was way too regular, and their trajectory perfectly predictable for the next few centicycles. Maneuvers were called for once they were in each other's shooting range, or what they mutually considered the enemy's shooting range.

The Brannock incident should have been a warning for them. Stingships weren't safe while in direct line of sight, regardless of their distance. They couldn't know whether *Assiduous* had its own pulse cannon—it didn't—even when *Raydancer* was out of sight.

Their bravery clearly exceeded their wits—after all, they were engaging a would-be ancient super weapon, weren't they? Shouldn't that deserve a little more respect?

She'd teach them.

The small corvette poked through her crotch lips, just enough to stick its bow out. Its pulse cannon fired twelve times in rapid succession. After all, *Raydancer's* power reserves should be good for something.

That hurt.

Speech was difficult in deep integration. She had to slow her thoughts down to trigger her mouth and tongue.

"Stephan . . . *Raydancer's* . . . pulse . . . cannon . . . needs . . . immediate . . . maintenance."

"Yeeeessss . . . Ssssiiiir."

By the time he arrived at the hangar floor, the corvette

would be safely docked again. Meanwhile, she checked her plot.

The stingships were no longer accelerating. A moment later, the battle cruiser deployed an evac shuttle. It would be left behind to pick up survivors.

Syreen wasn't sure if they'd find any. This time, she'd had to play it safe and target the small ships' main body, to take them out of the equation. Shooting a winglet wouldn't have ensured that.

Sadly, the stingship body wasn't much wider than a human body, so the probability of hitting the pilot, too, was above eighty percent.

Unless one had pulled his stick at the last moment . . . by luck or premonition.

Practice targets, Syreen noted. The battle cruiser had just launched three missiles at them, probably at their maximum effective distance, and most likely to get some more intel on her abilities. *So you guys have some wits left.*

– *We could evade them.* –

Smart missiles will follow our evasion maneuvers. They may have proximity triggers. Nasty bastards, swift and tough. I'd shoot them if it wasn't for the energy consumption.

– *There's no reason to worry about power yet.* –

I'd rather worry now than be caught with my pants down.

– *We're not wearing pants.* –

Duh.

There had to be another way . . . even if that meant wading through molasses again.

You know what? Those bastards are remote-controlled. You can change their mission after launch. Of course, that transmission protocol is encrypted – like Raydancer's *remote controls. Only, other than* Raydancer, *missiles are meant to be controlled remotely, without prior authorization. Get me?*

– *I understand.* –

The protocol could be difficult to hack. The inevitable

signal latency was another reason to worry — how long would they need to intrude, while the missiles with their dangerous proximity warheads came closer and closer?

Time too precious to waste. Fortunately, the first attempt penetrated all barriers and wiped out the missiles' memories.

The missiles stopped accelerating, thus blocking *APS Griffin's* path. They didn't have to hunt the battle cruiser down — it would come to them unless it stopped pursuit.

Griffin's crew quickly realized what had happened. They tried to send new commands and found them ignored. Next, their gunners had an opportunity for target practice.

They wouldn't try the same maneuver again soon.

With sorrow, Syreen watched *APS Harpy* approach *Griffin's* shadow. Once they could complete that maneuver, the battle cruiser would take all the beating, but would protect the light cruiser until it could come out for the decisive kill shot — unless the larger tank with its heavier guns could score first.

She could change her course and offer her flank to both ships and thus spoil their calculations, but that wouldn't improve her own situation much.

See the bright side — as long as the Harpy *is hiding away, it can't shoot.* She frowned. *Bright prospect indeed.*

Okay, the battle cruiser's stingship hangars were empty, and it wouldn't try to launch any more missiles soon, but it still had its lasers and heavy pulse cannons.

As they approached each other at a significant fraction of light speed, the battle would be very brief and fierce. She had a few more tricks up her sleeve — well, okay, up *Assiduous'* crotch — but hardly enough power to apply them all, even with RAK-11 continuously feeding her more, and even with the little bits *Raydancer* might contribute.

It was another slight advantage — the living ship didn't need sails. The entire skin could collect power and had done so since they had left the cavern.

APS Echidna had deactivated its beacon. Only from its drive emissions could Syreen tell its position and trajectory — and the remaining light cruiser was coming for her, too. If *Griffin* and *Harpy* could damage her, *Echidna* would arrive in time for the finishing shot. She'd have to be ready, then.

Two shots, and we must make them count.

— We will. —

Okay. Fuck me hard.

CHAPTER ONE-HUNDRED-EIGHT

Everyone could see the plot that Syreen let *Assiduous* project above the basin. Everyone could see where the projected trajectories met each other. Everyone could see the three fuzzy spheres Syreen had placed around their own symbol — green for easy-to-dodge shots, yellow for increased danger, red for . . . well, nobody dared to voice it.

Stephan had returned to his seat behind her. *Raydancer's* pulse cannon was ready, whatever that would be good for, and the corvette was thus positioned right behind the curtain.

They were approaching yellow. *APS Griffin* held its fire, as did *Assiduous*.

What was worse? Having to wait for cycles until the action started, or being aware of the enemy's presence in plain sight all the time? Having too much time to think of all the things that could go wrong, to wet one's own pants, to go mad with fear?

To *make it count,* Syreen had to wait until their enemy reached the red sphere, and she had to keep her ship intact until then.

She felt no longer sure whether she could really pull off this stunt. Perhaps her unrest also originated from the fact that she had already ridden this big cock for cycles — but couldn't ignore her continuing state of arousal either. Skirmisher pilots were trained not to go mad, instead, they were trained to enjoy sexual stimulation for cycles with or without getting off.

Or was she troubled by the ongoing feed of drugs?

She slowly moved in her seat, trying to elicit some

additional stimulation from either the big boner in her pussy or the plug in her butt. Nobody cared to lick her clit or kiss her tits though—and it was all too *clean.*

She'd have *dirty* soon.

Time to get ready.

"Brace yourself, guys."

She entered deep integration again.

For a few centicycles, the ships ran toward each other like unstoppable trains on the same track. There was almost no warning when *APS Griffin* fired all four forward heavy pulse cannons and all twelve heavy lasers together.

She felt the shots coming and stepped aside—barely quick enough, as the lasers had been meant to block her escape routes. Those shots would have missed had she kept her course and taken the pulse shots instead—but in that case, there'd be nothing left of her now.

One laser grazed her skin. *Ouch.*

She was already moving when the battle cruiser fired again, this time with more spread to its lasers. She ducked closer to the pulse shots, and then turned out of her course, rapidly accelerating forward—much faster than she had shown them before—and covered the distance to red with a growing tingling between her legs.

Four pulse shots went far past her, two lasers almost grazed her, and when *APS Harpy* moved into sight and *Griffin* spat out a cloud of missiles, she knew she was in deep trouble.

Herman stared at the spherical plot display. One moment, it had shown three quickly approaching enemy ships, one of which was still farther away than the others, the next moment, it filled with scores of new red symbols, and all symbols were pulsating and approaching, his shipmates were gasping, and their skipper was writhing and moaning in her chair.

His instincts told him to run, his training told him to search for cover, and his love told him to protect her at all cost — but what could he do?

He'd give her anything, everything.

Suddenly, he knew what to do. He jumped up and dashed toward her, leaned over her shoulder and offered his neck to her. Was it her arm or the seat that grabbed and held him?

"That's not the right moment for kisses, mate," Stephan called after him.

But Stephan couldn't know, and couldn't see, his commanding officer sinking her fangs into Herman's throat.

Sensing worries, dedication, and protective instinct, and commanding action were one for Syreen. She couldn't deny Herman's sacrifice when she needed it so much.

This was new, though — biting someone, sucking his blood, while having another one's cock in her pussy, sharing her arousal and her ecstasy with two other minds, while still in deep integration — reaching a higher level of consciousness.

The universe came to a halt around her.

Her mind was spread out — there was her own physical body, just an anchor for her own self, there was *Assiduous'* reassuring presence, Herman's devotion and his warm body, his throat at her mouth and his hand now grabbing one of her tits, the simple but familiar *Raydancer*, there was the central star singing its melancholic song, and finally there was hyperspace calling for her — and she couldn't go there before she got rid of a few nasty pursuers who didn't know their proper place.

She had the means to teach them.

Sadly, just stunning them wouldn't do — not with the third threat approaching fast. She could only afford to eliminate one, and she did.

The tension between her knees and her clit sprang to an

almost unbearable pain — the rod inside her felt like it was burning — and then, the charge shot away. *Ah!*

The gauge torpedo traveled toward *APS Griffin* at light speed. Shields didn't matter, and matter had to yield when its strong interaction was discontinued, when protons and neutrons no longer were. The battle cruiser simply disappeared.

She dodged the only pulse shot *APS Harpy* managed to toss at her and answered with another EMP strike, sending the enemy ship into darkness. *Ah!*

Meanwhile, *Raydancer's* pulse cannon harvested the hostile missiles one by one. There were only fractions of a blink left when she finally managed to wipe the controls of the three remaining threats and stepped aside.

One proximity trigger went off anyway. The warhead's blast hammered against *Assiduous'* body, shaking it to the core, burning skin, shattering a limb, destroying innards. Only her acceleration compensators protected the living beings inside.

Severely hurt, struck with pain, she sailed past their opponents' wrecks.

We must feed.

We must turn.

There was still another enemy quickly approaching. There was no time to lick wounds. If *APS Echidna* didn't strike sail at once, the battle had to continue.

They seemed unable to learn fast enough.

With the damaged leg, she lacked guidance for the next shot — and she could only afford one more shot.

But did she need guidance?

Her senses reached outward, felt the fabric of space.

We can do it.

We do it.

This time, there was no tingling in her knees, no tension rising between them. There was just her clit, and her mind to guide the charge that sprung from it. *Ah!*

CHAPTER ONE-HUNDRED-NINE

Slowly rising from deep integration, Syreen noticed a metallic taste in her mouth.

Herman?

He was alive and breathing, but weak. She withdrew from him and saw the bite marks shrink and disappear. This time, she wouldn't wipe his memory.

"Stephan," she croaked.

"Yessir!"

"Pick Herman up. He needs food and rest."

"Sure."

— We must feed. —

We will. Use Raydancer's *power supplies to navigate back. There's plenty of livestock to feed from.*

The most gruesome part was yet to come. *Assiduous* was severely damaged and almost entirely drained of his powers. The next Association ship arriving in the system could just pluck them away like a box of lost cargo.

"*Assiduous,* this is Lieutenant Marrassas of *APS Harpy.* Can you assist our evac maneuvers?"

She sighed deeply and felt her eyes water. It wasn't for the severe pain she felt in her leg.

"Lieutenant Marrassas, this is *Assiduous,* Lieutenant Syreen speaking. You were warned that without an advance declaration of war, any hostile activity was to be considered piracy. The Association nevertheless continued its attack, and thus all Association people in this system are collectively guilty of piracy — there will be no further ruling on the cause. Your resources — *all* your resources — will be used to compensate for the damages your actions caused. You may prepare a crew list for submittal to your government."

Drake rose from his seat, stretched his arms and legs, felt his head, and walked around the pilot chair to look for their pilot. She was bathed in sweat and — between her legs — her own juice. Her face was red and her eyes full of tears.

"A hell of a job," he said gently. "But you did it. Thank you."

She nodded.

"You must be tired," he went on. "Are you otherwise okay?"

"My leg hurts."

He looked down. "Which one?"

"Right."

"I can't see anything."

She looked down. Her true leg looked whole, but the pain was there. "Oh — no. Not mine. The ship."

"You can feel that?"

"I'm connected."

"Perhaps you should disconnect for a while."

"Perhaps I should . . . only, I can't. I can't move."

"Crow!"

His friend quickly came over.

"Yes?"

"We must help her out of the chair. Take her legs, I'll take her shoulders." He cautiously pulled her head out of the tight rest. Two small drops of blood at the neck pimples quickly disappeared. Drake placed one arm over her chest and reached around her back. From behind, he found firm hold on her lower arm and began to pull her away from the large boner that had impaled her far too long.

She let out a faint moan when the tool entirely left her. It was still shining from wetness. Crow took her ankles and helped lifting her out of the chair. Together, they placed her down on the floor.

"Do you know where to find a cover?" Drake asked.

Crow nodded and quickly left.

He kneeled down at her side and took her right hand. "Brave woman. It's over now."

"It's not," she disagreed. A tear ran down along her ear.

"Not?"

"This is a living ship." Her voice was just a whisper. "When it's hurt, it needs organic matter to heal itself."

He shook his head. "I still don't understand."

"Our enemies. They're made of organic matter."

Syreen saw understanding dawning in him.

"You mean, the ship will *eat* them?"

"Eat, consume, assimilate—call it what you like." She couldn't muster the energy to shrug. "If we want to get away from here before the next ship gets us, we have no choice."

"You defeated these—you surely could do it again."

"By defeating them, I spent every bit of power we had. Currently, we couldn't even shoot a cargo box." *Not entirely true. Raydancer has a little power left. Otherwise, we'd have no light in here.*

"And consuming those people would change that?"

"No. Consuming those people will enable us to collect starlight again, in sufficient amounts to get us away from here before the first Association dreadnaught arrives."

"A dreadnaught? Now you're exaggerating."

"They came to the Duchy with five dreadnaughts, on the slight chance they might find some ancient artifact. Now they know a place where they'll most likely find one. I'd expect them to arrive with everything they can muster."

"There's no other option?"

"Of course." She tried a smile, but judging by Drake's expression, she failed. "You all board *Raydancer* and leave me alone. *Assiduous* and I can commit suicide by diving into the central star. That way, the others can live. There's one drawback, though."

"Which?"

"Should they ever get their hands on another living ship, another Navigator, there's nobody to stop them. And until then, they continue to kill everyone in their way—like they did at our home."

He stared past her. "I see."

A moment later, he squeezed her hand—gently. "It would be a brave thing to die, in order to save these men, who committed so many bad deeds. It would save you. But it's a braver thing to bear what you have to do, for the greater good of others."

"It's always that, isn't it?" she said. "For the greater good of others. Such an easy excuse. I tell you something, Drake. I won't do that."

"No? But—then . . ."

"No, Drake." She felt stronger, now that she had made up her mind, and her own voice sounded firmer. "I won't commit suicide. I don't want to die, I'm far too young for that. I will do what I have to do, but not for a fucking greater good. I'll do it for myself, and for *Assiduous,* and perhaps for you, too. I'll do it because those bloody bastards don't deserve my sacrifice, and because I'm not done with that cursed Association yet. While this ship regenerates, I'll find out what they're really after, and once *Assiduous* is back at full strength, I'll kick their fucking ass all across this galaxy." She pushed her body up on her elbows and stared down to her pubes. "I will enjoy it. I'll have another orgasm each time I shoot one of them bastards."

She focused on his face, and he shrank back. Was her face so grim? "I'm Fleet, and Fleet won't give up. Welcome to the show."

To be continued . . .

You may also enjoy the following from eXtasy Books Inc:

Entrance
Valerie J. Long

Excerpt

"I hope you're not getting bored by the daily ferry tour," I said to Freddie while we were approaching Gladstone harbor. "Meanwhile, I regret having torn you from your peaceful life."

"I could have left long ago if I had no good reasons to stay." He pointed at Beate, who was taking a sunbath on the fore-deck, her bikini in easy reach at her side. "She's the most important reason for me personally. Sorry if I'm so honest. I'm completely supporting your mission, that's another reason, but for me it comes second."

I placed one hand on his shoulder. "That's okay, Freddie. I started my mission for personal, egoistic reasons, too, and I'm still in primarily for the many good people. I think what matters is being in wholeheartedly. You know why Beate is here?"

He nodded. "She once said, here she counts as a human. Her task as Mamba is important, but she knows—don't ask me how—that she'd be welcome here without those abilities, too. For that, for the respect she enjoys as a person, she likes to be here."

"Tess once put it the same way. I still think she's here for your sake."

"Maybe." He shrugged. "I won't put her in conflict by proposing to go elsewhere. I believe she doesn't want to show you less determination than Jasmine. You're her role model, and she doesn't want to risk you thinking bad of her. Aside from that—even if I take the same route every day, it's never boring."

He pointed forward. Two men who didn't belong to our team were waiting at our jetty. I recognized them anyway—Jack from Gladstone Observer and Flip from Oz Flash.

"Ah, the press," I commented for Freddie, who didn't have the advantage of nano-enhanced eyesight.

"Oh." He knocked at the windshield, and Beate looked up. Then she smiled and began to dress. I looked down my body and wrapped myself in shorts and a top.

"Hello, guys," I greeted the two reporters, who struggled to take their gaze away from Beate's barely covered bum.

"Hello, Jo. We had hoped you'd come across," Jack began.

"Hello, Jo," Flip quickly chimed in.

Jack went on, "Can you spare a moment of your time for us?"

"I'll take it. Here, or at Niko's?"

"It needn't be right in the middle of the jetty."

"Oh, we can go aboard. There we're alone."

"Gladly."

Jack and Flip followed me into the spacious lounge of Freddie's yacht. Flip dropped into one of the chairs next to the counter, Jack on the opposite couch. I walked behind the counter and opened the fridge.

"Are we taking someone's place now?" Flip asked.

"That's okay. Freddie and Beate are busy loading."

"Oh, fine." He looked at Jack.

Jack nodded when I held a can of Fourex up, and then caught it swiftly. Flip took a second one from my hand. I opened a third, and then took seat on the counter. "So, what's up? New protests?"

"You could say so," Flip confirmed.

"Sports," Jack said.

"Sports?"

"Sports. Your Ironman record."

"Ah—that's about to shake, isn't it? The men are close on my heels."

"It's not that." Jack shook his head. "It's about your record and how you achieved it. Flip?"

"A few people are debating on the Internet whether your Dragon skills played a role—that is, if you had an unfair advantage, so to say had been doped. They say without this mean trick—not my words—you could never have won." Flip took a sip. "Can you say something about that?"

"Sure." I drank, and placed the can down at my side. "First, yes, the Dragon skills were involved. Second, no, I don't see an unfair advantage. Third, no, I wasn't doped, as opposed to my competitors. Fourth, although I think I could have won without my Dragon skills, I don't know whether I'd have wanted to win so determinedly."

"I don't understand that," Jack followed up. "You admit having used your Dragon skills, but at the same time claim not having been doped. How does that fit?"

"How could you know the others were doped?" Flip asked almost simultaneously.

"My Dragon skills allow me to judge and watch my own body in more detail. I used this skill to such an extent that I didn't have to fear dropping down dead during the race. That only came later."

I could see in their faces that they had questions on that topic, too. "Let's briefly put that aside. Now it's about doping. I can judge my body, and I know how good I can be. I can align my training efforts very well without machines. My competitors could have the same, and that has nothing to do with consuming illicit substances. I trained very, very hard, and from that alone, I took my body to a performance level that hardly anyone else could reach. Admitted. I also must clearly admit that I had the chance to enhance my performance significantly further without health risk for me and without any possibility to prove it from outside. In which case I'd only need half the time of my own record for the entire competition—or less."

The reporters glanced at each other.

"Half?" Flip then echoed.

"Sure. No four hours. I'd probably be faster if I carried that bike instead of struggling with a ridiculously low gain ratio."

"Well, then," Jack said. "You might have held back deliberately, though."

"Right, I can't prove that wrong, although I didn't hold back at all."

"What about your claim of the others being doped?" Flip asked. "Can you prove that? How could you tell in the first place?"

"I can watch and judge others as well as myself. My closest competitors were definitely not enough in shape for the performance they showed."

"Which you can't prove." Flip slid around in his seat so that he didn't have to turn his head as much.

"No, I can't."

"Then you have a problem."

"I participated in and passed all official doping tests," I disagreed. "The opposite is true—nobody can provide evidence about me doping. Back then, I already said that I don't care what others think about it, that I only care how I appear to myself. Watch the recordings."

Jack placed both hands around the beer can. "Maybe that's enough for you. But as part of a bigger smear campaign . . ."

ABOUT THE AUTHOR

I am Valerie J. Long, born in 1963. I live and work in Germany as an IT project manager. I like role playing games, and I like putting my ideas on paper. I like all kinds of Science Fiction and Fantasy, I like music, and I like making you bite your nails off.

www.ingramcontent.com/pod-product-compliance
Lightning Source LLC
Chambersburg PA
CBHW071304200626
46813CB00015B/38